Taps For Private Tussie

JESSE STUART has also written

MAN WITH A BULL-TONGUE PLOW
HEAD O'W-HOLLOW
BEYOND DARK HILLS
TREES OF HEAVEN
MEN OF THE MOUNTAINS

♣

E. P. DUTTON & COMPANY, Inc.

TAPS FOR PRIVATE TUSSIE

•

JESSE STUART

ILLUSTRATED BY

THOMAS BENTON

E. P. DUTTON & COMPANY, INC. • NEW YORK

TO

JESSICA JANE

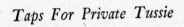

Taps For Private Tussie

CHAPTER I

GRANDPA'S brogan shoes made a noise like whettin two rocks together as he shuffled them back and forth on the witherin school-yard grass. I stood beside Grandpa and watched him work his feet in his crumple-toed brogan shoes while the hot July wind played with Grandpa's white beard. The wind lifted Grandpa's white corn-silk beard up and down but it couldn't tear it away from his face. His beard grew to his pale face for I could see it growing there when the wind lifted it up and down. I stood beside Grandpa and looked up and down his tall body; he looked as tall as a tree to me. But Grandpa didn't look as straight as a young tree. He was bent like an old tree weighted down with branches.

"Will Mott ever get outten that coalhouse?" Grandpa asked me.

"I don't know, Grandpa," I said.

Then Grandpa rubbed his brogan shoes across the thin school-yard grass again. He put his hands behind his back and locked them together. He'd look at the coalhouse door, then he'd look at the ground. He pretended that he was a-walkin and he couldn't get anyplace. He walked in the same steps all the time and when he looked at the ground he'd squirt a mouthful of ambeer on the withered grass. It would stain the white beard around Grandpa's mouth. And it hurt my stummick to see the long slivers of ambeer hangin to Grandpa's white beard that he would catch with his tongue and pull them back into his mouth and spit them out again.

"Trouble, trouble, trouble," Grandpa whispered after he'd spit a mouthful of ambeer on the wilted grass. Then he cleaned the beard around his mouth with the elbow of his clean blue work-shirt sleeve—a sleeve that had faded with many washins. "Man born of woman is full of trouble!"

I thought Grandpa was talkin a little crazy but I could see that he was worried about somethin. I knew that somethin was wrong or there wouldn't be so many people at our house. They were our blood kin but for many days they hadn't come to see us. Some of them had never been to see us. But they had come now. The schoolhouse yard was filled with them. They'd come on the razor backs of plug horses and mules whose ribs I could have counted easy enough where they stood trying to pull the limbs of the school-yard oaks down to the hot wilted grass so they could pick them a mouthful of somethin to eat. I saw a mule nearly get one down low enough to get him a bite. But the limb wouldn't give any more and the bridle bits pulled the mule's mouth open and showed a set of bad teeth. They looked a lot like Grandpa's teeth when he opened his mouth to put a brown burley leaf behind his beardy jaw. All the mules and horses tied to the school-yard trees had bad teeth and razor backs, crooked legs and sores and some sort of afflictions about their bodies.

"Grandpa, what are you a-waitin on?" I asked him.

Just then the coalhouse door came open and Uncle Mott came out with a screwdriver in his hand.

"Is it Kim, Mott?" Grandpa asked.

"It's Kim all right," Uncle Mott said. "But, Jesus Christ, I'm sick at my stummick. I'm ready to throw up every vittal I et for my dinner!"

Uncle Mott's face had lost its sun-browned color. His face was almost as white as the milkweed furze that I've tried to catch on the meader. But the wind lifted it like it lifted Grandpa's beard—it lifted it higher and higher and I ran under it and couldn't reach it. Uncle Mott's face was nearly that white. I'd say it was more the color of a yellow clay road when it dries out in the spring. His face had the same color of dried clay where the sun has left big cracks in it. Uncle Mott's hand was tremblin too—the one he held the screwdriver in. I thought he was a-goin to punch the sharp end of the screw-driver into his new overalls.

"How do you know it's Kim?" Grandpa asked Uncle Mott.

"That was very easy to find out, Pap," Uncle Mott said.

"Tell me how you told," Grandpa growled like a hound dog. "I want to be sure it's my boy!"

"Remember the gold upper front tooth in Kim's mouth?"

"Yep, I remember it!"

"It was there. Kim didn't have no lips and it was easy to see! Remember the two lower front teeth that Cousin Hester Tussie knocked out of Kim's mouth with a rock?"

"Yep, I remember that very well."

"They were out."

"Then you could tell it was Kim by his teeth!"

"That was not all the way I could tell it was Kim."

"What other ways could you tell?" Grandpa asked, his lips tremblin while the July wind played with his white beard, liftin it up and down so I could see where the little fine white hairs grew into Grandpa's pale lean lantern jaws—flesh the sun couldn't brown because there was too much shade on it.

"Remember the middle finger on the right hand that Kim had ground off in the cane mill?"

"Yep, I was just a-thinkin about that finger."

"Well, it was gone. I took the coffin lid plum off. I took the screws out and I lifted the lid! Then I unwrapped Kim's blanket down to his navel. That was as fur as I wanted to see. I'd seen enough when I got that fur."

"I oughta gone in there with you, Mott," Grandpa said.

"It wasn't no place for you, Pap!"

"I guess it wasn't at that!"

The screwdriver shook more and more as Uncle Mott talked to Grandpa. I didn't get close to Uncle Mott for I thought he might jab the sharp end of the screwdriver into me.

"Pap, don't go in the coalhouse," Uncle Mott warned Grandpa. "Stay outten there. That scent will knock you down. Let the wind carry the scent out through the knot-holes of the planks before the funeral!"

"I aint a-goin, Mott," Grandpa said, his voice tremblin as he spoke. I thought maybe the beard around Grandpa's mouth was a-catchin Grandpa's words and tryin to hold them. "I don't want to see Kim like that. I want to remember 'im like he was the day he left. Like the day I saw him get on the bus for Fort Thomas, Kentucky. I didn't think Kim would get back. I had some sort of a token that he wouldn't. He was a-gettin too fur in years to make a good soldier. Kim was forty-four years old the day he left!"

We could hear a few screams now and then back in the schoolhouse. They must have come through the holes in the winderpanes the boys had knocked out with rocks before we moved into the schoolhouse. One good thing we'd done for the county school system, we had stopped the boys' knockin the winderpanes out with rocks. That's what Grandpa told a member of the County School Board when he ordered Grandpa to move outten the schoolhouse.

"It will soon be time for the funeral," Grandpa told Uncle Mott. "We'd better be a-moseyin back over to the school-house!"

We started across the wilted school-yard grass toward the schoolhouse that had once been painted. The grass felt soft and warm to my bare feet and the little puddles of sand were hot enough to burn my toes. The hot July air was smothery to breathe except when the wind blew.

"We'll haf to get Kim in the ground soon as we can," Uncle Mott told Grandpa. "Atter I opened the coffin and let fresh air into Kim—I could see more flesh a-goin. It was a-goin fast!"

"I know it," Grandpa told Uncle Mott. "But I just wanted to be sure it was my boy. I didn't want to bury some other mother's son and think he was my own. When I lay a bunch of wild roses on his grave, I want it to be on Kim's grave. God only knows what makes a body feel that way. But that's the way I feel. I want the bones to be Kim's bones that I put flowers on and keep the briers and sprouts cleaned away!"

Grandpa pulled a big blue bandanna from his overall hip pocket and wiped sweat from his turkey-wattles red sunburnt neck just as we reached the schoolhouse doorstep. After Grandpa had wiped the sweat from his neck and pressed his sweaty beard down like fine rain-wet corn silks against his bony face, he put the bandanna back into his hip pocket and walked slowly inside the door, holdin to the door facins with his big bony hands to help himself into the house. Uncle Mott followed Grandpa into the house, nervous as weeds shaken by the wind. I had to keep clear of the sharp end of the screwdriver as I followed Uncle Mott into the schoolhouse.

"Poor Kim, he's out there in that coalhouse," Aunt Vittie wailed, wavin her arms high in the air and lettin them fall on a schoolhouse desk. "I don't know whether it's Kim or not either!"

"Don't take it so hard, Vittie," Grandma said, pattin Aunt Vittie on the back. "Take it easy, honey. These things haf to come to a body. I brought Kim into the world! I give him nourishment from my breasts. I know that it's hard to take. But we must be able to bear up under the things that the Lord sends down on us!"

Grandma was sittin on the schoolhouse seat beside Aunt Vittie. The hair on Grandma's head was white as Grandpa's beard only it wasn't stained with terbacker juice. It was clean and white as sheep wool hangin to a cluster of sawbriers where many April rains have washed it clean. That's the way Grandma's hair looked to me.

"It's Kim all right, Vittie," Uncle Mott said, his voice tremblin like the dry hickory leaves rustled by the July wind on the school yard.

I felt a little ashamed to be among so many people in the schoolhouse. My feet were a little dirty; my overalls were patched. My shirt was slit across the back and the sleeves were out at the elbows. The schoolhouse was filled with people; but they were our people. They were the Tussies. Many of them I had never seen before. They had never been to our house and we had never been to their houses. They had come to Uncle Kim's funeral.

Now on one side of the schoolhouse we had taken the seats up so we could put the few pieces of furniture down. In the corner of the schoolhouse we had our stove. It was the schoolhouse stove, a big pot-bellied stove. We used the teacher's desk for our eatin table. And we had our beds in the front part of the schoolhouse where the long hard seats used to be. But we had carried them out and put them under the schoolhouse floor. This was the best house that we had ever lived in. We didn't even haf to chop wood here, for the coalhouse had a lot of coal in it when we moved here. That was just after school was out last January. And it was the warmest house we had ever lived in.

"How do you know it's Kim?" Vittie asked Uncle Mott.

"He's got the gold tooth in front and the finger off," Mott told her.

"I want to see 'im," Aunt Vittie screamed, hittin the desk top with her lean shriveled hands.

"But you mustn't see 'im," Uncle Mott said. "I warn you, Vittie, not to look at Kim! It's Kim all right—that's all you want to know!"

"For three years I aint seen 'im," she wailed like wind in the hickory tops around the schoolhouse in February.

I looked over the schoolhouse. In many of the seats young people were a-sittin and whisperin to one another. There were big smiles on their faces. That was what Grandpa called "sparkin." There was a lot of sparkin a-goin on at Uncle Kim's funeral. Old people sat with their faces restin in their hands and their elbows braced on the desk tops. I didn't see many tears shed. Just a few of the old women shed tears when Aunt Vittie carried on. Aunt Vittie was a-doin most of the weepin and Grandma was tryin to coax her from weepin. She had her arm around Aunt Vittie and she was a-callin her "honey" every time she spoke to her.

"Kill 'im in a war and send his bones back to me," Aunt Vittie screamed again.

"But that's war, Vittie," Grandpa said. "You are lucky if you get Kim's bones back to the mountains! They had a fur piece to bring 'em!"

Everybody in the schoolhouse got quiet when Brother Baggs McMeans got up from the front seat with a Bible in his hand. It was so quiet that we could hear the lazy July wind a-rustlin the drought-dry hickory leaves on the trees that shaded the schoolhouse.

"I aint a-takin long for this sermon," Brother Baggs McMeans told us. "I know that Kim Tussie was a fightin man! I know that he was a good soldier! That's what our country wanted and that's just what she got when she took Kim Tussie. I knowed 'im from the time he was a leetle boy. I know how he could shoot. I've squirrel hunted with 'im and watched 'im bark squirrels from many a tall walnut tree in Womack Holler!"

Then Brother Baggs opened his Bible and read slowly. He had a time readin the Scripture, for Brother Baggs, so Grandpa said, didn't know his A.B.C.s until after the Lord called him to preach. Then he got the Light and his A.B.C.s come to him so he could read the Word. But Brother Baggs stumbled over the words just like when you try to walk among rocks barefooted. You stumble over them and hurt your feet. Brother Bagg's face looked like it was in much pain as he tried to read some of the big words in the Bible.

But it was different when Brother Baggs started usin his own words. They come hot and fast from his mouth. Great pieces of foamy spittle flew outten his mouth with the words he said. And he hit his hands down on top of our eatin table to drive his words home to us. He said he wasn't a-goin to

preach long, but atter he got goin I thought he never was
a-goin to stop. I thought that it would be all right for him to
preach a long time and give the wind time to carry the scent
through the knotholes in the coalhouse planks.

"The Lord will forgive Kim fer every man he's kilt,"
Brother Baggs said. "Don't ye doubt it! Like David of old,
who slew the Philistines with the jawbone of an ass, Kim
barked our enemies with his rifle. I know that Kim has entered
the pearly gates of Heaven!"

That made all the women feel better. It made Aunt Vittie
stop her weepin for a while.

"If we all live right, folks," Brother Baggs said, slappin his
big hands down on our eatin table, "we'll meet Kim in the
starry skies one of these days. We'll walk with 'im on the
streets of gold!"

The few old women and Aunt Vittie who had been sheddin
tears didn't shed any more tears after Brother Baggs said these
words. But I wondered if Uncle Kim would be happy walkin
on streets of gold in the starry skies. I remembered Uncle Kim
how he used to come home drunk and throw the few pieces
of furniture out of the house, break the dishes and winders,
break the chairs over the stove and run Aunt Vittie off. She'd
come to Grandma's a-cryin. I remember how Uncle Kim
used to fight and hunt and drink—how he carried two big
pistols with 'im and slept with 'em under his pillow at night.
All these thoughts went through my head and I couldn't keep
them out while Brother Baggs finished his sermon. I remember
how the Law used to threaten Uncle Kim because he wouldn't
pay his debts and how he'd take to the woods with his pistols
when the Sheriff would come to get 'im. I didn't think that
heaven with golden streets and good people would suit Uncle
Kim.

I sat thinkin about these things while everybody was
a-singin, "We'll Meet You in the Mornin Over There." Soon
as the singin was over, we followed Brother Baggs out of

the schoolhouse. Grandpa was the last one out for he had a big auger hole bored through the schoolhouse door and one through the wall. He had a chain through these holes and a big padlock on the chain. He had it locked so the Law couldn't come and throw our furniture out of the schoolhouse while we were gone to the funeral. Grandpa stayed behind and locked the padlock. He kept the windows locked down all the time. Enough air whistled through the broken panes for us to get fresh air all the time.

"B-gad, that'll hold 'em out till we git back," Grandpa said as he hurried to catch the crowd walkin slowly toward the coalhouse. "They can't get the house plunder out while we're gone to plant Kim on that lonesome mountain."

As we walked across the wilted grass, grass so hot and stringy that it was like wires when it hooked around the people's shoes, it tripped Uncle Mott. He fell flat on his face, jumped up real quick and brushed his white shirt and his clean pressed blue pants. Many of the young Tussies laughed when Uncle Mott was tripped by the stringy grass; Uncle Mott didn't like it either. He looked at them with mean blue eyes. But the air was so hot when you breathed it you felt that you were short of breath all the time. It made me wonder why we hadn't buried Uncle Kim in the mornin. We had slept in the schoolhouse with him all night and moved him to the coalhouse so Uncle Mott could open the coffin to see if it was Uncle Kim.

"Christ, it's hot," Grandpa's brother, my Great-Uncle Will said. "It's might' nigh too hot to get upon that hill this atternoon! But I guess Kim has to be buried! Shoulda been done in the mornin!"

Six of Uncle Kim's first cousins left their wives and went inside the coalhouse. There was Sid Tussie, whose big-muscled arms swelled his shirtsleeves tight enough to split them when he contracted his arms; there was Enic Tussie, with big arms and long legs and a small red face; Bert Tussie who could kill a beef with his fist but who never had done a day's work in his life; Mort Tussie, short and heavy with a red mustache; Sebie Tussie, whose shoulders were broad as a corn-crib door; and "Mule" Tussie who could pull a plow through new ground beside a mule.

"Take it easy, boys," Sid said to his first cousins as they came through the coalhouse door, with the coffin upon their shoulders. "Easy, easy, easy! Watch yourselves. Don't bump against the sides of the door!"

"It's a load," Mort Tussie said.

The coffin was covered with a flag.

"Oh, my Kim," Aunt Vittie screamed.

"Now, don't worry, honey," Grandma said as she walked along beside Aunt Vittie, with one hand a-hold of her arm, the other hand around her back. Uncle Mott walked on the other side of Aunt Vittie and held to her arm. Uncle Mott said soft words to Aunt Vittie as the great procession of us followed the six men carryin the coffin up the hill. Brother Baggs McMeans walked next to the coffin, then Grandma, Aunt Vittie and Uncle Mott followed Brother Baggs; Grandpa walked behind Grandma and the rest of us followed. Many of my kinfolks I didn't know and some I did know walked in the procession behind with their arms around their girls' backs, laughin, talkin and whisperin words of love into their ears. It was the greatest bit of excitement that I had ever seen, just to walk in the great procession and hear the people laugh and talk. I had been to one or two funerals before, but I had never seen one like this funeral. Everybody seemed happy but Aunt Vittie, Grandpa, Grandma and Uncle Mott. They seemed to be a little sad. But I'd never seen Grandma and Grandpa nor Uncle Mott shed a tear. Just Aunt Vittie was the only one who was a-sheddin any real tears!

With the big black coffin restin on their shoulders, I watched these men pull big bandannas from their pockets with their free hands and wipe sweat from their red, sun-

tanned faces. Mort, Sid, Enic and Bert Tussie had beardy faces and the sweat was drippin from their beards. I could see the sweat drops shine on their beards betwixt me and the sun as we walked up the narrow path where there were wilted clusters of smelly sawbriers, greenbrier stools, wild grapevines, sassafras sprouts, huckleberry vines and rock cliffs on each side of the path. I saw a crow fly over and heard his caw-caw above us. And I heard the dry weeds rattle and I saw a lizard scurry across the leaves and disappear among the wilted weeds. The heat came down hot enough to burn our backs through our thin shirts as we climbed the mountain path. I wondered what it would be to carry a load up this mountain when it was all I could do to walk up it.

Before we had gone far upon the mountain, Brother Baggs turned around, faced us and said, "Brothers and sisters, let us sing 'Beulah Land'!"

If you don't think it's hard to climb a mountain and sing, you try it one of these days. Try it when the July sun comes down upon your back with blisterin heat and the lizards are scurryin over the dead leaves a-huntin a wisp of shade on the backbone of a mountain that is steamin in the swelterin heat like a pan of bread in an oven. Everybody tried to sing; even Grandpa and Grandma. If Aunt Vittie was singin, I couldn't hear her voice. But I know some of the heavy Tussie women could hardly get their breaths when they sang. Their words were short. They sang with little puffs of breath and held to the sassafras sprouts along the path to help themselves along. Brother Baggs led the procession, singin with his heavy voice like low thunder that rumbles over the mountain skies before a rain. We marched toward the mountain top with Uncle Kim on the shoulders of his cousins, with "Beulah Land" on our lips—the great procession of Tussies a-goin to bury one of our dead.

Maybe Brother Baggs was right when he had us to sing. Our climbin wasn't so hard as we sang "Beulah Land" over and over with words fast as an April mountain stream that pitches headlong over the rocks, down, down into the valley. It was great to walk behind Brother Baggs and sing and to see the six powerful Tussie men—the strongest among the Tussies—carry Uncle Kim to his last restin place, a country where Uncle Kim used to bark the squirrels and listen to his fox hounds chase the fox around the mountain.

Brother Baggs turned again and faced us, a-raisin up his hands for us to stop singin.

"Brothers and sisters," Brother Baggs said, with short puffs of breath. Then he pulled his bandanna from his pocket and wiped the sweat from his beardy face. "While we're a-gettin near this mountain top, up among these rocks, let's sing 'Rock of Ages.'"

Brother Baggs started the song; we joined him. We marched and sang. I looked on each side of my path now and there wasn't much but jutted rocks. There were a few sourwood sprouts, scrubby pines and masses of greenbriers a-growin among the moss-covered rocks near the mountain top. I didn't see a sassafras sprout higher than a mule's back. The mountain was too high to grow anything but a few briers and sprouts. But I don't believe I'd ever seen as many rocks and gray lizards scurryin over the rocks a-huntin greenflies. My feet didn't get so hot up this high on the mountain and the high wind cooled my face, makin the sweat dry on my neck.

All of a sudden the singin stopped and the Tussie men took the big black coffin from their shoulders. They sat it on the ground by a mound of fresh dirt. Five Tussie men with long beards on their faces, a-wearin sweaty-damp work shirts opened at the necks and with sleeves rolled up, stood with shovels and coal picks in their hands. Thad Tussie was Grandpa's first cousin; there was Fiddis Tussie, a cousin of Uncle Mott; Add Tussie, a brother to Bolivar; Cy Tussie, a brother to Add; and Wade Tussie, a second cousin to Cy and Add. They had come early that mornin while it was cool to dig the grave. Now they stood beside the grave and looked at the long procession of Tussies walkin slowly up the hill singin with breaths so short they could hardly sing.

I hurried up to the grave to look down in it. It wasn't as deep as I was tall. It looked shallow to me. But I looked at the dirt they had shoveled from the grave and there were big rocks in it that I knew the men had to lift from the grave with their hands. One of the rocks would have broken a shovel handle. And near this grave was a row of Tussie graves that looked like tater ridges, for they weren't marked with stones. On another grave was a tattered flag, that the wind had faded until you could hardly tell what it was. Parts of it had been beaten off by the strong mountain wind and had caught on the huckleberry vines.

"Oh, my Kim," Aunt Vittie screamed as she tore loose from Grandma and Uncle Mott and fell on her knees with her face down on the coffin lid. "I love you, Kim! I couldn't help it. I love you! Kim! Kim! Kim!"

"We'd better get 'im buried, Brother Baggs," Grandpa whispered in Brother Baggs's ear. "Vittie'll take on until she makes herself sick!"

Everybody was hot climbin the mountain and Grandpa thought that Aunt Vittie would be cooled by the mountain wind and that it would make her sick. I thought, maybe, Grandpa didn't want to hear Aunt Vittie a-carryin on. No one but Aunt Vittie was a-carryin on—not even Grandpa and Grandma, and Uncle Kim was their boy. Everybody else seemed to be havin a good time. It was better than pitchin hoss-shoes on Sunday or a-ridin the mountain paths on mules a-shootin at the lizards with their pistols as they scurried over the rocks and up the sprouts.

"Now, now, honey," Grandma said to Aunt Vittie. "No use to take it like this. You want to live yerself, don't you, honey?"

"I'd as soon be dead and buried beside Kim as to go on

a-livin without 'im." Aunt Vittie cried hard as I ever heard anybody cry in my life. Tears ran down her cheeks and wet the flag in two tiny places.

I'd never noticed before that Aunt Vittie was so pretty. Her blue tear-stained eyes looked soft, her long hair was the color of the broom sedge that had ripened high on the mountain in the drought long before its time. She had prettier teeth than any of the Tussies that I had ever seen. I thought Aunt Vittie was pretty as she lay with her head upon the coffin, her knees on the dry mountain earth where she wept like the sound of wind a-cryin among the fine huckleberry briers on the mountain top. It touched me to hear her weep; maybe that was why that I thought she was so pretty.

"All right now, honey," Grandma said, a-pattin Aunt Vittie on the shoulder, "you're a-takin it too hard! Come, Mott, hep me lift her up!"

Grandma and Uncle Mott lifted Aunt Vittie up from the coffin while Fiddis and Add Tussie brought two pairs of leather check lines and slipped them under the coffin. Fiddis and Add held to one end of a pair while Cy and Thad Tussie held the other end; Sid and Enic Tussie grabbed one end of the other pair while Bert and Mort Tussie grabbed the other end of the pair of lines.

"Ready, boys," Mort said.

They lifted the coffin over the grave hole while Grandpa pulled the flag from over the coffin. They lowered Uncle Kim down into the mountain earth to the bottom of his shallow grave. Then Brother Baggs crumbled a clod of clay into the grave and said, "Ashes to ashes and dust to dust." He quoted more from the Word that I don't remember. But Grandma and Uncle Mott had to lead Aunt Vittie away while the men started shovelin the lumpy clay and loose rocks over Uncle Kim.

Now the great procession of people moved down the mountain faster than they had climbed it. There was more talkin and laughin than I had ever heard in one crowd of people. I wondered as I walked among my kinfolks how Aunt Vittie could love Uncle Kim the way she did after the way he used to run her outten her own house. But she did love him; they were real tears that she had shed.

Before we had reached the schoolhouse at the foot of the mountain, I noticed that Uncle Mott walked real close to Aunt Vittie, with his right hand a-hold of her right hand and his left arm around her back. He had her squeezed over close to him but that was because she had climbed the mountain and she had wept a lot and she was tired. Grandma walked on the other side of Aunt Vittie and held her left hand. I walked beside of Grandpa a-holdin to his hand. Many sang songs as we walked down the mountain, a mountain so steep that it made the knees creak to hold us back.

CHAPTER II

❧

"I SEE 'EM," Grandpa said to Grandma. "They are back. It's a good thing that I padlocked the house before we left!"

I looked down at the schoolhouse, where I saw four men a-waitin for us.

"We're a-goin to haf to get out of that schoolhouse, Press," Grandma said. "School begins next week!"

When we reached the school yard there was a lot of hand-shakin among the Tussies before they parted. They invited each other to come and see them; I saw Tussies a-shakin hands that wouldn't speak to each other before Uncle Kim's death. I wondered what Uncle Kim's gettin killed had to do with it. They had never liked Uncle Kim. Why would they come now and be so friendly? Grandpa talked friendly with his kinfolks; then he would look toward the schoolhouse where the four men stood waitin on us.

"Don't be in any hurry, Arimithy," Grandpa whispered to Grandma. "Maybe that pack of buzzards will leave."

"They won't leave, Press," Grandma said. "They'll haf to see us before they leave! You know the Law. You've had too many trials and tribulations with it not to know it!"

"I guess you're right," Grandpa said. "We'll haf to face 'em."

It was fun for me to watch a big strong Tussie man jump astride of his mule that didn't have a saddle on its back. Then his wife would come up and put her foot upon his foot and he would take her by the hand and pull her and she'd sling her leg over the mule's back, catch her husband around the waist and off they'd go, the lean mule a-kickin up little clouds of dust as he ran down the road like a rabbit. We watched men and women a-gettin into their buggies and jolt wagons; and a

28

few of the young Tussies had old run-down cars that they
piled in long as the car would hold another person, long as a
person could swing on—and down the road each would go,
the car a-clatterin like a mowin machine. The big day was
over now; the Tussies had come and they had gone. We had
to go back to the schoolhouse for the night.

"You remember me, don't you, Press Tussie?" a big man
with a pistol in his hip holster said to Grandpa.

"Yep, I remember you, Sheriff Whiteapple," Grandpa said.
"I ought to remember you. I hepped elect you!"

"But you didn't heed me," Sheriff Whiteapple said. "That's
why I brought my deputies along! Why aint you outten that
schoolhouse?"

"I aint found a place to go," Grandpa said.

"You'd better find a place and find one quick," Sheriff
Whiteapple said as he wrinkled his face and squinted his eyes.

"Guess I could've found a place this week," Grandpa said,
lookin the Sheriff squarely in the eyes with his soft blue eyes,
"but my son Kim has been shipped back here and we buried
'im today! He died for his country. How many boys did you
have to die for our country?"

Sheriff Whiteapple looked at Grandpa. He didn't speak.

"I lost one in the last war," Grandpa said, "and I've lost
one in this war!"

"Now, Mr. Tussie," Sheriff Whiteapple pleaded, "can't you
clear outten this schoolhouse before next week? The County
School Board members have been after me again. They've been
after me to get you outten this schoolhouse since last January
when you first moved here. You've been a-promisin me that
you'd clear out but you won't do it. I've lost confidence in
you!"

Sheriff Whiteapple talked to Grandpa in a soft voice since
Grandpa had asked him how many boys he had in the war.
Everybody knew that his boys, Pert and Harley, got out be-

cause they had flat feet or something; yet they worked all the time—went away to Baltimore and made a lot of money buildin ships. I held to Grandpa's hand while he talked to Sheriff Pearse Whiteapple. Sheriff Whiteapple's deputy sheriffs stood by and listened. They had pistols in their holsters with big leather belts around their middles holdin their pistol holders. While Grandpa talked to Sheriff Whiteapple, Uncle Mott got the key from Grandpa, unlocked the padlock, and Grandma, Aunt Vittie and Uncle Mott went inside the schoolhouse.

"Atter tonight I'll know more about when I can get outten this schoolhouse," Grandpa said. "I've got a little business to talk over with my daughter-in-law, Vittie!"

"Business or no business, Press Tussie," Sheriff Whiteapple demanded, "we've got to have this schoolhouse! Superintendent Ott Rashburn said he wouldn't place an indictment against you for burnin the school's coal, if you'd only vacate the house. It will save you a fine if you'll go now!"

"I don't dread the fine," Grandpa said, his lips partin his fine beard when he laughed. "You could fine me ten or ten thousand dollars and it would be the same to me. I couldn't pay the fine; I'd be fed and clothed in jail. You tell Superintendent Ott Rashburn to do as he pleases about it. I'll ask 'im why his boy wasn't in service overseas. Why didn't a big able-bodied boy like he's got haf to go to yan side and fight when they took my Kim over?"

"You'll have to ask the govern-ment about that," Sheriff Whiteapple said. "I've come out here to see when you're a-goin to get outten this schoolhouse?"

"I told you." Grandpa spoke soft as the lazy wind that lifted the white corn silk beard on his face.

"I'd a put your house plunder outten that schoolhouse to-day," Sheriff Whiteapple said, "but you've padlocked the door and locked the winders!"

"I expected you to be here today," Grandpa said. "You're

the kind to come when a man is a-buryin his boy that died a-fightin for his country so your boys could go to Baltimore and make a fortune!"

"I don't like that," Sheriff Whiteapple told Grandpa, lookin him squarely in the eyes with his hard mean brown eyes.

"I don't care what ye like," Grandpa said. "I'd like to have someplace to stick my head. That last rock cliff that we lived under had several leaks that we couldn't stop. No way to plug up the holes. We don't want to move back to it."

"That's too bad," Sheriff Whiteapple said.

"It was awfully bad," Grandpa said.

"I'm a-goin to give you until Wednesday to get outten this schoolhouse," Sheriff Whiteapple said. "If you aint out, I'm a-goin to throw your house plunder outten the schoolhouse. I've fooled with you long enough!"

Sheriff Whiteapple walked away, his three deputies that hadn't spoken a word walked away with their high sheriff. They walked down to the car they had parked beside the narrow dusty road. Grandpa and I watched the yellow clouds of dust a-risin from the windin road.

"He didn't want to arrest me," Grandpa said. "He didn't want to haf to feed me. He knows I didn't care. I'd about as soon eat jail grub as relief grub. It don't matter to me. One's about as good as the other!"

I'd seen people come and ask Grandpa to work; but he'd always tell them that he was down in his back. He'd tell them that he'd never be able to work. And Grandpa wouldn't work for anybody. Soon, people quit askin Grandpa to work. Uncle Mott wouldn't work either. He'd send me to the woods to find sticks for kindlin to start the fire in the coal stove while he lay under the shade of the hickory trees and picked his banjer. Uncle Mott was a good banjer picker, so everybody said when he played at the square dances. But everybody said he ought

to be a good banjer picker since he hadn't done a day's work
in his life. He was just too old the reason the draft didn't get
him.

But I guess it was all right that the draft didn't get him,
since Grandpa needed help to carry our relief grub home.
Uncle Mott didn't mind goin to town and carryin a sack load
of relief grub home on his back atter he'd traded the prunes
for a couple of beers. I used to go along with Uncle Mott and
go into Hadden's beer jint with him. I'd watch him put the
beer bottle back into his mouth. I'd hear 'im gurgle a few
times and watch the Adam's apple run up and down his hairy
throat; then he'd set the bottle on the table, wipe the beer
foam from the beard around his mouth. Uncle Mott would
call for another bottle and put it down his gullet the same way.
Then we'd get our sacks of relief grub; Uncle Mott would
carry the big sack and I'd carry a little sack and we'd start
home. By the time we got home, Aunt Vittie, Grandpa and
Grandma would be a-gettin a little hungry. Because Uncle
Mott was so slow about goin to town and gettin back,
Grandma used to send Aunt Vittie with Uncle Mott.

I remember the time we lived in the rock cliff. That's the
first house I ever remember. I remember the big place inside.
It was in Eif McCallister's pasture field. Eif had let his cattle
stand under this cliff until Grandpa took it over. Then
Grandpa whipped the cattle out. Grandpa and Grandma carried some loose planks they'd found some place and set them
up against the side of the cliff to keep the winter wind out.
But it was good and warm back under the cliff. I remember
Grandpa complained because we didn't have a plank floor so
we could have dances. He said you couldn't have a square
dance on a dirt floor. And we didn't have any dances there.
We lived there a long time. Eif McCallister hated to run
Grandpa outten the cliff; though we knew he wanted it for
his cattle.

"Better the cattle sleep out under the pines than people,"
Grandpa said.

So we stayed under the cliff for a long time. Then Grandpa rented a house and some land to farm. But Uncle Mott wouldn't plow. He said he couldn't stand plowin. Said he sweated too much and drank too much water. Grandpa said he was too old to use a hoe. Said he wasn't able to work. Grandma said it wasn't a woman's place to do the farmin. So the weeds took the corn we planted and Mr. York made us leave the place. He didn't fool with sickin the Law on Grandpa. He brought his gun and three of his boys brought guns and they put our things out on the ground at the point of guns. Then Grandpa went over the mountain where no one had heard of us. He rented another house. He told Mr. Snodgrass that he was a good farmer.

And while we lived there, Aunt Vittie came to stay with us. Uncle Kim was drafted into the army. Aunt Vittie would work and I would work with her; but we couldn't do enough farmin to please Mr. Snodgrass. Uncle Mott and Grandpa laid in the shade. They wouldn't work.

"I don't haf to work," Grandpa said, "long as the government feeds me. Why should I work!"

Sheriff Whiteapple came and set our house plunder out in the big road since Grandpa wouldn't move. That was in January too. Grandpa was supposed to move in September but he beat the Law until January. That's why we saw an empty schoolhouse and carried our house plunder to it. No use to move our old rattletrap of a stove that didn't have any legs. We had to put it upon rocks for legs. There was a good stove in the schoolhouse, so Grandpa told us, and there was plenty of coal in the coalhouse. Grandpa was right when he said throw our old ax away. Each bit was worn off to the eye anyway, not where we'd done a lot of choppin but where we'd chopped it into the ground so much.

We moved to the schoolhouse and Grandpa said it was the best house that he had ever lived in. Said he didn't haf to get wood and all he had to do was walk to town and get his grub given to him. We didn't like the grub much and Grandpa always complained why they didn't give us better grub. But we could have square dances in the schoolhouse. Uncle Mott made music on his five-string banjer. It was a big floor. We just moved the seats back and had big times. Most all the people that came to our dances were our kinfolks. It seemed like we were akin to a lot of people too. There were from eight to fourteen youngins in some of the Tussie families.

Soon as we'd had supper, I pulled off my overalls and crawled in bed in my shirttail. My bed was in the corner of the schoolhouse by the winder. It wasn't so hot near the winder. I slept with Uncle Mott but he hadn't come to bed yet. When the night cooled a little, Aunt Vittie put a lump of coal in the stove. She opened the door and let the light flicker out to light the schoolhouse. I couldn't go to sleep, for I thought something was a-goin to happen. I saw Uncle Mott, Aunt Vittie, Grandpa and Grandma all sittin around the stove. Grandpa and Uncle Mott were chewin terbacker and spittin on the stove. I could hear the ambeer sizzle on the hot stove like meat a-fryin in a skillet. And Grandma sat there a-smokin her pipe.

"Now you stay right with us, honey," Grandpa said. "We'll take care of you just like you was our own daughter. You are our daughter by marriage ties!"

"Honey, you can't leave us now," Grandma said. "We've kept you while Kim was over yander. Now, honey, you want to stick with us!"

"Aint no use for you to go on like that Ma," Uncle Mott said. "You and Pa talk like Vittie's a-goin to leave us. She's never had that kind of a thought. Have you, Vittie?"

"No, Mott, I aint," Aunt Vittie said.

"That's fine, honey," Grandma said.

"I'm glad to hear you talk like that, Vittie," Grandpa said.

Then Grandpa spit on the stove and I heard the ambeer sizzle.

"Kim was our boy same as he was your husband," Grandma said. "I know who felt the pangs of birth for 'im. Didn't have a doctor either. I know who suckled these breasts of mine. That's why I feel that somethin's a-comin to us!"

"I know somethin's a-comin to you, Ma Tussie," Aunt Vittie said.

"But now if you marry agin," Grandpa said.

"Oh, don't say that to me, Pa Tussie," Aunt Vittie said. "You know that I'm not a-tryin to get married again after the way I loved Kim. My love is a-sleepin on top the mountain with the Stars and Stripes like a quilt over his fresh-dug grave tonight!"

"But a woman's comb gets red again," Grandpa said, "when she is still young and pretty and don't have her a man!"

Grandpa laughed and spit on the stove again.

"Shet up, Press," Grandma said. "What do ye know of women's combs a-gettin red again?"

Then Uncle Mott spit on the stove and I heard a lot of ambeer sizzle. I could see the clouds of smoke go up from Grandma's long-stemmed pipe.

"You don't haf to worry about me," Aunt Vittie said. "I'm a-stayin right with you."

"Then it means we can rent a house and pay our rent," Grandpa said.

"It means we can have new house plunder too," Grandma said.

"And it means we don't haf to eat relief grub no longer," Uncle Mott said.

"And we can vote any ticket we want to," Grandpa said. "B-gad, I's allus a Republican until this relief thing come along. It looked like too good a thing to pass up. I didn't mind to cross over to the other side and makin my cross!"

"It means we'll get outten this schoolhouse so they can have school here next week," Grandma grunted. "Let old Whiteapple have the schoolhouse!"

CHATER III

SOON as Grandpa had swallowed his last sup of coffee, he pushed his schoolhouse seat back from the table, wiped his coffee-stained beard with his big bony hand. His long skinny fingers played with his crow's nest of white beard like pitchfork tines slippin into a mow of timothy hay.

"Get the egg offen your shirt bosom, Press," Grandma told him.

Then Grandpa dug the yellow stains of eggs from the bosom of his shirt with the black ends of his finger nails. Grandpa had to dig and dig to get it off.

"Allus like to put a chaw of burley behind my jaw soon as I finish eatin," Grandpa grunted, "and I like to just let it lay there until dinner. I like the feel of terbacker aginst my jaw. Just love the taste of it."

Soon as he had finished cleanin the stains from his shirt bosom by wettin his index finger in his mouth and rubbin his shirt with spittle until it come clean, he reached into his overall hip pocket and pulled a long-dried burley leaf, crumpled and broken where he'd sat on it, pushed it through his beard into his mouth and lodged it behind his jaw. It was big as a hen's egg behind Grandpa's jaw.

"We'd better be on our way to Greenwood," Grandpa said. "Want to get there while the mornin's cool."

"There's no sign of rain today," Mott said as he looked through the schoolhouse window at the sky. "Mare tails in the sky aint a sign of rain no more. All signs fail in dry weather."

I thought Uncle Mott was right for I could hear the early morning wind rustlin the dry green leaves on the hickory trees. It made a funny sound like rubbin two pieces of glass together. Grandma sat smokin her pipe after she'd finished her last cup of coffee.

"You'd better be on your way, Press," Grandma said with soft words.

I'd never heard Grandma talk like this to Grandpa before. She had always fussed when he went to Greenwood on relief days. Grandpa had often come home stewed to the gills on rotgut whiskey; then he raised a fuss with Grandma or tried to fight Uncle Mott. Never but once did he try to bother me. I thought it was in fun until he pulled his terbacker knife from his pocket and made at me with the blade open. "You damned little woods colt," he yelled, "I'll cut your damned throat." I took to the bushes and slept out all night on the dry leaves. I waited for Grandpa to sober. I knew he'd be all right then; I went back to the rock cliff and he didn't even remember what he had said to me.

"Are you ready, Vittie?" Grandma asked.

"All but my hat," Aunt Vittie told Grandma.

Aunt Vittie got up from the table and went after her hat.

Grandpa got up from the table, spit on the stove; then he stood watchin the ambeer sizzle until it disappeared, leavin a little stained ring on the stove since Grandpa had spit in a place where it wasn't already stained.

"Wait a minute, Press," Grandma said. "You'd forget your head if it was loose."

Grandma got up from her seat and walked over to the corner of the schoolhouse.

"I'll be dogged," Grandpa said with a big laugh, "if I wasn't a-forgettin my relief sack."

"It's tolerable dirty," Grandma said.

Grandma was right too. I remember when the sack was white; but now you couldn't tell what color it was.

Grandma gave Grandpa the sack; then she tiptoed and kissed his beardy mouth. I'd never seen Grandma do this before. I could tell she was as happy as a hen redbird in the spring. When she kissed Grandpa, his dim blue eyes sparkled and he spit on the stove again.

"If they come to put our plunder out today, Arimithy," Grandpa said, "tell 'em we've rented a house and will move into it shortly."

"All right, Press," Grandma said. "Not a stick of the plunder we've got'll be moved. It'll be here when you come back."

Grandpa, Uncle Mott, Aunt Vittie and I started to Greenwood. We walked down the little yellow clay path to the turnpike.

"We want to hotfoot it while the dust is laid," Uncle Mott said as he set a fast pace.

I didn't say anything to Uncle Mott for I was afraid to cross him. But it wasn't the dust that bothered Uncle Mott. I'd seen him take his time and walk in clouds of dust—he'd be the same color as the yellow clay turnpike when he got home. Uncle Mott wanted to get to Greenwood to get to the beer jint. I could tell Uncle Mott was wantin a drink.

From the schoolhouse to Greenwood it was seven miles.

"It's a fur piece to haf to walk after your grub," Grandpa said. "If a man votes for it, b-gad, they ought to deliver it to his door."

"You're right, Pap," Uncle Mott said as he pulled his bandanna from his hip pocket and wiped the sweat from his long red neck.

"But it won't be this way long," Grandpa said. "We'll soon be livin like other people."

"Only a hell of a lot better," Uncle Mott said with a nod.

"We'll look down on some of the polecats that've looked down on the Tussies," Grandpa said. "People have called us a breed of cats and a lot of stuff like that. They won't be a-callin us that long."

"You've got the papers, aint ye, Vittie?" Uncle Mott asked Aunt Vittie.

"I sure have," Aunt Vittie said.

To our left as we climbed the Crump Hill, we saw Snider and Pratt Crump workin and suckerin their terbacker. They straightened their backs, looked at us with mean eyes from their rows of shoulder-high terbacker.

"It's a fragrant weed," Grandpa said, pointin to the terbacker, "but damned if I'd like to bend my back in one of them long rows. Wouldn't suit me to look at the ground all day and pull big juicy green terbacker worms in two. It would sorta turn my stummick too. I like to chaw it, smoke it and have snuffed it. It's a wonderful fragrant weed."

Uncle Mott pulled a pack of Bull Durham from his shirt pocket and rolled a chicken-billed cigarette as he walked along. He pulled a match from his hatband, where he kept his matches to keep them dry, struck the match on his shoe, and with cupped hands around the flame to keep the wind from fannin it out, he stuck the fire to his cigarette and puffed a small cloud of smoke.

"Did you notice the look them polecats give me?" Uncle Mott asked me.

"I thought they's a-lookin awful hard at us about somethin," Grandpa said.

"They tried to get me to help 'em in their terbacker," Uncle Mott said. "I told 'em 'nothin a-shakin.' Told 'em I wouldn't work for two bucks a day!"

"They even tried to get me to help 'em," Grandpa said. "I told 'em I wasn't a-goin to lose what I's a-gettin. Told 'em I's too old to work and was pensioned."

Grandpa laughed a wild laugh, spreadin his mouth so wide I could see a few terbacker-stained teeth with spaces between them in his mouth. Then Grandpa slapped his overall knees with his long skinny hands. It was always a lot of fun to walk to Greenwood with Grandpa and Uncle Mott. They always laughed and talked about people workin. They had a good time a-goin places together until they got tanked on rotgut and fursed with one another. Sometimes they tried to fight.

Grandpa would tell Uncle Mott he was the best man and Uncle Mott would tell Grandpa he was the best man and they kept on this sort of jourin until they struck each other. I always liked to be with them when they didn't have rotgut in 'em; when they got full of rotgut, I was afraid of 'em. I hated to see them bloody one another's noses.

We passed the clean cornfields along the county road. I liked the smell of wilted corn; I liked to hear the wind rustle in the corn blades. And I thought that I would like to plow corn, to hoe corn, to raise it. It looked so pretty in tall straight rows with tassels a-noddin to one another. Every time we passed a cornfield, I whiffed the wind from it into my nostrils. I never liked the stare men gave us as we walked home a-past these cornfields with our sacks of relief grub on our backs. Men and boys looked at us with hard mean eyes. They never bothered about speakin to us. Many times I heard 'em a-cussin somethin; maybe it was their mules 'r their hoes. I didn't stop to listen but hurried toward home.

It was nine o'clock when we reached Greenwood. There was a little yellow dust on Aunt Vittie's hat. She pulled it from her head and brushed it with her hand. Uncle Mott dusted his loose pant legs, rolled him another cigarette. Grandpa shifted his terbacker from one jaw to the other.

"I'd better go to the post office first," Grandpa said. "Our checks are there."

We waited on the outside while Grandpa went into the post office. He came out a-wavin a long gray envelope. There was a big smile on Grandpa's face as he ripped the end from the envelope, poked his thumb and long index finger into the envelope and pulled out his check.

"Get it cashed now, Pap," Uncle Mott said.

"B-gad." Grandpa laughed until some people passin the post office stopped on the street, looked at Grandpa and started laughin.

"Get it cashed, Pap," Uncle Mott asked him. "I don't like to ask you twice."

"B-gad," Grandpa laughed again, "I know what Mott wants!"

We went to the bank with Grandpa. I watched him hold the tip end of a pencil while the young banker wrote Grandpa's name. Then he had another man, who was standin by, to sign as a witness. The young banker shoved a ten-dollar bill and a one through the little winder in Grandpa's face. Grandpa gave Uncle Mott the one dollar and he put the ten in his overall pocket.

"It's like gettin money from home without workin for it," Grandpa laughed as we trailed out the bank door.

"Bankers aint friendly people," Uncle Mott said. "Did you see the looks on that young devil's face when he had to sign your name for you, Pap?"

"Yep, I saw it," Grandpa said. "I always notice them things. If you'll be with us in about an hour, you'll see a different look on that banker's face. B-gad, he'll have a smile on his face."

Grandpa laughed like a drunk man; but I know he wasn't drunk. He waved his relief sack high into the air with one hand, with the other he played with his fine white corn-silk whiskers.

"But I won't be with you, Pap," Uncle Mott said. "I got some business to tend to down the street."

"Listen, son," Grandpa said without laughin, pointin a tremblin finger at Uncle Mott, "you be damned sure when you leave that beer jint you can hit the street with your hat! We've got a lot of grub to tote home. Heerd we'd get some extra provisions today!"

"I'll be able to hep," Uncle Mott said. "Don't worry about me. I aint no virgin. I've been down this street before."

We watched Uncle Mott go down the street, turn the corner.

"He's gone," Grandpa said. "Couldn't go to the court-house with us. He knows what we're a-goin after. Damned if I couldn't put off drinks on a day like this. I could do it one day—I'd be ashamed of myself if I's Mott!"

I didn't ask Grandpa why he gave Uncle Mott the dollar. Aunt Vittie didn't ask him either. But I knew why he gave 'im the dollar; he did it to keep from havin a furse with Uncle Mott on the Greenwood street. That's where Uncle Mott always asked Grandpa for some of his pension check. He'd get 'im before people and ask 'im. He knew that Grandpa wouldn't refuse 'im then.

We climbed the courthouse steps where there was a tall steel pole with a big flag on it. I looked up at the flag to watch the wind unfold its wrinkles. I watched it flutter in the wind —the broad red and white stripes and the blue corner filled with white stars. Honest, it was a pretty sight but it hurt me to watch it—I thought about the big flag that we'd spread over Uncle Kim's fresh mound of dirt. The flag above this courthouse seemed so much alive blowin in the wind, and the flag that covered Uncle Kim's grave would soon be splattered with rain, tugged at by the wind—it would be a dead flag. It would be dead—dead with Uncle Kim. He had died for the flag and the flag would die over his grave.

"Come on, Sid," Grandpa yelled, "quit a-watchin that flag!" Grandpa and Aunt Vittie were on the top steps ready to go inside the courthouse. I hurried up the steps with blind spots before my eyes where I'd looked up toward the sun to see the great livin flag.

"A lot of people like this newfangled structure," Grandpa said, "but danged if I didn't like the old house better. All the old men did. It had been here since we whopped the British in 1812, I heard a man say. But had to tear it down and give the men work. They put me on that WPA job but they took me off on account of my back. I'd rather have what I got."

Grandpa looked at the smooth walls down a long hallway with doors on each side.

"I guess it's a right pretty courthouse after all," he grumbled, "but it looks too much like a damned goods box to me!"

It was square like a box.

"They even cut the shade trees down around it," Grandpa said, "so a body'd haf to sit in the sun and blink his eyes like a fox when it sees daylight."

We walked to the far end of the courthouse to the last door on our right.

"There's the lawyer to see about our papers," Grandpa said. "I hepped elect 'im."

Aunt Vittie walked in first; we followed her.

"Lawyer Landgraves," Grandpa said to a young man wearin a white shirt, striped tie and glasses, sittin in a big chair behind a smooth polished table with a cigarette in his mouth, "I've brought my daughter-in-law to see you about some important papers. We want to know how to go about gettin some money."

"You're Mr. Tussie, aren't you?" he asked Grandpa.

"Yep, I'm him," Grandpa said with a cackle.

"And this is Mrs. ——?"

"Tussie, too," Grandpa said. "Vittie Tussie. She married my son Kim that was kilt over yander!"

"Too bad he was killed," Lawyer Landgraves said softly.

I thought the reason Mr. Landgraves was so kind to Grandpa that he was wantin the Tussie vote. It was the biggest vote in our county. Every man that ran for office came to see Grandpa since he was the oldest livin Tussie and what he said among the majority of Tussies was law. If a Tussie wanted relief, Grandpa got it for him. If he didn't get it, that Tussie was mad at Grandpa. That's the reason a lot of Tussies came to Uncle Kim's funeral that I didn't expect to see and many came that I'd never seen before. They wanted to get in good with Grandpa. They, too, wanted to get relief. Relief had split the Tussie family miles apart. Our branch of the family was known as the Relief Tussies. Grandpa headed the Relief Tussies and Uncle George, Grandpa's brother, we hadn't seen but had heard a lot about on the other side of the county, was head of the Tussies. He still voted the way his people had voted before him.

"It aint so bad that Kim died," Grandpa said, "since he died a-fightin for the Stars and Stripes. They are back yander on his grave on top of the mountain."

Aunt Vittie looked at Grandpa with tears in her eyes, holdin the paper in her hand. Lawyer Landgraves looked silently at Grandpa, workin his lips like he was tryin to say somethin but the words wouldn't come out.

"It would've been bad," Grandpa said, "if Kim hadn't had enough sense to take a little insurance. What would the little gal a done! She'd a had to a stayed with us and et relief grub 'r got out and got 'er another man!"

Grandpa pointed to Aunt Vittie, who had turned her eyes away from us.

"Let me see your papers, Mrs. Tussie," Lawyer Landgraves said.

Aunt Vittie reached him the paper, turned her face from him, took her handkerchief from her pocketbook and wiped tears from her eyes.

"Poor Kim," Aunt Vittie wept.

"Now, Vittie," Grandpa said, "you want to bear up under the strain."

"But it was the way he come back to me," she wept as if her heart would break. "I never got to see 'im. Kept 'im in that coalhouse!"

"All you have to do to get this money," Lawyer Landgraves said, "is to show your marriage license and have someone with you to identify you as Vittie Tussie."

"I've got my marriage license right here in my pocketbook," she said. "I don't know anybody here in Greenwood."

"I'll go over to the bank with you," Lawyer Landgraves said.

When we reached the bank again, Grandpa had been right

when he said the young banker would be friendly. Lawyer Landgraves whispered to the banker and told him who Aunt Vittie was.

"Oh, yes, Mrs. Tussie," he asked in a friendly way, "what do you want to do with this money?"

"Want to take a hundred dollars with me," Aunt Vittie said. "I want to leave the rest in the bank!"

"That's fine, Mrs. Tussie," he said in a sweet voice. "Do you want it on savins or a checkin account or do you want it on two accounts?"

"Checkin account, Vittie," Grandpa tried to whisper but you could hear him all over the bank.

"Checkin account," Aunt Vittie said.

The young banker counted out a hundred dollars to Aunt Vittie, tens, fives, ones.

"That leaves you nine thousand and nine hundred dollars in the bank," the banker said with a smile as he looked at Aunt Vittie with bright eyes. He gave her a bankbook showin how much she had deposited. We left Lawyer Landgraves a-talkin to the banker. They were whisperin to one another through the little bank winder. I think they were whisperin about Aunt Vittie.

"Will we get relief now, Pa Tussie?" Aunt Vittie asked.

"B-gad, the relief grub is free and we'll get it," Grandpa said. "Just as well have it as the other feller. I wouldn't feel at home unless I got it. Been a-gettin it ten years and I'll get it ten more if I can. That's the way I feel."

Grandpa waved the dirty sack into the air as we went down the street past the courthouse toward the relief office. The street was hot and dusty; swirls of dust followed the few cars that drove by on rationed gasoline. There was a loud boom when a tire blew out on a passin car. The driver pulled into the curb and parked his car.

"If we could buy a car, Vittie, you'd buy one, wouldn't you?" Grandpa asked.

"I've always wanted one," she said. "But it's too late now."

"Yep, it's too late," Grandpa said. "Might get a second-hand one if we could find one with good tires."

"But what about gasoline?" Aunt Vittie asked.

"That's right," Grandpa cackled like a rooster. "Never thought about gasoline."

We crossed the street, turned to our left down the alley by the jailhouse.

"Durned if this street aint got as many people on it anymore," Grandpa said, "as it used to have when we swapped plug hosses here. Don't allow hoss swappin on this street any more. Men come with sacks now instead of ridin their plugs up and down the streets doped with high-life powders with their gray fetlocks polished with black shoe polish—curried, brushed and saddled—men a-ridin their plugs and a-shootin their pistols. Great days I've seen on this old street. Never started shootin until we got tanked on moonshine! We'd leave the town a-ridin our plugs and a-shootin our pistols!"

Men had come to this street with sacks. There were women among the men a-carryin coffee sacks, meal sacks, flour sacks and big baskets. I had never seen as many people before and I had been comin to the relief office with Grandpa ever since I was big enough to tote a sack of apples. It was an army of people; I looked at them as we walked among them to get on the end of the long line from the relief-office door to the end of the street. There were people scattered over the streets a-holdin their empty sacks and baskets talkin and laughin. I couldn't see inside the relief office but it must have been full.

"I remember a few years ago," Grandpa told Aunt Vittie, "when the relief office was over yander in that little house. Look at it now! Look what a house! It's one industry that keeps a-growin right through good times!"

Then Grandpa laughed at the words that he had said.

"Good times," he repeated to himself to hear how the words sounded.

I thought Grandpa was a-thinkin about the money Aunt

Vittie had in her pocketbook and all the money she had in the bank.

It was tiresome to stand in the long line that moved slowly toward the door. My bare feet got hot on the concrete street. The sun came down with all the power it had—tryin to blister our backs. I watched the old men chewin their terbacker and spittin on the streets—laughin, tellin jokes and slappin each other on the shoulders after they'd finished tellin a joke. It would have been wonderful to see these people and to have heard all they said but the concrete burnt my bare feet until I nearly cried. I kept wigglin my toes on the concrete to keep them from roastin. Men swarmed around me that looked like Grandpa. And some of the old women looked like Grandma. Some of the men were afflicted, lame, one-eyed—but they were very few. I saw young strong men with big arms and bull necks. I saw Mort, Enic, Thad, Fiddis, Cy, Bolivar, Add, Wade, Sebie, Sid, Bert and Mule Tussie in the crowd. They were powerful men. I'd seen them carry Uncle Kim in his big black coffin to the top of the mountain where they had dug his grave through the rocks on the mountain top.

It was an hour before we got inside the relief office. But Grandpa had us wait. I wanted to tell Aunt Vittie to go to the store and buy us some store grub so we could find Uncle Mott and go home. But I was afraid to say anything. I didn't like to have my toes burnt by the hot street and wade through so much spittle and step on so many hot ends of cigarettes and cigars on the relief-office floor. I didn't like the quash of terbacker cuds under my bare feet either after I'd thought about the ugly mouths that had spit them out onto the floor, the lean beardy jaws they had been coddled behind and the dark terbacker-stained pokin-stick teeth that had munched them.

"Mr. Tussie," the referral agent at the desk greeted Grandpa with a smile more than any groceryman would smile at a man that had bought a lot of groceries.

"Looks like business is good today," Grandpa said.

"It's a-pickin up every day," she said, laughin, showin two rows of pretty teeth.

Grandpa didn't stop at the referral agent's desk since he already had our card. We had to pass this way to reach the big relief storeroom. Grandpa had our card that listed six people in our family while there were only four. "Relief for two extras takes care of our company," Grandpa said. We walked slowly, in line with the other reliefers, through the big door into the vast storeroom, that was made of corrugated tin with winders on each side and chimneys in the roof to let fresh air in.

"Just a minute, Uncle Press," Gilbert Tussie said. "I'll be right over to hep serve you."

"Take your time, Gilbert," Grandpa cackled, swingin his sack with one hand, rubbin his sweaty beard with the other. "There's a lot of folks ahead of me."

Before Uncle Gilbert Tussie could finish waitin on Eif Patton and get over to us, Tim Snodgrass, who had married my Aunt Belle Tussie, had hurried over to wait on Grandpa. Each had tried to get to Grandpa first and I guess Vic Wampler, who had married one of Grandpa's nieces, would have been there first if he had seen Grandpa. But Uncle Tim Snodgrass had the honor of waitin on us. I'd never been in but a few grocery stores; then I hadn't gone in them to buy anything. We'd always come to the relief office. It was the place where we'd done our tradin. But I'd never seen friendlier clerks than our kinfolks in this relief office. They felt over the apples to find the ones for us without bruised spots. They found us the best cabbage heads—cabbage heads that looked fresh and hadn't any brown spots on them. And we got the best peaches and apricots.

"You're a-goin to have a load, Uncle Press," Uncle Tim told Grandpa as he wiped sweat from his red-bearded face with his sleeve. "Where's Mott? Didn't he come with you?"

"He's in town someplace," Grandpa said. "Don't know whether he'll be able to hep us much with the load back home."

"Too bad about Kim, wasn't it?" Uncle Tim said as he finished fillin Grandpa's sack.

"Not so bad," Grandpa said. "He died a-fightin for his country! I'm proud of Kim. Never amounted to anything until he got in the army!"

"Never looked at it like that," Uncle Tim said, "but I guess you're right, Uncle Press!"

When Uncle Tim agreed with Grandpa, that pleased him. Uncle Tim had better have agreed with Grandpa or he wouldn't have held the job he now had in the relief storeroom. There would have been another one of our kinfolks in his place. And it wasn't so bad after all, for Aunt Vittie had money in her pocketbook and money in the bank. I knew that Grandpa thought of this too. If Uncle Kim hadn't carried insurance, it would have been a terrible thing.

"We have a lot of good things today," Uncle Tim told Grandpa. "I'll get you a sack for Sid and one for Vittie."

"Can you tote a load home, Vittie?" Grandpa asked Aunt Vittie.

"Sure I can," she said.

He didn't ask me; he just loaded it into the sack—all he thought I could carry—and told me to swing it across my shoulder. I had salt pork, raisins, lard, cheese, fresh peaches and pears. I had all I could tote in my sack. It was so full I could hardly get a handhold to hold the sack across my shoulder.

Aunt Vittie had the fresh eggs in a paper sack, cans of milk, beans, oatmeal and dried fruit in a small white sack. Grandpa had a load much as an old mule could carry. Grandpa was too old to carry such a load. Uncle Tim told him he was. He had flour, apples, oranges, cabbage, he had more cans of milk, more cheese—he had his sack loaded until people stood in the warehouse to watch him shoulder his sack. Grandpa grunted a few times and swung the sack onto his shoulder with ease.

"He's more powerful than a mule," I heard an old woman say, who hadn't any front teeth.

"Haf to carry it seven miles, boys," Grandpa bragged.

Everybody looked at us as we left the warehouse. Before we reached the door Grandpa turned to Aunt Vittie and said, "Maybe I'll carry it seven miles. There's more ways to kill a hound than to choke him to death on hot butter."

My load was all I could carry. I didn't think I'd ever go seven miles with it without fallin flat in the middle of the road under the broilin sun. I wondered where Uncle Mott could be? Why wasn't he here to help us? He would be there when Grandma and Aunt Vittie served it on the table. I didn't think Aunt Vittie would get very far with her load for she wasn't as big as the other Tussie women. She had small bird legs, small arms and small hands. And her face didn't have much color. But her marriage to Uncle Kim had tied her to us. That's why she wouldn't quarrel with Grandpa or Grandma. She'd do about anything they told her to do.

We walked past the jailhouse where the men stuck their hot beardy faces up against the iron bars and yelled at us. Asked us up to see them. They yelled at Aunt Vittie and told her she was "good-lookin." But we didn't answer them. We kept on walkin under our heavy loads up the dusty street.

"There's a lot of people worse off than we are," Grandpa said, soon as we had passed the jail. "I'll tell you that jail is hot in July. It doesn't pay you to fool with moonshine when you can git something like this. It doesn't pay to run the risk."

"But this is not the street that leads us to the turnpike," I said.

"Now you never mind," Grandpa said. "Follow me."

We followed him. I was at his heels. Aunt Vittie walked next to me. We crossed Main Street where the farmers come to town and park their cars when they trade at the grocery stores.

"There's Alvin Pennington's car," Grandpa said. "Come on. Let's lay our loads in!"

"Won't he care, Grandpa?" I asked.

"No, he hides out to dodge me, but I find 'im," Grandpa said. "I just thought he'd put his car about here on relief day. It won't be all the loads of relief he'll haf to haul."

When Alvin Pennington laid by his corn, he got a job on the state highway. He drove his car to town—to the state garage—then he drove a dump truck out on the state highway and came back to town and picked up his car and drove it home. Grandpa had managed to catch 'im several times.

"This is what I call good luck," Grandpa roared as he opened the unlocked door and threw his load upon the back seat. I laid my load beside Grandpa's for I was glad to get it off my shoulder. Aunt Vittie laid her load inside the car and wiped the sweat from her pale face with her handkerchief. But the heat had flushed Aunt Vittie's cheeks pale pink, the color of early wild-plum petals.

"We've kilt a lot of time in here today," Grandpa said, "but we'll go home tonight with the bacon!"

"Reckon Alvin won't care to haul us and our loads?" Aunt Vittie asked Grandpa.

"Shucks, no," Grandpa said. "He can't complain. He can't grumble. Look what he makes from the state! He's on the gravy train!"

We waited until Alvin Pennington came to his car. He was a short red-faced man, wearin overalls, a overall jumper, pin-striped cap and brogan shoes. He was a-wheezin hard on his pipe when he walked up to the car.

"We're a-waitin on you, Alvin," Grandpa chuckled, tryin to be friendly.

"I see you are," Alvin said. He pertended to be friendly

but his smile soon disappeared from his face. "Get in and we'll be a-goin."

"See, I told you," Grandpa said, nudgin me with his elbow.

Grandpa got in the front seat with Alvin; I got in the back seat with Aunt Vittie. We sat on the back seat but there wasn't room for our feet so we put them on the sacks. We were off over the dusty turnpike toward home. I talked to Aunt Vittie. She never talked very much; she was almost as silent as a terrapin. But she'd always talk to me more than she would any of the Tussies. Grandpa rattled like a dry fodder blade on a cornstalk in the December wind to Alvin Pennington. He told him how he had hepped to keep Alvin's party in power so that Alvin would have a job on the state highway and make him a few dollars each year after crops were laid by. Alvin Pennington agreed with him and once or twice slapped Grandpa on the shoulder with one hand and told him he was a fine man. That pleased Grandpa and it made Aunt Vittie and me feel good. Not many people said kind things about my Grandpa. Just part of his own people did. Part of them called him bad names when they met him on the turnpike.

We passed men leavin their cornfields and terbacker fields. They looked tired, dirty and sweaty. Many we passed staggerin on the turnpike with full sacks of relief grub over their shoulders. I know that's what they had in their sacks because I'd seen them gettin them filled at the storeroom. Many of the men were staggerin under these loads—not from the weight of them, for Uncle Tim didn't fill their sacks like he had filled ours. They had sold their fresh eggs for less than the grocery stores sold them and they'd bought beer or rotgut. They could get rotgut anyplace on relief day, hoss-sale days and Saturdays. I'd heard Grandpa say many times that he had counted as many as twenty-eight bootleggers in town on these days.

I kept lookin out to see if I could see Uncle Mott. I thought he may be with some of this crowd. Every time we passed a crowd I looked them over but Grandpa didn't look for Uncle Mott. I guess he thought he'd lived a long time, that he had managed to take care of his own self and Uncle Mott could do the same. Maybe Grandpa thought if Uncle Mott was tanked he couldn't do anything with him anyway. Uncle Mott would try to start a fight with him if he could get Alvin Pennington to stop the car to pick him up. We just rolled along and passed everybody up until we were nearly to the schoolhouse. There was Uncle Mott plain for us to see in front of the car, pitchin headlong into the dust, gettin up again and takin in both sides of the turnpike. We passed him up, got our sacks out so fast that we forgot to thank Alvin Pennington for the ride. We wanted to beat Uncle Mott home so we wouldn't have trouble with 'im.

CHAPTER IV

W HILE Uncle Mott laid flat on the schoolhouse floor and
snored in his drunken sleep, Aunt Vittie showed Grandma the hundred dollars she had in her purse.

"Let me have my hands on a hundred dollars once in my lifetime, honey," Grandma said to Aunt Vittie.

Grandma fondled the money like I thought she'd fondled Uncle Mott when he was a baby.

"Kim money," she called it, feelin of it like it was silk. "It's Kim money, honey!"

Grandma was pleased to look at this money and to feel of it. She took each bill separately and looked at it.

"It's a pile of money, Press," she said, turnin to Grandpa.

"I'll say it is," Grandpa said, laughin a wild laugh.

"It means we'll leave the schoolhouse, won't it, honey?" she asked Aunt Vittie, lookin her straight in the eye with her cold blue eyes that were surrounded by dark wrinkled skin.

"Yes," Aunt Vittie said.

"Wonderful," Grandma said.

Grandpa put a new leaf of burley behind his beardy jaw.

"Money's like manna from heaven," Grandma said. "I've always dreamed of findin a pot of gold where a shootin star fell. Pap ust to tell us gold was there. I've dug with a mattock but I never found it, honey. This is the pot of gold that I've always looked for!"

Grandpa spit on the stove and laughed.

"That's one thing you won't do when we get moved into a big new-painted house," Grandma said.

"What do ye mean?" Grandpa asked.

"A-spittin on the stove!"

"Ah, shucks," Grandpa said. "I like to hear spit sizzle."

"But I don't like the stain of spit on a stove," Grandma said. "Why don't you smoke like I do?"

"Love the taste," Grandpa said. "Smoke aint got enough taste for me."

Then Grandpa laughed until Aunt Vittie started laughin.

"Where can we find a big house with paint on it among these hills?" Grandpa asked.

"I've already got the house picked out," Grandma said.

"Where?"

Aunt Vittie looked at Grandma.

"That big Rayburn house about three miles this side of town," Grandma said. "I've always wanted to live in that house!"

"So it's that big hotel," Grandpa said. "Enough room in it for ten families."

"But it's a pretty house," Grandma said. "It is painted white with green trimmins and it's even got a green shingled roof!"

"It will cost something to rent that house," Grandpa said. "Doubt that George Rayburn would let clodhoppers like us have it."

"He'll rent it for fifty dollars a month," Grandma said.

"But they'll stop my relief," Grandpa said. "I'm not able to work!"

"Vittie will be a-rentin the house," Grandma said.

"Oh, I see," Grandpa said, slappin his big hands together.

"Don't you think that's the kind of a house we want?" Grandma asked Aunt Vittie. "You know it'll be our Kim money that's a-payin the rent."

"It will be better than this schoolhouse," Aunt Vittie said. "Sheriff Whiteapple won't be after us there!"

"He won't have the pleasure o' settin our house plunder out in the school yard," Grandma chuckled. "We'll beat 'im to it!"

"That's the right place to move," Grandpa said suddenly as if the thought had just come to him.

I thought it had just dawned on Grandpa how much closer to town he would be. And I knew Uncle Mott would want us to rent the house—that is, if he had been sober enough to've told us. It would be close to town for Uncle Mott. He could go to town every day. Grandpa could go to town every day.

"Will you go rent the house tomorrow, Press?" Grandma asked.

"Daylight will find me on my way to see George Rayburn in the mornin," he answered Grandma.

That night while Uncle Mott snored on the schoolhouse floor, makin funny noises and tryin to fight a man named Bill, I couldn't go to sleep. Grandpa's snores would go up high and come down with a wheezin noise like a wind-broken horse makes. And Grandma laughed a lot in her sleep. I think Aunt Vittie was too tired to make any noise. But Uncle Mott was the one that kept me awake. "Goddamn you, Bill," he'd say, "I'll cut yer goddamned throat with my knife. You gypped me, Bill. You took more than your part of the bottle. You leave me a-wantin a drink, Bill. Goddamn you, if I could just lay my hands on you, I'd fix you!"

I laid in bed and thought of the new house we would rent. It was a big house. I'd seen it so many times walkin from town with a sack of relief grub over my shoulder. I'd stagger along under my load with sunspots before my eyes in the summertime, with the icy winds of winter tryin to dry the sweat on my face in the wintertime. And I'd look toward this house and wonder what rich people lived in it. I'd wonder about the kind of grub they ate and if they had a white table-cloth on their table or an oilcloth or if they didn't have no cloth at all. But I knew they didn't eat from a teacher's desk in a schoolhouse or a big flat rock under a rock cliff. I wondered what it would be like to be somebody and live in a big house like the George Rayburn house, for it was the biggest house on the turnpike to town. It was the house that I'd always wanted to see inside; I'd never dreamed that I'd ever be a-livin in this mansion.

I rolled and tossed on the bed. I couldn't sleep. Grandpa's and Grandma's snores didn't bother me. I knew Grandma must be a-havin pleasant dreams 'r she wouldn't laugh so much in her sleep. And maybe she was dreamin about the house, I thought, that I was a-thinkin about. But Uncle Mott's vile oaths made my blood run warm. He was a-rollin on the floor a-cussin Bill. I didn't know whether it was these things that kept me awake or the big supper that I had eaten of the good relief grub that Grandma had prepared for us. It was somethin that kept me wide awake and almost made me cry.

I heard the wind in the dry-leafed hickories around the schoolhouse that would soon shade the school children again. Their slitherin sounds against the wind like rubbin two pieces of glass together bothered me. Their sounds made me think of Kim and why we were a-movin from the schoolhouse. We'd get the jump on Sheriff Whiteapple. He wouldn't have the pleasure of throwin our house plunder outten the schoolhouse. I laid on the bed and thought these crazy thoughts. Then I started thinkin about Uncle Kim and how we had carried him from the coalhouse to the mountain top on that hot day. It was the money that we'd got from Uncle Kim that was a-takin us to this mansion. It may not have been a mansion to some people but it was to me. And it was a mansion to Grandpa and Grandma.

"Kim money," I thought as I rolled over in bed and put my hands over my ears to shut out the vile curses a-comin from Uncle Mott's lips and the sound of the July winds among the dry hickory leaves. They made me think of Uncle Kim. They made me think of the lonesome mountain that we carried him up on and all the lonesome songs that we sang as we sweated up the mountain where the gray lizards scurried over the dry leaves. It was the money from Uncle Kim's blood and dust. It was a bullet—just a little bullet through Uncle Kim's brain or through his heart that was a-puttin us in this mansion. I thought about Uncle Kim. I didn't want to think about him but I couldn't help it.

I thought about the days when I used to walk across the mountain from Grandpa's rock cliff to the two-room shack where Uncle Kim and Aunt Vittie lived. I'd want to talk to Uncle Kim but he never had much use for me. I don't know why. Once he grabbed my shoulder with his big hand and almost pushed his fingernails into my skin. "You damned little devil," he said, "I don't like you and I never will. I'd like to claw a handful of meat from your shoulder."

Aunt Vittie made him let go and shamed him. "Kim," she said, "aint you ashamed of doin Sid like that?" Uncle Kim didn't say anything. He looked at me with mean eyes and walked away.

No matter what Uncle Kim did to me I liked him. He was big and rough with a face the color of an October leaf after the frost had hit it. He had big hands and big fence-post arms. And he cussed and shot his pistols around the house. He'd shoot at the crows as they flew over the shack and he'd shoot redbirds, bee martins 'r any kind of birds on the wing or alighted in trees. And he'd laugh when he saw one fall. That was Uncle Kim. He loved to kill. He'd go to the woods and hunt the year around. There was no huntin season for Uncle Kim. He kept wild meat on the table all the time. That was about the only kind of meat Aunt Vittie and Uncle Kim had on their table.

Aunt Vittie was afraid of Uncle Kim but she loved him. I think she was afraid when he'd go to bed with her and sleep with two pistols under his pillow every night. And when people would come from town and try to collect money that Uncle Kim owed them, she was afraid that he would shoot them, for he'd run from the house to the hills and shoot back over the house. The men that had come to collect money from

Uncle Kim would leave almost as fast as they'd come. Then Uncle Kim would come back to the house a-laughin. Uncle Kim was so alive then, so big and strong, and his hawk-gray eyes could almost look holes through you. I'd never seen a man like him. He was a man you couldn't forget in life and now it was hard for me to forget him in death. I couldn't keep from thinkin about holdin a man like 'im in a big black box. I just wondered if a coffin could hold Uncle Kim. I wondered if the mountain could hold him forever.

Grandpa had gone to see about the George Rayburn house before I got outten bed. Grandma had got him up, got his breakfast and had sent him in a hurry. Grandma was gettin around the schoolhouse much faster than Aunt Vittie. Grandma was young again. Uncle Mott was at the desk a-drinkin coffee when I washed my face and sat down for breakfast. Uncle Mott's eyes were bloodshot—little red streaks not as big-lookin as thread crossed and crisscrossed his blue eyeballs. He didn't even say good mornin to me when I sat down.

"Cheer up, Mott," Grandma said, "we'll be a-goin to our new home tomorrow."

"That's right, Mott," Aunt Vittie said.

"I'll be glad to leave here," Uncle Mott said. "I'm tired of this damned schoolhouse. I'm tireder of it than I was that rock cliff on the McCallister place! This schoolhouse is the closest to eddication that I've ever come!"

Then Uncle Mott blew his breath on his coffee to cool it. He looked at Aunt Vittie and smiled. I'd never seen Uncle Mott look at many people and smile before. I remember how, two years ago, he cussed more than he had cussed last night, when Grandma told him that she was a-goin to bring Aunt Vittie to live with us since Uncle Sam had taken Uncle Kim. Uncle Mott didn't want her to come and Grandma told Uncle Mott that sometimes when you did a kind deed for a person you'd be paid twentyfold.

Now Uncle Mott was a-smilin at Aunt Vittie.

"More coffee, Vittie," Uncle Mott said.

Aunt Vittie brought the coffee biler from the stove and poured hot black coffee into Uncle Mott's cup. Then Uncle Mott looked at her and smiled again. And Grandma stopped and looked at Aunt Vittie and Uncle Mott. But Grandma wasn't pleased the way they smiled at each other.

Before I'd finished my breakfast of salt pork and fresh fried eggs, Grandpa bolted inside the schoolhouse, his big umbrella hat in one hand fannin his hot beardy face. With the other hand thrust before him, he sliced the wind as he talked.

"Th' George Rayburn house is rented, b-gad," Grandpa said with a cackle. "I've hurried there and back and I'm hot as a roasted tater!"

"You've made a quick trip, Press," Grandma said.

"Just as you said, Arimithy," Grandpa said. "He wouldn't talk no business until I showed 'im the money! Had to pay 'im a month in advance. Th' money talked instead of me. I told 'im it was my daughter-in-law a-rentin the house. Told 'im about Kim. He said we could move in any time!"

"Glory! Glory!" Grandma shouted.

"What do you think about it, Uncle Mott?" I asked.

"It's the very thing to do," Uncle Mott said. "I'll tell you I'm pleased."

"Yep, I've closed the deal," Grandpa told Grandma. "Fifty dollars closed it."

"That means Vittie and I will haf to go to Barton's furniture store in Greenwood and buy new furniture," Grandma said. "I aint a-takin any of this old plunder to that fine mansion!"

Grandma and Aunt Vittie left the schoolhouse in a hurry for town. Grandpa sat on a seat and fanned his beardy face with his umbrella hat. With one hand he fondled his sweaty beard. He rubbed his beard together; then he pulled wisps of it apart after it had stuck together. Uncle Mott didn't do anything but roll cigarettes and smoke them. Through the long hours of waitin for Aunt Vittie and Grandma to get back, Uncle Mott took a dirty deck of cards from his hip pocket and beat old Sol. He cheated Sol to beat 'im.

It was after four o'clock when Aunt Vittie and Grandma came strealin up the turnpike from town, covered with yellow dust. Dust had settled on their faces and necks where they had sweated; grains of yellow dust sparkled around the roots of their hair above their foreheads and on the backs of their necks. Grandpa laughed when he saw them; Uncle Mott didn't laugh until Aunt Vittie pulled her little hat from the top of her head and brushed the yellow dust from the wisp of red roses.

"Uh-uh, Vittie," Uncle Mott said, "you got your roses dirty!"

Then Uncle Mott looked at Aunt Vittie and smiled and smiled. He wanted to say something kind and sweet to her so he joked her about the dust on her roses. Grandma didn't do much brushin. She just let the dust stick to her. Grandma was tired but she was happy. She kissed Grandpa again; and I thought Uncle Mott was a-goin to kiss Aunt Vittie. He stood up close to her and he smiled at her but Aunt Vittie didn't smile at him.

"Got my roses dirty," Aunt Vittie told Uncle Mott, "but Ma Tussie and I got a lot of pretty furniture!"

"Lord, but I can't believe all this," Uncle Mott said. "It seems like a dream to me that we're a-goin to move into a mansion and be somebody!"

"No more of this old house plunder," Grandma said. "I'm so tired a-lookin at it nohow!"

"Everything new-fangdangled," Grandpa said. "B-gad, I aint so sure that I'll like it. Won't have no place to spit!"

"Yes, you will," Grandma said. "We bought you some flowered spittoons!"

"Oh, you did," Grandpa cackled.

"Furniture will be hauled to our new house in the mornin," Aunt Vittie said.

"Did it cost a lot?" Uncle Mott asked.

"A big slice of money," Aunt Vittie said. "When you buy good furniture to furnish sixteen rooms it amounts to big money."

Uncle Mott didn't even seem pleased. It was Aunt Vittie's money, I thought, and she had the right to spend it as she pleased. It wasn't anything to Uncle Mott how she spent her money. Grandpa and Grandma had been tellin her how to spend it and they were enough. Uncle Mott, I thought, wanted Aunt Vittie's money, the way the frown came over his brown face after Aunt Vittie said the new furniture had cost big money.

Grandpa, Aunt Vittie, Uncle Mott and I carried the big three-cornered cupboard from the schoolhouse corner out into the school yard. Uncle Mott went to the coalhouse and brought back the dull double-bitted ax. Uncle Mott swung it over his shoulder a few times until he'd busted the walnut boards in the cupboard to pieces.

"We'll have a rip-roarin fire tonight," Grandpa laughed, "and we won't be burnin the county school system's coal either!"

Grandpa gathered him a load of the cupboard kindling into his arms and carried it back into the schoolhouse.

"Don't see no use a-carryin this old furniture out in the yard to bust it up for kindlin," Grandpa said. "Haf to carry it right back in the house."

"You're right, Press," Grandma said.

Uncle Mott brought the ax into the schoolhouse. He knocked the beds down after Grandma and Aunt Vittie had taken the shuck ticks offen 'em. He busted 'em to pieces on the schoolhouse floor. He had a time a-choppin the ropes apart that corded the bed to hold the ticks. Uncle Mott cussed and sweated but he stayed with the job until he had it finished.

"We've moved this old plunder around until it's got the rickets," Grandma said. "Thank God we won't haf to move it again. It's too old to move nohow!"

I remember that Grandma had said once that her mother had given her the cupboard and that Grandpa's mother had given them the two beds when they went to housekeepin. And I guess it was time they were a-doing something with it since Grandma was tired of it. She'd used it all her life—had raised a family of fourteen with it. It was ready for the ax if age makes anything old and ripe enough for the ax.

"I want everything destroyed before we leave here in the mornin," Grandma said.

That night we burned the cupboard and bedstead kindlin in the stove and cooked our suppers. It burned like powder. Just a flash and an armload of it was gone. Just had to keep fillin the stove. After supper we slept on our shuck bed ticks on the schoolhouse floor. The floor was a leetle dirty but that didn't matter. Next mornin we'd burn the bed ticks anyway.

We worked by the light of an oil lamp next mornin a-carryin bed ticks, dirty quilts, sheets, pillowcases, old clothes, and odds and ends of house plunder out into the school yard where Grandpa struck a match to the heap. Then we worked by the light of this big fire that lighted up the schoolhouse winders and made the schoolhouse bright as day.

"Shucks," Grandma said, "I wouldn't wash them old dirty clothes and patch 'em for all they're worth!"

"I fired that heap o' junk while there's dew on the grass," Grandpa said. "Don't want fire to get out and burn this schoolhouse."

By the light of the great fire, Uncle Mott and I carried broken dishes, cracked dishes, stained dishes, pots, pans, a coffeepot and kettles down to the edge of the school yard and threw them into a gulley.

"School youngins'll dig 'em out," Uncle Mott said, "and

make playhouses outten 'em. They'll do somebody some good!"

We carried out so much old junk, I wondered what we'd have left. I didn't think we'd haf to carry anything to our new house. That mornin we'd put on our best clothes and we'd carried out all our old clothes and piled them with the bedclothes, shuck ticks, quilts and sheets. We wouldn't have any clothes to take, only what we had on our backs. But soon as we'd finished carryin the junk outten the house, I found out what we had to take. Grandpa had all our relief grub sacked. He had it sacked in the same sacks that Uncle Tim had sacked it in. And we had the same sacks to carry.

"We must take something for our stummicks," Grandpa said. "And I must take my sack of dry burley."

Grandma had saved a few pictures of men with beardy faces and old women with wrinkled faces. They were some of our kinfolks but I didn't know them. They had lived before my time. She had saved a few dishes. Grandma took the pictures and dishes. Uncle Mott had a load of guns and huntin knives. Aunt Vittie had her relief grub and a picture of Uncle Kim. I had all the relief grub that I could carry. It was good daylight when we were ready to go. This was the earliest that I could ever remember of our gettin outten bed.

We didn't bother to sweep the schoolhouse floor before we left. We'd even burnt our old stub of a broom. The schoolhouse looked like a pigpen floor. And we'd never bothered to put the schoolhouse seats back in order. We left them torn up just like we'd torn them up to get plenty of livin quarters in the schoolhouse. But we left the big pot-bellied stove in the corner of the schoolhouse just like we had found it only it had more terbacker-spittle stains on it than any stove I'd ever seen. Grandpa had had a good time spittin on the stove when it was hot, to hear his ambeer sizzle. I would have hated to have been the one to scrub this stove. And we left the coalhouse empty.

When we left, the big junk heap was a pile of thin warm ashes on the school yard with a tiny stream of smoke risin from the ashes toward the sky. The sun wasn't up and the mornin wind hadn't risen to stir the dry hickory leaves around the schoolhouse. The sound the wind made in these leaves always made me want to cry. I was glad to leave these sounds. I was glad to be away from this place and I didn't mind a-carryin a load big enough for a mule colt to carry to get away.

"It's a good time to go," Grandpa said. "I like to walk when the dew has laid the dust. It don't get into a body's whiskers and keep eachin 'im all day!"

We hotfooted it down the road, prayin silently for a ride, swayin under our loads. We were a-goin to our new mansion. We didn't look like people that had money in the bank. We didn't look like people that were movin into a sixteen-room house.

CHAPTER V

WE REACHED the house an hour before the first truck-load of furniture came. Grandma and Aunt Vittie had the truck driver and his helper to help Uncle Mott and Grandpa carry the furniture into the rooms where they wanted it. It was pretty new furniture—clean and bright—the like of fine furniture Grandpa, Grandma, Aunt Vittie, Uncle Mott and I had never seen before. Grandpa complained with his back but he nearly had to work. I thought he could surely help carry the furniture into the house after Aunt Vittie had bought it and was a-payin the house rent. I could tell Uncle Mott wasn't pleased to be caught in a trap and haf to work.

All day we carried new furniture into the rooms and placed it where Grandma and Aunt Vittie wanted it. We unrolled big flowered rugs and spread them over the floors. The house was clean as a pin, the floors were varnished, the walls were papered with a pretty flowered wallpaper. I had never seen a house like it. There was even a privy inside the house. We wouldn't haf to go to the brush like we did around the schoolhouse. It's all right to go to the brush except on dark nights, winter nights and rainy nights. Then one has to take a lantern and the folks back in the house can watch your lantern and see just where you are a-goin. And when you sit down, if you don't blow your lantern out they can watch you. And if you blow your lantern out, you can't get it lit again for the wind a-blowin your matches out or the rain a-puttin 'em out. This would be a handy thing. No more watchin me and laughin; the game we used to play on one another at the schoolhouse when one of us had to take a lantern and run.

All day we worked harder than we had ever worked. Grandpa and Uncle Mott had wet their shirt collars with sweat. It was about to kill Uncle Mott and Grandpa. But they got a rest when we ate a bite of dinner that Aunt Vittie hastily prepared for us. All day the truck driver rolled the furniture to us and helped us carry it into the house. I could tell that it had cost a big slice of money: new beds, new bedclothes already made, mattresses with springs in the middle of them, dressers, tables, stand tables, chairs, rockin chairs with brown leather backs, new dishes, new pots, new pans and kettles. I'd never seen anything like this. Aunt Vittie had told the man at the furniture store she wanted him to furnish the house for her. And that's what he'd done. I wondered if he hadn't sold her too much. But I don't guess he did, for we put it in the sixteen rooms and they weren't too crowded. It was too much furniture for five people.

At the end of the day, long after the last truck had come and gone, we were sittin around in the new chairs in the front room a-feelin of the new leather and whiffin the good smell of it into our nostrils. Uncle Mott reached over on the wall and fooled with a little thingamygig and a big yellow light came on over my head.

"My God," Mott said.

"Yep, we got lights too," Grandma laughed. "No more old oil lamps. Didn't you know that, Mott?"

"No, Ma, I didn't," Uncle Mott said.

Uncle Mott sat with his legs across the big rockin-chair arm and played with the light like it was a toy. He flipped it on and off and laughed while he did it. Grandpa got so tickled at the light that he missed one of the flowered spittoons and spit on the soft flowered carpet. Aunt Vittie ran out and brought a cloth and wiped it up.

"Don't bother about doin that, Vittie," Grandpa said. "It'll get dirty anyhow!"

"Oh, I don't mind, Pa Tussie," Aunt Vittie said.

"But I don't want ye a-cleanin spit up for me after all ye've given us," Grandpa said as he watched Uncle Mott play with the light.

That night I went to the inside privy first. And after I'd finished I didn't know what to do until I pulled a little lever; then there was a great roar and water flushed the place clean— the great roar of water inside a house. Then I went to a room that was all my own—a room where I was to stay—and Aunt Vittie had a room of her own and Uncle Mott had a room of his own. Grandpa and Grandma had a room of their own. And the big beds with mattresses that had springs in the middle of them were soft to sleep on. It was wonderful for me to put my naked body between these cool clean sheets. It was a great feelin and I loved it. When I first climbed be- tween these sheets I couldn't go to sleep for thinkin about the privy inside the house.

I wondered what we'd do for something to laugh at on moonless nights when one of us used to take a lantern and go. We'd even watched Grandpa and Grandma. They were part of the fun too—especially Grandpa. And he'd never blow out the lantern on a windy, rainy or cold night or any other night. He'd keep it lit all the way. Grandpa wouldn't bother to blow it out so he could sit in the dark in a patch of brush on the school yard—sometimes he wouldn't get to the brush; I guess it was too much trouble for Grandpa and besides he didn't mind. It pleased Grandpa to hear us laugh at him from the schoolhouse. But Grandma always got mad. She'd come back to the schoolhouse mad as a hornet and call us a lot of foul names. When she got mad she could say a lot of foul names that I had never heard before.

Now I laid in bed—a clean new bed for the first time in my life—and I couldn't go to sleep. It was worse than hearin the wind among the hickory leaves. My brain was so excited over these new things and our livin in this big house that I couldn't sleep. I wondered if it was a dream that I was dreamin or if it had happened. And I'd think about Uncle Kim and Aunt Vittie. I'd think about the shack they used to live in and wondered, if Uncle Kim was alive now and a-livin in this

house, if he'd enjoy it. Then I'd think that he wouldn't for he wouldn't have as much brush around this house and as many broom-sage fields for huntin ground. He wouldn't have as many places to shoot his pistols. I'd first think that Uncle Kim would like the inside privy, the water and the lights. Then I'd think there would be so many things that he wouldn't like that he wouldn't be satisfied in a house like this.

Then I thought our clothes didn't go with this house and relief grub didn't go with it. And I wondered what Aunt Vittie and Grandma would do about our clothes. I wondered if they wouldn't dress us in new clothes from head to foot and if I wouldn't get shoes to wear the comin fall and winter like other boys wore. I wondered if I'd haf to wear brogans like I'd done every winter since I could remember. Now I wondered if Grandma and Aunt Vittie wouldn't buy me new shoes and new clothes. I'd never had a suit of clothes in my life. I wondered if I'd get all these things from the blood and dust of Uncle Kim.

And before I could close my eyes in sleep, I wondered if this good life would go on forever. And if something happened to it how hard it would be to go back to the old life after a taste of this kind of life. I wondered why Uncle Mott smiled so pleasantly when he spoke to Aunt Vittie. He couldn't have love in his mind when Aunt Vittie was his dead brother's wife. I wondered if he wanted money from Aunt Vittie to buy beer. He had never been so kind to her before. I wondered about these things as I slipped into the darkness of sleep.

CHAPTER VI

W HEN I awoke my first mornin in the new house, I couldn't believe that I was Sid Tussie. I thought I was somebody else. I thought I was one of the boys that I had seen in town drivin a big car. But I looked in the lookin glass and I was myself all right. I could tell by the long hair on my head. I could tell by the old clothes I had to put on in this new house. I was the same Sid Tussie that had lived in the schoolhouse. I was just in a different shell. I was in a white shell that had green trimmins—a big undreamed-of shell with lights and water and a privy inside—a shell where a person could live winter and summer and never get out unless he wanted to go.

I went to the privy and turned on hot and cold water and washed my face. I looked in the lookin glass on the wall and combed my hair. I looked a lot better to go down to breakfast. Then I looked at myself several times before I went downstairs. It was hard for me to find the "dinin room" but I heard a lot of fussin. I heard Grandpa swearin at Grandma, then I knew that I was a-goin in the right direction.

"These clothes are good enough for me," Grandpa said. "B-gad if I'll be cornswaggled into anything more."

"Not for this house," Grandma said.

"I've seen a lot of men wear old clothes and live in fine houses," Grandpa said. "Have seen 'em do it right in town. Look at Jedge Whittlecomb!"

"I'll leave it to Vittie," Grandma said.

"Do I need new clothes, Vittie?" Grandpa asked.

"Yes, you do, Pa Tussie," Aunt Vittie said.

"Then I'll get new clothes," Grandpa said.

Then Uncle Mott, Aunt Vittie and Grandma laughed.

"I need new clothes too," I said as I entered the dinin room.

Uncle Mott, Aunt Vittie, Grandpa and Grandma were a-sittin around the breakfast table.

"Your old jumper sleeves will dirty the white tablecloth," Grandma said. "You aint a-eatin offen a teacher's desk this mornin."

"It's wonderful to live in a house like this," Grandpa said, "but I'll be damned if the McCallister rock cliff didn't have its advantages for a man. I may want to go back to it someday. I may get fed up with this rich livin. I don't know whether a mansion is a place for a reliefer or not."

Then Grandpa laughed, pulled a dry leaf of burley from his overall pocket and crammed it behind his beardy jaw.

"Be sure you don't spit on this floor," Grandma said.

"I'll be careful as I know how to be," Grandpa said.

Uncle Mott rolled him a cigarette and Grandma lit her pipe. This was what they had always done after they'd finished breakfast. This was one thing that hadn't changed. It was so strange for me to sit down at a table with a white cloth spread over it. This was the thing that I had wondered about when I had walked up the dusty turnpike in summer and through the icy winds in winter with a load of relief grub and looked at this house and wondered about it.

"But let me tell you one thing," Grandpa told Aunt Vittie and Grandma. "I'll take the new clothes but damned if I aim to give up my rights to my relief. Not as long as it's here for me to get. I don't care how much money we have and what kind of a house we live in."

That day we walked to town and Aunt Vittie got more money outten the bank. I don't know how much money she got but she had a big roll of bills when we went to Zachery's clothin store. She bought Grandpa, Uncle Mott and me two suits of clothes apiece. She bought us two pairs of shoes apiece, a pair to wear every day and a Sunday pair. And she bought us shirts, socks, underwear, neckties and handkerchiefs. She bought dresses and coats for her and Grandma and she bought

them a hat apiece. And she smiled on Uncle Mott so he
wouldn't run off to a beer jint or go out and get tanked on
rotgut licker. Uncle Mott stayed with us and walked back
home with us and helped carry the load of clothes.

"Mott, you've acted real nice today," Grandma said soon
as we got home.

"Have I, Vittie?" Uncle Mott asked Aunt Vittie with his
mouth spread from ear to ear in smile, showin two rows of
terbacker-stained teeth.

"Yes, you've been real nice, Mott," Aunt Vittie said.

All that week we helped Aunt Vittie and Grandma in the
house. We didn't work hard but we helped 'em put up window
curtains. And we mowed the yard and did things around the
house that Grandma and Aunt Vittie asked us to do. We
worked all but one day. That was Thursday—relief day. And
Uncle Mott and I went with Grandpa to the relief office and
carried out a big load. Not a one in the office questioned our
gettin relief. I knew that they'd heard about our gettin all the
Uncle Kim money and that they had heard about our movin
into the sixteen-room George Rayburn house. They were
kinder to us than they had ever been and even quarreled over
who would fill our sacks in the storeroom. Grandpa was more
pleased than ever with his success. He didn't know whether
the new suit of clothes, new shoes and white shirt and tie had
made the difference or if our gettin the money had made the
difference. He talked about it all the way back home. He was
really proud of his new clothes.

We not only had relief grub in the house but we had store-
bought grub. Aunt Vittie sent me to the store to buy it. The
waiters in the grocery stores were not near as kind and polite
to me as the referral agent in the relief office and the kinfolks
in the storeroom had been. And the groceries I'd bought at
the store didn't look any better than the things I'd got with
Grandpa at the relief storeroom. One could get many more
things in the grocery store was all. We were all fixed to live

now. We had money, the house, the clothes and the grub. I didn't know how much it had cost Aunt Vittie but it had cost her a pile of money.

Uncle Mott was a-pickin the banjer; Grandpa, Grandma, Aunt Vittie were a-talkin and I was a-listenin to the things they were a-sayin about the Tussies. Grandpa was a-talkin about the Tussies that were his friends and the Tussies that weren't. He was a-tellin Grandma about the Tussies that would hurt him if they ever got a chance. They were the Tussies that still voted the way they pleased, scratched the hills for a livin, made moonshine, sold tanbark, crossties, raised terbacker and dug ginsing. Grandpa said they picked up a dollar here and there, anywhere and any way they could make one. He was chewin his terbacker, reared back in a big bright leather-covered rockin chair, dressed in his best clothes. Aunt Vittie and Grandma were takin in every word that Grandpa said.

"I wish I could compromise with 'em," Grandpa said.

"But they'll never compromise with you, Press," Grandma told him. "You've sold your party out. They aint."

"But they would have sold the party out if I hadn't a-beat 'em to it," Grandpa said.

Grandpa hit the flowered spittoon center as a die with a gob of ambeer spittle soon as he had spoken the last word; then he laughed and slapped his thin thighs with his long skinny hands.

"Yep, I beat Brother George," Grandpa said.

Then Grandma and Aunt Vittie laughed while Uncle Mott played "Careless Love" on his five-string banjer.

"I've learned to look after number one first," Grandpa said. "Look where we are today. Look where Brother George is!"

"Where is he, Grandpa?" I asked.

"The last time I saw 'im," Grandpa said, "I heerd George was in a bad fix. I walked a whole half a day to get to his shack upon Lost Creek. Before I went inside the shack, I heard a pistol a-barkin. One shot was fired right after the other so fast I couldn't count 'em. I didn't know what was a-happenin. I waited until the shootin was over and I went inside to see what the racket was about."

"What was it about, Pap?" Uncle Mott asked.

"Brother George was a-layin flat of his back in bed with his pistol out, a-shootin rats," Grandpa said.

"Rats?" Aunt Vittie asked.

"Yep, rats," Grandpa said. "They were a-runnin over some loose planks he had laid over his jists for a loft. While I was there I saw 'im kill two rats. I said to 'im, 'George, why don't you put rat pizen out? It would be a lot cheaper than cartridges for your pistol.' He just laid there flat of his back in the bed with his pistol in his nervous hand and he said, 'I'm a-practicin with my pistol for the son of a bitch that stole Lucinda.' I didn't say anything more to Brother George. He was in sich a spell of wind that I was afraid of 'im. He looked wild outten his eyes."

"Who was Lucinda?" Aunt Vittie asked Grandpa.

"She was his fifth wife." Grandpa said.

I remember it was Uncle George that I had heard Grandpa talk about before. I had heard him tell Grandma about his brother that left the mountains when he was a boy. My Great-Grandpa Tussie didn't know what had become of him. After fifteen years Uncle George got somebody to write a letter back home from New Mexico and tell my Great-Grandpa Tussie that he was well, that he was married and had five sons. After another ten years had passed my Great-Grandpa Tussie got another letter from Uncle George and he said that his wife in New Mexico had turned out bad and that he was now in Oklahoma, that he had been married to his second wife nine years and that he had four sons by her. Said that Oklahoma was a great country and that he loved it. Twelve more years passed before Great-Grandpa Tussie got another letter from Uncle George and this time it came from Idaho. Uncle George said that his second wife, who was a righteous

and good woman, was dead and that he had moved further west to Idaho, and had been married eleven years to another woman and that he had seven boys by her.

Great-Grandpa Tussie never got to see Uncle George while he was alive. He had been dead and in his grave five years when the last letter came from Uncle George. He had divorced his wife in Idaho and had married a woman in South Dakota. They didn't have any children. If they had any, Uncle George didn't mention it in his letter. But he told Great-Grandpa Tussie that he was a-gettin homesick for the mountains of Kentucky, that he wanted to drink the sweet water from a Kentucky well before he died. Told them in his letter to look for him when possums got ripe, when the corn was in the crib, meat in the smokehouse and taters holed in the ground and fruit was in the cellar and sorghum was in the barrel. Uncle George got home in October but didn't bring his South Dakota wife. When Uncle George came home he married Lucinda Abrahams, widow of Tom Abrahams. He sold the timber from her farm—everything from a hoe handle to a saw log. He spent every dollar that she had saved. And he tried to sell her farm but it was in her name, and to get rid of Uncle George, she had run away with Enic Crabtree and left Uncle George in her house, with her furniture, a-livin on her farm. That's where Grandpa found Uncle George a-shootin at the rats.

"George married too many times to be a happy man," Grandma said.

"I aint so sure about that," Grandpa said.

"He must've had a man's nature to have sons planted all over the West," Grandma said.

"But the Kentucky woman broke Brother George's heart," Grandpa said. "She was a lot younger than Brother George! He told me, before I left the shack that day, that he loved Lucinda. But he couldn't hold her. Brother George's pride was hurt to think another man had taken a wife that rightfully belonged to him."

Grandpa looked sad as he spoke about how Lucinda had treated Uncle George. He pressed his fine beard against his face with his big hand and looked at a picture on the wall. Aunt Vittie started laughin. She laughed harder than I had ever heard her laugh.

"Why are ye a-laughin?" Grandpa asked.

"At your brother George," Aunt Vittie said.

"You won't laugh if you ever see Brother George," Grandpa said. "Women take to George. He's a big fine-lookin man and he can make a fiddle cry 'r laugh. Wait till you see Brother George."

"I have a feelin that we'll be a-seein 'im one of these days," Grandma said.

"What makes you think that, Arimithy?" Grandpa asked.

"He'll starve out since he don't have a wife to make 'im a livin," Grandma said, wheezin on her long pipestem.

"It was wrong for me not to get relief for Brother George," Grandpa said. "I've always hated it. But all his youngins are some'ers in the West. He don't have no influence here. If all his youngins had been here to vote, Brother George's life would be a different story."

There was a big rap on our door.

"Listen," I said.

"Somebody a-knockin," Grandma said.

"It's Brother George, I'll bet," Grandpa said. "I just felt that he'd be here tonight all the time I was a-talkin about 'im."

"Talk about the devil," Grandma said, "and he's sure to appear!"

Rap! Rap! Rap!

"Sid, let Brother George in," Grandpa said before I left my chair to open the door.

Before I had walked over to the door, I heard a fiddle playin.

"I hear a fiddle outside," I said.

"Listen," Grandpa said.

Uncle Mott stopped playin his banjer.

"That's George, all right," Grandpa said. "Wait a minute, Sid, I'll open the door."

Grandpa got up from his comfortable chair and went to the door. He switched on a porch light over Uncle George's head. I could tell it scared Uncle George, for his fiddle stopped playin.

"Does Press Tussie live here?" we heard him ask Grandpa.

"This is Press Tussie," Grandpa said.

"This is not you, Press?" the voice said.

"It's the same old Press only I'm in different clothes," Grandpa said, then he laughed a cacklin laugh.

"I'm yer brother George!"

"We knowed it was you," Grandpa said, "soon as we heard your fiddle cryin."

"I heard about your fine success," Uncle George told Grandpa. "I heard about you a-gettin all that money. Since you are a rich man I wonder if you'd let an old tramp like me come in your fine house and bring his fiddle!"

"Come in, Brother George," Grandpa said.

Uncle George could barely walk under the door he was so tall. He pulled off his slouch black hat as he entered the house with his fiddle under his arm. His hair was white and clean as sheep's wool washed by spring rains and he had eyes like Grandpa. Blue eyes that looked at you and soon looked away. He was a big man that you looked at the second time. And his overalls were ragged—holes torn in the legs until you could see the white flesh through the holes. His blue, faded work shirt was worn at the collar.

"Arimithy, this is Brother George," Grandpa said.

"I've heard about you, George," Grandma said, "but this is the first time I've ever laid eyes on you."

"Vittie, this is my brother George," Grandpa introduced him to Aunt Vittie.

"Howdy, Uncle George," Aunt Vittie said, her eyes sparklin as if she had always known Uncle George.

"She's my boy Kim's wife," Grandpa said.

"Kim was your boy that was kilt?" Uncle George said.

"That's right," Grandpa said.

Then Uncle George looked at Aunt Vittie again and Uncle Mott looked at Uncle George.

"This is my boy, Mott," Grandpa told Uncle George.

"Glad to know you, Mott," Uncle George said, shakin Uncle Mott's hand quickly.

Uncle Mott didn't seem pleased to hold Uncle George's hand. He dropped it like you'd drop a hot tater.

I waited for Grandpa to introduce me but he didn't notice me.

"Press, you had a boy kilt," Uncle George said, "and you got a big lot of money. I know some of my boys are in the army and I don't know whether any of 'em has been kilt 'r not. Wished I knowed. There might be something a-waitin for me. The West was a man's country when I went there. But it aint any more. I've come home to die among the mountains where I was born."

"You look like you're good for many years yet, George," Grandpa said. "Don't talk about dyin. I'm just two years older than you and I'm beginnin to live for the first time in my life."

Grandpa laughed after he'd said these words.

"It looks that way to me, Press," Uncle George said. "I've never been in a finer home in my life. Look what pretty furniture! I'll bet you selected that!'

Uncle George looked at Aunt Vittie.

"I helped her, George," Grandma said.

"Oh, to live in a house like this one," Uncle George said. "I'd like to spend a few of my old days here since I can't get the old-age pension—not even relief—and I aint able to work."

"Why can't you get the old-age pension?" Grandma asked. "You are old enough."

"Aint been in the state long enough to establish my residence here," Uncle George said. "Can't get relief because my brother wouldn't have me put on it!"

"I've been sorry about that, George," Grandpa said.

"Just because I wouldn't vote your way, Press," Uncle George said.

"Not that, George," Grandpa said. "You don't have your sons here to vote. You don't have enough influence. It's your influence that counts any more. It takes influence to get things you want."

"George, have you been to supper?" Grandma asked.

"I'm so hungry I could eat shoe leather," Uncle George told Grandma.

"Then I'll set you up some supper," Grandma said.

"No, I'll fix Uncle George some supper," Aunt Vittie said. "You're tired, Ma Tussie. Sit down and rest and talk with Uncle George."

After Uncle George had eaten a big supper, he played his fiddle far into the night. Grandpa was right when he said that Uncle George could make a fiddle cry and laugh. Uncle George could almost make it talk. He would pet his fiddle like it was the dearest thing on earth to him. He told us he had taken it to the West with him and he had brought it back, that every place he had been his fiddle had been with him. I thought it was strange that he would bring his fiddle back from the West and leave his sons there. And I wondered if he had ever had a son by any of his wives that he had called as many pet names as he had his fiddle. His fiddle was scarred and ugly but after you heard Uncle George play it you loved his fiddle. You forgot that it was old and scarred. Aunt Vittie had asked Uncle George to play a lot of "pieces" for her and she couldn't name a tune that Uncle George didn't know. He'd pat his foot and play his fiddle, like he'd rather do it as anything he'd ever done. And you didn't have to ask him but once to play a piece.

Uncle George even played the "Mockin Bird" for me. I asked him to play it—and Uncle Mott looked funny. I could tell Uncle Mott didn't like it. I used to beg Uncle Mott to

pick his banjer for me and he'd make me fetch him a drink
of water 'r go get him a match before he'd play. Now there
was somebody in our house who could play music besides
Uncle Mott and he didn't like it. He didn't act like he cared
for Uncle George the minute he walked into our big house
with his fiddle under his arm. But Uncle Mott pretended that
he was glad to meet Uncle George and he played a few pieces
with Uncle George. But Uncle Mott didn't know half as
many tunes as Uncle George. When Uncle George rested
his fiddle, Uncle Mott would pick a piece on his banjer. And
we had music until midnight. Grandpa said that he could
hardly keep his feet still. Said they nearly got out of his control
when he heard the fiddle music.

And after the music, Grandpa brought Uncle George to
the room beside mine. Uncle George brought his fiddle to
the room, then he stepped outside his room and started to go
outside. I thought he'd do something like this and I watched
to see if he would. And when he walked outside of his room,
I showed him the inside privy and Uncle George didn't know
how to use it. After he'd been everywhere I thought he'd
a-been up on things but he wasn't. And when I showed Uncle
George the inside privy and showed how to use the gadgets
and levers, he said: "This is some place. I wish I could live in
a place like this and play my fiddle until I died. I'd die a happy
man." I left Uncle George in the privy and went into my room
and went to bed.

While I laid in bed, the tunes that Uncle George had played
kept a-going through my brain. I couldn't get them out. I
wanted to get me a fiddle and learn to play pieces pretty as
Uncle George played them. And I thought about what Grandpa had told us that Uncle George was a big fine-lookin man.
And Grandpa was right. He was a man that everybody would
take to. Then it made me wonder why he had left all his
wives in the West and why Lucinda had left Uncle George
and why he'd be flat of his back a-shootin rats from the loft

when Grandpa went to see him. I wondered about the places Uncle George had been and all the things that he had seen. I couldn't go to sleep for thinkin about 'im.

It was a crazy thought to go through my mind but I wondered if Grandma and Aunt Vittie would let Uncle George stay in our fine house and wear the old clothes that he was wearin. He hardly had enough clothes on his tall body to hide his nakedness. I wondered if Grandma and Aunt Vittie wouldn't be ashamed to have a man in our house, livin among our fine furniture, where everybody dressed well as we were dressed, wearin old clothes like Uncle George was a-wearin. I didn't believe they would. I thought that they would take Uncle George to town and buy him new clothes. And then I wondered if they'd let Uncle George stay with us. I could tell that Uncle Mott didn't like him. I wondered if he'd hot-foot it away the next day or if he'd stay with us. And if he went away, I wondered where he'd go.

And before I went to sleep, I thought about how everything had changed. Visitors didn't used to come to our house when we lived in the rock cliff. Visitors didn't come to our house when we lived in the schoolhouse unless somebody died or the Sheriff came to throw our house plunder outside. And now I wondered if we wouldn't have a lot of visitors since we lived in a fine house, had good furniture and a privy and runnin water inside the house and fine clothes to wear. I thought about the wind in the hickory leaves and Uncle George's fiddle. Everything came to me; my brain was stirred and I couldn't sleep. I laid in bed and tried to forget these things so I could go to sleep, for I wanted to be awake next mornin to see if Uncle George stayed with us; I wanted to see if he stayed and if Grandma and Aunt Vittie would take him to town to buy him clothes.

CHAPTER VII

W HEN I awoke next mornin I heard the redbirds in the
locust trees in the back yard. I didn't know whether I
was a-gettin up early or not. I didn't hear a voice in the
house. All I heard was Uncle Mott's banjer downstairs. I
washed my face and combed my hair, dressed in my good
clothes and went downstairs to the front room. There was
Uncle Mott a-sittin in a brown leather-backed rocker
a-whangin away on his banjer strings.

"Where's everybody?" I asked Uncle Mott.

"Gone to town," Uncle Mott answered.

"But it's not relief day," I said.

"Went to buy Uncle George clothes," Uncle Mott said.
"He was almost naked. Was a-runnin around here like a picked
chicken. You could come near in daylight a-seein his nakedness!"

Then Uncle Mott plucked his banjer strings slowly. I could
tell that he was hurt about something. He always played his
banjer after he'd had trouble or he'd gotten over a big toot.

"I wanted to hear 'im play his fiddle again this mornin,"
I said.

"He can't play a fiddle," Uncle Mott said. "He just goes
around a-bluffin his way with that old fiddle. Calls it pet
names and says that he took it to the West and brought it
back with 'im. I'll bet that old box never saw the West. It
looks like a Lost Creek fiddle to me. I've been on Lost Creek
to square dances and that's the kind of fiddles they have!"

Uncle Mott plucked his banjer strings a few more times,
then he said:

"Uncle George is a sponge. He goes around and stays wher-
ever people will keep 'im. He has no home. He goes around

a-playin his old fiddle. I don't see why Pap ever let 'im come here. He'll stay as long as we have a good bed for 'im to sleep in and plenty of grub on the table."

I could tell that Uncle Mott didn't like Uncle George. I could have told Uncle Mott that he wouldn't work either and it was just as fair for Aunt Vittie's money and Grandpa Tussie's relief grub and pension check to help keep Uncle George as it was to keep Uncle Mott. And I could have told Uncle Mott that Uncle George was a kinder man than he was. But it wouldn't do for me to tell Uncle Mott this. I knew why Uncle Mott felt the way he did toward Uncle George. I'd seen Uncle Mott smile pleasantly upon Aunt Vittie—and he didn't do that until she got her money. When Uncle George came, Aunt Vittie fixed his supper and she smiled at Uncle George and asked him to play her favorite tunes on his fiddle. I thought that was the reason that Uncle Mott didn't like Uncle George.

"Did they leave me any breakfast?" I asked Uncle Mott.

"Your breakfast is on the table," Uncle Mott said.

While I ate my breakfast, I wondered if Aunt Vittie would get Uncle George one suit of clothes or two suits of clothes like she'd got for Grandpa, Uncle Mott and me. And I wondered if she'd buy him two pairs of shoes, socks, shirts, underwear, handkerchiefs and neckties. Uncle George had cast his kind smile upon her and he looked at her all the time she wasn't lookin at him and he looked at her with kind blue eyes when she was a-lookin at him. Aunt Vittie liked this, since kindness hadn't been shown her at our house until she got her money. Then everything had changed. She had always been the best to me of all the Tussies. She had often smiled on me. And many times, I thought she was a-goin to kiss me; but she never did. Before she got her money Uncle Mott had been cross with Aunt Vittie; now he was as sweet to her as long sweetnin.

It was noon when Grandpa, Grandma, Uncle George and Aunt Vittie got back to the house. There was a big smile on Uncle George's face. His lips were spread apart, showin two rows of broken, discolored front teeth. He carried a big bundle under his arm. Aunt Vittie carried a small bundle.

"I never thought there was a Santa Claus before," Uncle George said to Uncle Mott, "but now I know there is."

Uncle Mott didn't say anything. Uncle George saw that Uncle Mott was peeved when he saw Aunt Vittie lay down two pairs of men's shoes. Uncle George opened his bundle and took out three suits of clothes. He laid them on the bed and looked at them. Then he felt the cloth in them. He fondled each suit of clothes like Grandma fondled the first hundred dollars that she had ever seen.

"Best clothes I ever had in my life," Uncle George said. "Just to think last night I came here hungry, weak and tired. I wanted a bite of grub, a bed to sleep in for the night and a roof over me—not a roof of sky and stars—but a good house roof. I was given plenty to eat, a good bed to sleep in and today you clothed me. Aint there something in the Word about clothin a man? Doesn't it say in the Word that you'll be rewarded in heaven for sich a kind deed?"

"I don't know, Brother George," Grandpa said. "I can't read the Word. Aint been to church in a long time—not since they fell out over the church house and fit from one end of the creek to the other!"

Uncle George looked at his shirts, neckties, socks and underwear. He went over each garment carefully with his big hands, feelin of it, admirin it with his soft blue eyes. He was as proud of his clothes as I had been of mine. He fondled his clothes like I had fondled the first marbles I ever had. Uncle George was a happy man and Aunt Vittie was happy. I thought she was happy because she had made Uncle George happy. Uncle Mott hadn't been near so happy when Aunt Vittie had bought clothes for him.

"Now I want to get these rags off and wash my body clean

as a hickory sprout is washed in a spring rain," Uncle George said, "and put on these new clothes and new shoes and know how fine they'll feel against my skin."

"Wait until after dinner, George," Grandma said. "It's too near dinnertime now."

"Then I'll take the afternoon to wash my body and dress in my new clothes," Uncle George said.

Grandma and Aunt Vittie prepared dinner while Uncle George sat in the kitchen and played his fiddle. Uncle Mott stopped pickin his banjer; he sat in the leather rocker with his legs across the chair arm, mad as a wet hen. Uncle Mott's face would get red when Uncle George played a tune on his fiddle for Aunt Vittie and Grandma. When Uncle George stopped playin his fiddle, Uncle Mott's face would get white again. Now I knew that Uncle Mott didn't like Uncle George, and they were livin under the same roof. I knew that Uncle Mott was bad to fight. I'd heard Grandpa say that Uncle Mott had a temper like a copperhead when he got riled. And if I'd ever seen a man riled, Uncle Mott was riled now. Uncle Mott was riled but he wasn't a-sayin anything; like a copperhead quiled among the weeds, he was a-waitin for his time to strike. Uncle Mott would strike when everything was to his advantage, and he would strike hard.

While we were eatin dinner, Uncle George looked across the table and said to Aunt Vittie: "Vittie, you've bought clothes for all of us, and we're a-goin to dress up and look pretty, now why don't you dress yourself with the best clothes? Why don't you have your fingernails polished a deep dark red, the color of the inside of a September red-oak ink ball? Why don't you put store-bought red on your lips and cheeks and why don't you have your hair curled? You'd be a much prettier woman!"

Aunt Vittie smiled and looked at Uncle George, but he didn't have time to look at her for he was a-shovin a ball of mashed taters big as a June apple from the pint of his knife back into his mouth. Uncle George didn't look at Uncle Mott, who was eatin at the end of the table; but Uncle Mott looked at Uncle George. I think Grandma saw him look and she understood. Grandpa didn't see it for he was too busy dippin soup beans from his plate with a big tablespoon and shovin the spoon through his white whiskers into his mouth.

"I think a little paint on the toenails is right pretty," Uncle George said, "if you wear slippers that don't have any toes in 'em. You don't wear stockins any more and I think red is a pretty color."

"I don't agree with you, George," Grandma said. "It's real sickenin to me."

"You're right, Ma," Uncle Mott said.

Aunt Vittie didn't say anything but I wondered what thoughts were in her head. Her face beamed when she looked at Uncle George. Maybe Uncle George had given her some ideas.

"You know I'd rather see a woman smoke a cigarette as a pipe," Uncle George said. "I just love to see women a-smokin cigarettes!"

"I think they are coffin tacks," Grandma said.

"You say that, Arimithy, because you smoke a pipe," Uncle George said. "Your pipe is strong enough to knock a body down. But the smell of cigarette smoke a-comin from between red lips is a pretty sight! A long-stemmed pipe may be all right for old wimmen with wrinkled faces but it doesn't look good in a young woman's mouth."

"I'd rather see 'em smoke pipes," Grandma said.

"You're right, Ma," Uncle Mott said.

Soon as we had finished dinner Uncle George got up from the table and went upstairs. We hadn't left the table when Uncle George came back to the dinin room.

"That bathtub looks too much like a white coffin," Uncle George said. "I couldn't bear to get into it. Is there a hole of water deep enough for a tall man to take a bath in around here someplace?"

"I know where one is that's over your head, Uncle George," I said. "It's where Uncle Mott and I go in swimmin."

"That's where I want to go," Uncle George said. "I want to bathe in runnin water. I want to feel free."

"That's funny," Grandpa laughed.

Uncle Mott didn't say anything; Grandma and Aunt Vittie smiled.

"Will ye show me where that hole is, Sid?" Uncle George asked me.

I thought he was waitin for Uncle Mott to go with 'im but Uncle Mott wouldn't have done it. Since Uncle Mott didn't offer to go, Uncle George wouldn't ask him.

"I'll be glad to go with you, Uncle George," I said.

I jumped up from the table and followed Uncle George outten the house. He had a bundle of new clothes under his arm and a new pair of shoes, a bar of soap and a bath towel in the other hand. We walked from the house across the field that lay between our house and a timbered hill.

"It's not a half mile to it," I told Uncle George.

"I don't care if it's five miles," Uncle George said. "I love to walk. I've done a lot of walkin in my day. These old legs have carried me over many miles of strange roads."

I walked behind Uncle George and told him which path to take where the paths parted. We followed the cattle path across the pasture toward Shackle Run.

"I'd break the ice in the wintertime and take a bath in Shackle Run," Uncle George said, "before I'd scrouch down in one of them newfangled bathtubs. It's the same color of my beard and they are both the same color of a coffin and I'm a-gettin old and I love life and don't want to think of a coffin. I don't like the looks of the swans painted on the bathroom walls a-lookin down at water lily blossoms and the little fishes with big mouths and thin tails and little fins painted everywhere over the walls. It didn't look like the right kind of a place for an old codger like me to wash the dirt from his body."

I thought Uncle George was right after we reached the Shackle Run swimmin hole. I saw 'im pull his old brogan shoes off and throw them over among the wilted horseweeds. Then he pulled off a pair of socks, thick with dirt, without toes and heels, and tossed them the way he had thrown his shoes. Then he ripped the rotten rag of a shirt from his back without even botherin to unbutton it and threw the strings over among some willows that grew on the creek's edge. He pulled off his overalls and threw them among the willows. I had taken my good shirt, pants, shoes off. I was ready to peel off my new clean underwear when I saw Uncle George a-comin outten his. I thought of a snake a-sheddin its skin in the spring. And I thought the new clothes that Uncle George would put on his body would be his new skin. But I had to watch Uncle George.

Uncle George waded out into the water, slappin the water with his hands and then rubbin his hands over his body. In one hand he carried a bar of soap. He waded out where the water came to his navel, then he started soapin his body. Great flecks of soap lather covered his arms, hands, shoulders, neck and beard. While Uncle George bathed, I swam from bank to bank, up and down the length of the swimmin hole. When Uncle George had finished bathin, I was tired of swimmin under the hot July sun, in the milk-warm creek water. I walked out on the sand and watched Uncle George rub the towel over his body. I let the water run offen my body, for it wasn't woolly like Uncle George's body, and after the water ran off, the sun would soon dry me. I shook the water from my hair so it would soon dry in the sun.

"Whose boy are you, Sid?" Uncle George asked me.

"Grandpa and Grandma's boy," I said.

"You aint a brother to Mott, are you?"

"I guess I am," I said.

I'd never known anyone but Grandma and Grandpa. I could remember them from the first time I could remember that I was alive and there was a world about me. I could re-

member Grandpa a-holdin me on his knee and trottin me up and down and sayin, "Git up, hossie! Git up!" He'd ride me on his knee and hold my hands. He'd trot me awhile; then he would move his leg from side to side and tell me the horse was a-tryin to throw me. I'd lock my legs around Grandpa's leg and hold on. Grandpa would take me every place with him. He'd lead me by the hand. He'd take me when he went to visit one of his relatives, then he'd bring me back to the Mc-Callister rock cliff with him. I thought he was my father; I thought Grandma was my mother.

"You don't look like a Tussie," Uncle George said. "You've got more sense than any Tussie youngin I ever saw!"

Then Uncle George laughed a little like Grandpa laughed. I could tell, by the way that Uncle George laughed, he liked me. I knew that I liked Uncle George. I let the sun dry my hair and body while I watched Uncle George put on his new underwear, his new shirt and one of his new suits of clothes. Then Uncle George went down beside the creek, stood on a rock and washed the sand from his bare feet. He laid his handkerchief down on the rock, sat down on his handkerchief to keep from gettin his new clothes dirty while he slipped his long white clean feet into his new socks. He put on his shoes and laced them while I put on my clothes.

"No, you don't act like a Tussie," Uncle George said. "I went to bed last night a-thinkin about ye."

As we walked along the path together toward home, I didn't tell Uncle George that I had gone to bed and couldn't go to sleep for thinkin about him. I didn't tell him that I wondered if Grandpa and Grandma would let 'im stay and if Aunt Vittie would take her money from the bank and buy 'im more clothes than she had bought for Grandpa, Uncle Mott and me. I didn't tell 'im that the fiddle pieces he played, I heard long after I'd gone to bed and that they brought back to me the sounds of the wind in the hickory trees around the schoolhouse that stirred the dry hickory leaves with a lonesome sound.

CHAPTER VIII

✠

WHEN Aunt Vittie wanted something done about the house, all she had to do was call on Uncle George. He was always ready and willin.

"The reason George is so good to help you womenfolks," Grandpa told Grandma, "is he's proud of his new clothes and his good keeps!"

"I aint so sure about that, Press," Grandma told Grandpa, lookin him straight in the eye. "A woman sees things a man never sees!"

When Aunt Vittie worked around the flowers in the yard 'r sickled the grass, Uncle George helped her. Once Uncle George, Uncle Mott and Aunt Vittie worked in the yard together before the mornin sun was too hot. Each one took orders from Aunt Vittie. But Uncle George didn't speak to Uncle Mott and Uncle Mott didn't speak to Uncle George. I carried the grass from the yard that they sickled. That was the day Aunt Vittie told me to stop sayin "privy" and to call it a "bathroom." I thought it was funny to watch the three a-working together while Grandpa sprawled under the shade of a locust tree in the back yard with a cud of terbacker in his mouth. He laid there flat of his back to let the wind blow over him and play with his whiskers.

"Our good times won't go on forever, Press," I heard Grandma tell Grandpa one day while Uncle Mott, Uncle George and Aunt Vittie were out in the yard a-walkin under the locust shade.

"Why won't they go on?" Grandpa asked.

"Company will come," Grandma said.

"More company?" Grandpa asked.

"More Tussies will come," Grandma said.

Then Grandpa laughed like he didn't believe a word Grandma had said.

"You know the nature of the Tussies," Grandma said. "When one family has plenty, the kinfolks come to live with 'em until everything is gone."

"Who will come here?" Grandpa asked.

"It won't be the relief Tussies," Grandma said. "It will be the Uncle George Tussies!"

"Don't think so," Grandpa said.

"See if my words aint true, Press," Grandma said. "They will come like locusts come in their seasons and eat up the trees. The Uncle George Tussies will be here. They will see George in town in his new clothes and see how well he's a-farin and they'll come and pound on our doors until we let them in."

It was an evenin in early August when Uncle George sat in our front room with his beardy face against his fiddle and with one hand drew his bow slowly across the resined strings, tryin to make the mournful sounds that the beetles made in the dewy grass on August evenins. As Uncle George slowly drew his bow across the strings, I could hear the lull of the beetles, that drowsy lull that makes one want to cry when he walks across a dewy cornfield on an August evenin. It was wonderful to hear Uncle George mock the beetles and the katydids on his fiddle. And he would put the sound of the night wind a-rustling the corn blades with the sound of the beetles and the katydids.

"Where did you larn that song, George?" Grandpa asked him.

"By a-goin out in the cornfield on an August night and a-listenin," Uncle George said. "This aint no song. It's just somethin that I copied from the katydids, beetles and wind in the corn at night."

"It makes me think of a thousand cornfields that I've seen," Grandma said.

"It makes me think of a corn patch Kim used to have beside our shack," Aunt Vittie said, wipin a tear from the corner of her eye. "I used to sit on the porch and listen to the whippoor-wills and the beetles while I waited for Kim to come home from a hunt."

I didn't tell Uncle George how it made me feel. I could see the dewy corn with crabgrass-covered balks in the August moonlight; I could hear the wind and the beetles and the katydids and feel my bare feet a-touchin the wet crabgrass, a-gatherin the crabgrass seeds between my toes as I walked along. Every evenin Uncle George played for us; he played us the old songs, the dance songs, the love songs, and he played his fiddle like he'd heard the wind among the willers and the pine-tree fingers. Grandpa was right when he told us that Uncle George could make his fiddle laugh or cry. While Uncle George sat playin his fiddle, there was a knock on our door.

"Some of the Tussies," Grandma said. "Open the door, Sid, let's see who it is!"

I got up to open the door; Uncle George stopped his fiddle. Before I reached the door there was another loud knock.

"He's in a hurry," Grandma said, wheezin on her pipe.

I opened the door.

"Does Press Tussie live here?" a tall man with a beardy face asked me while he jostled a baby in his arms to keep it quiet. Beside him stood a woman a-holdin the hands of two small children.

"Yes, Grandpa Tussie lives here," I said.

"He's sure got a mansion to live in," the man said. "Wonder if he'd keep a few of his poor kinfolks that he wouldn't help get relief?"

"I don't know," I said. "I'll ask 'im. He's a-sittin right here."

I turned around and left the door open, walked across the room to where Grandpa was a-sittin.

"Grandpa, it's some of our kinfolks," I said. "They want to see you."

"What did I tell you, Press?" Grandma reminded him, shakin a tremblin finger toward 'im. "I told you the locusts came in their season and they devoured the trees, leaves and grass when they came."

Grandpa walked nervously to the door.

"Uncle Press," the voice said, "I'm Ben Tussie, your brother Ben Tussie's oldest boy. I've followed you to your mansion. I wondered if you could keep us all night. I aint a relief Tussie but I heard about your good fortune so I've come to share a little of it with you."

"Well, it aint exactly all mine," Grandpa said. "I aint got no money; my daughter-in-law's got a little."

"But you've got Uncle George Tussie," Ben Tussie said, "in your house and you've bought 'im new clothes. You are a-keepin 'im and I thought that I might as well come and share your riches for a night."

I had heard Grandma say that when the Tussies went to stay with one of their kinfolks who had raised a good crop they told 'im they were a-coming for one night only; but after they'd spent that night, they'd spend another night and another. Grandma said that to stay a night for a Tussie meant that he stayed with you until all your grub was gone. Now Ben Tussie, his wife and three youngins had come to spend the night with us.

"Yes, Brother George is with us," Grandpa said. "He's an old man without a home. He's a-traipsin over the country with his fiddle."

"He's got a home on Lost Creek," Ben Tussie said. "Uncle George played his fiddle while his wife danced with the other men. I'm entitled to as much as Uncle George!"

"Oh, yes, yes," Grandpa said softly, a-lookin back at Grandma as if he didn't know what to do.

"Then we'll come in," Ben Tussie said.

"We don't ask for clothes, kinspeople," Ben Tussie said. "We just ask for a place to sleep and three good meals a day."

Grandpa introduced Ben Tussie and his wife to Grandma, Aunt Vittie and Uncle Mott. He didn't introduce them to Uncle George for Uncle George knew them. He spoke to them and shook their hands. Ben Tussie was a big man with locks of winter-colored broom-sage hair hangin down from around his cap's edge. He was a big man with broad shoulders, with two rows of crooked teeth that showed every time he opened his mouth. Effie Tussie, his wife, was a short woman with black hair and brown eyes. Her too-thin dress showed the ugly shape of her body. Their children cried when they walked inside the big room. Maybe there were too many people around them; maybe they were afraid of the pretty room, with the big cluster of electric lights that hung like a pod of overgrown white grapes in the center of the ceilin.

"Have you been to supper?" Grandma asked.

"Aint had a bite since this mornin," Ben Tussie said. "We're awful hungry."

"Your youngins act like they're hungry too," Grandma said. "I never could stand to hear a hungry youngin squall!"

Grandma got up and started toward the kitchen.

"I'll fix their suppers, Ma Tussie," Aunt Vittie said.

"I'll fix this supper," Grandma said, walkin toward the kitchen. "You can fix the next one."

While Ben Tussie and his family ate supper, I wondered if Grandpa hadn't wished he'd have gotten relief for Ben Tussie. But I had heard Grandpa say that he couldn't get relief for all the Tussies. Said if he got relief for all who wanted it he'd haf to get relief for all the Tussies, and something would be said about it. Said they didn't need all their votes, just enough to swing the balance of power and that the Tussie family was the biggest family in the county and he was the oldest Tussie and all the power was put in his hands. I heard him tell Grandma that he had wished a thousand times that he could've had his relief without foolin with the balance of power. Said he'd made so many of his people mad at him.

But they didn't act mad at Grandpa after he took them into our new home. They seemed quite friendly with Grandpa. Uncle George, Grandpa thought, was mad at him until after Grandpa took him in and gave him a good bed, good grub, and Aunt Vittie bought him new clothes. I wondered if Aunt Vittie would haf to buy clothes for Ben Tussie and his family. I didn't believe she would. They would keep a-comin just like they went after Grandpa to help 'em get relief, until Aunt Vittie would haf to stop. She couldn't go on and buy for all the Tussies; there would haf to be a stoppin place sometime. Aunt Vittie's money wouldn't hold out.

Grandpa had been right when he wouldn't give up his relief. What if the Uncle George Tussie's branch of Tussies would come to live with us as long as Aunt Vittie's money lasted? Grandpa had held onto his relief but how much longer would he be able to hold on, I wondered, since he was a-wearin good clothes, a-livin in this fine house furnished with new furniture? I had heard Grandpa talk so much about relief, and the laws that governed it, I knew that when somebody would keep you, you didn't get relief; I knew that when you owned your own farm, you couldn't get relief. And many Tussies had given away the few acres they owned or sold them for a few dollars to get relief. Said the food was better they got from relief and they didn't haf to work to make it, so they sold and gave away their poor hill acres. I knew that when they owned land they couldn't get the old-age pension or when some of their children promised to take care of 'em. I knew that many of the Tussies deeded their farms to their children and lived with them and got old-age pensions from the state.

They either had to do that or deed their farms to the state; so it was better, they thought, to deed their farms to their children.

That night Grandma put Ben Tussie and his family in the room between the bathroom and my room. She took them upstairs and showed them how to use the bathroom and they thought it was a wonderful thing. They thought about it as I thought when we first moved into the house. Now I didn't think about it. I'd gotten used to it. And Uncle George was a-gettin used to it. White coffin or no white coffin, he cramped himself down into the bathtub and took a bath instead of walkin to my swimmin hole in Shackle Run. Uncle George had been well fed and he was a-gettin lazy. He didn't like to walk a half mile to take a bath.

And that night was the worst night of all. It wasn't a fiddle, nor the wind in the dry hickory leaves that kept me awake; but it was the cryin of their youngins in a room filled with new furniture. Maybe they were afraid of the light, or the rug on the floor. Uncle George told us that Ben Tussie had lived in a rented house that didn't have a wooden floor— said the house had a dirt floor. If it wasn't their baby a-cryin it was one of the other youngins a-cryin all night. I'd doze off to sleep and then I'd awake. We hadn't been used to any babies around our house. I laid in bed and tried to sleep but I couldn't. I wondered if Uncle George was bothered by their youngins a-cryin for I heard his door open two or three times and I heard 'im a-goin to the bathroom.

I laid in bed and wondered if Grandpa would try to get relief for Ben Tussie and his family. But I didn't think that he could get it if he wanted to. And if he didn't get it, he'd haf to open up a store account. We'd haf to carry grub from town on our backs in coffee sacks and in baskets on our arms if we didn't get it. The relief grub that Grandpa was still gettin was enough to feed Grandma, Aunt Vittie, Grandpa, Uncle Mott, Uncle George and me; but it wasn't enough to feed us since Ben Tussie was a-livin with us. I'd never seen people that could eat like Ben Tussie, his wife and three youngins. They were like hollow barrels to fill. They didn't turn their hands to do any work around the house. They were a-livin with us and enjoyin the riches that we were enjoyin.

It was exactly two days after Ben Tussie and his family had come to spend the night with us, Dee Tussie, a brother to Ben, and his wife came, bringin their four youngins. Grandma put them in a room next to Uncle Mott's room. They didn't wear good clothes; but Aunt Vittie didn't buy them clothes. She did them the way she did Ben Tussie and his wife. Ben asked Aunt Vittie to clothe him and his wife same as she had clothed Uncle George, Grandpa, Grandma, Uncle Mott and me. Ben told her he was entitled to as much but Aunt Vittie wouldn't listen to 'im.

"You'll do well to get your grub and a bed to sleep on, Ben," she told him. "You came to stay one night but you are still here."

Next day after Dee Tussie came, Uncle Ben Tussie and his wife, Aunt Vie, came to stay with us. Uncle Ben was Grandpa's youngest brother.

"You wouldn't get relief for me," Uncle Ben told Grandpa. "You did help me get a job chislin rock to make the courthouse. That's what's the matter with me now. I lifted rocks and sprained my back. Aint able to work a lick. Can't get relief. You're the cause of it, Press."

Uncle Ben and Aunt Vie roomed across the hall from Uncle Mott. Now it was hard to get into the bathroom when you wanted to go. There was always Dee's or young Ben Tussie's youngins in the bathroom a-playin with the gadgets and levers. They'd play with the electric lights, switchin 'em on and off, just like Uncle Mott did the first night after we'd moved into the George Rayburn house. It made Uncle Mott ashamed of himself now to see little youngins a-doin what he'd done when he'd first moved into a house that had all these fixtures.

"Grandma, it's a-gettin awful upstairs," I said. "Can't use the bathroom for the youngins. Will soon haf to use our lanterns again."

"Shucks, it aint nothin what it will be, Sid," Grandma said. "The locusts are a-comin. I ain't been in the Tussie family fifty years for nothin. I know 'em too well."

It kept Grandma and Aunt Vittie busy a-tryin to keep the new furniture in its place after the youngins ran through the house a-playin like they did when they ran over the hills, through the brush and briers around the shacks where they had lived before they came to live with us.

"A body just can't keep the place clean," Grandma said. "Shucks, we's happier back yander in the schoolhouse than we are here a-tryin to pertect our new furniture."

I wondered why Grandma hadn't thought about this when she had Grandpa to rent this big house. Why did she and Aunt Vittie buy all this new furniture if she thought Uncle George Tussie's branch of the Tussies would come to live with us? Then I thought Grandma wanted to have new furniture once in her lifetime and she had better take it while she could get it. And I had the thought in my mind that maybe Grandma thought Aunt Vittie might marry again and spend her money on a worthless man. Maybe that was the reason Grandma thought she had just as well reap the benefit of some of the money paid for Uncle Kim's death for his service to his country. Once I had heard Grandpa say that Aunt Vittie's comb would get red again. Puttin all these things together made me think that Grandpa and Grandma thought they'd as well help Aunt Vittie spend her money while they had the chance.

There were nineteen in our family now and we were all Tussies. We had two sittins at the table. Ten people at the first table, nine at the second. We drew straws who would wait for the second table and who would eat at the first. I was lucky to get the first table. Uncle George got the second table and he didn't like it.

"No use to get huffy about it, George," Grandma said, "for you may be a-eatin at the third or fourth table before the end of August."

Grandpa made young Ben Tussie and Dee Tussie go to the relief office with 'im and help 'im carry relief grub home. They didn't want to do it but Grandpa told them if they didn't he'd see they didn't get a bite to eat. "Them that don't work, can't eat," Grandpa told them. And when they got home with the bulgin sacks of relief—for Grandpa had the sacks filled long as a can of beans 'r milk could be put into the big sacks— young Ben Tussie and Dee Tussie would lay sprawled flat of their backs on the yard grass under the locust trees a-moanin and a-carryin on like they'd done enough to kill 'em. They even complained because Grandpa didn't make Uncle Mott, Uncle George and me go to the relief office and carry home the bacon to feed 'em.

CHAPTER IX

B UT it took more than the relief grub we got to feed nineteen people. Aunt Vittie had to go to Perk Marcum's grocery store and open an account. They had a delivery route out
the turnpike and they would haul the provisions right to the
house. The truck came every mornin a-bringin store-bought
groceries. Aunt Vittie would tell the delivery boy what she
wanted and he would make a list and bring them the next day.

Two days after Uncle Ben and Aunt Vie came to spend
the night with us, Starkie Tussie and his family came.
Starkie Tussie, who was Grandpa's first cousin Ceif Tussie's
oldest boy, brought his wife and three youngins and Grandma
put them on the first floor. They wanted my room which was
near the bathroom, but Uncle George told me not to let them
have it. Told me to hold on and let them climb the stairs to
the bathroom or go outside. He said there were too many brats
now on the second floor that were a-makin a playhouse outten
the bathroom. I held to my room and told Grandpa and
Grandma that I didn't want to give it up. Aunt Vittie talked
to Grandpa and Grandma about my havin first rights to the
room so I held it.

Starkie Tussie brought his family because he had heard that
Uncle George was a-livin with us and a-fairin well, a-goin to
town with new clothes on his back, a-laughin and talkin with
his old friends from Lost Creek, a-tellin them how lucky he
was, that for the first time he had found a place where he could
live and play his fiddle all he wanted to play it. After Starkie
and his family had spent their first night in our big house,
Grandpa and Grandma went around all day a-doddlin their
heads. They were so sleepy they could hardly stay awake.
Grandpa went to sleep in his chair after he'd finished his din-

ner but Aunt Vittie shook his shoulder and told him to get up so the second sittin could get to the table.

"They're a-comin so fast it's hard to get acquainted with 'em," Aunt Vittie said.

"All the rooms will be filled before this thing is over," Grandma said. "One Tussie tells the other about what a good thing he's got, and after you take one to spend the night, you'll haf to take the others until the house is filled. They'll come as long as there's an empty bed."

Watt Tussie came and brought his wife and five youngins. It was hard to crowd them into one room but Grandma said they hadn't been used to anything but a one-room shack and she put them in one room. They were on the first floor next to Grandpa and Grandma's room. Watt Tussie was one of the biggest men that I'd ever seen. He was larger than Uncle George, with a nest of red whiskers on his long hatchet face. He had shoulders almost as broad as the bathroom door. "He's powerful on a lift," Grandpa said. "The trouble is, he doesn't want to lift. When he tries he can lift the butt end of a small saw log upon the ox cart."

Watt Tussie was one man that I didn't get around. He didn't look right outten his eyes and I was afraid of him. I think Uncle George was afraid of him too. He didn't belong to either clan of Tussies. He just heard about the big house where all the Tussies were a-comin, so he brought his family to jine the rest in peace, rest and comfortable livin. Grandpa figured for hours to find out if he was any kin to Watt Tussie and he finally figured he was a son of his second cousin, Trueman Tussie. Watt Tussie wore brogan shoes laced with groundhog-hide strings.

A-buyin clothes for all the Tussies was outten the question with Aunt Vittie now. I wondered if she wasn't a-thinkin how she would be able to feed them. Each trip the truck came, it had to bring more supplies. When Grandpa went to the relief office, he took more men and brought back more sup-

plies, though he was a-gettin supplies from the relief office for
only six people. But Grandpa's kinfolks ran the relief office
and he had a pull with them. Watt Tussie could carry a load
on his back large as a mule could carry. Grandpa took Watt,
Starkie, Dee and Ben Tussie and they all came home with
sacks of grub. That was a great help and cut down Aunt Vittie's expense at the store. I wondered if Grandpa didn't wonder how long Aunt Vittie's money would last. August was just
half over and we had many of our kinfolks gathered around
us. We had so many that Grandma put another table in the
dinin room and we still had two sittins for breakfast.

In the evenins our front room was packed. We gathered to
hear Uncle George play his fiddle. Uncle George had a big
audience now and the more he had the merrier it was for him.
He liked to play for people; he'd play the fiddle until his arm
got tired; then Uncle Mott would pick his banjer to enter-
tain our guests. That's about the only time the youngins would
stop runnin through the house. It was the only time some of
them wasn't a-cryin. Then Uncle Mott and Uncle George
would get together on a few fast breakdowns. They'd play
"Sallie Goodin," "Hell Among the Yearlins," "Birdie" and
"Susie Ann." All the Tussies would pat their feet and clap
their hands. Every now and then a Tussie would let out a wild
yell.

"We've got enough here for a square dance," Grandpa
said. "Believe we've got enough for two sets. Aint no use
a-losin this good music. My feet are a-gettin outten control."

"Let's get to the dance hall upstairs," Grandma said.

Uncle Mott and Grandpa played for the dance. I've never
seen sich a dancin in all my life. Grandpa danced with
Grandma. I didn't see anything wrong with his back when he
started dancin. He was one of the most active men on the floor.
I wondered how he'd stayed so active. But that wasn't hard
to figure out. Grandpa had never done any hard work in his
lifetime. He hadn't done anything that would hurt him. His
hair had turned white with old age but that was all. And

Grandpa wasn't short of wind. He'd call the dance sets until you could hear 'im for a mile, jump high into the air and crack his heels together three times as he swung Grandma around and around. I'd never seen anybody that loved to dance like Grandpa. He wouldn't take time to wipe the sweat drops from his white whiskers. He'd let sweat run down his beard and drip off to the floor.

We had to have some kind of exercise around the house, I thought, and dancin was about the best exercise we could have. Just a few of the men got exercise. They got it a-carryin relief grub from town. And they didn't get that exercise when they could find a car comin out the turnpike. They loaded their sacks into the car and waited for the owner to come. Grandpa was wise on this sort of thing. He knew the men who owned cars, when they went to town, and about the time they left town and the places where they kept their cars parked. Dancin would give us exercise and we loved to dance. I'd never seen a Tussie that didn't like to dance; I'd never seen one that couldn't dance. Watt Tussie was the poorest dancer I'd seen among them. He was almost too big to dance well.

When we coupled off to dance, every man with his wife, there wasn't anybody to dance with Aunt Vittie. Uncle George would let Uncle Mott pick a dance tune on the banjer while he danced a couple of sets with Aunt Vittie. Then Uncle George would play dance pieces on his fiddle while Uncle Mott danced with Aunt Vittie. Each wanted to dance with her and they played the music for our dances. I often wondered what would happen if somebody else had played the music and had left both Uncle Mott and Uncle George free to dance with Aunt Vittie. I wondered which uncle she would have danced with. I wondered if there wouldn't have been trouble between my uncles. Now each counted the times the other danced with her while he played the music and he in his turn danced the same number of times while the other played the music. It worked out very well.

One hot afternoon Aunt Vittie and Uncle George went to

town together. I could tell that Grandma was worried. I heard her call Grandpa out into the yard so the other Tussies wouldn't hear. I heard her a-talkin about George and Vittie. I couldn't understand what she was a-sayin; but I thought I knew what she was a-talkin about. Uncle Mott sat in the shade of a back-yard locust tree and whanged lonesome songs on his banjer. Uncle Mott was worried.

Before sundown Aunt Vittie and Uncle George walked up the road a-laughin and a-talkin. Aunt Vittie laughed more than I had ever heard her laugh. And when she reached the house we hardly knew her. Aunt Vittie had been made over. She was a pretty woman. Uncle Mott lifted his downcast eyes to look at her; then he couldn't drop his eyes again. Aunt Vittie's curled brown hair, her red lips and her painted nails kept Uncle Mott's eyes strained toward her while Uncle George laughed and talked with her. Grandpa and Grandma looked at her and talked secretly to one another. Aunt Vittie was talkin more than I had ever heard her talk to anybody. She was a-talkin and a-laughin with Uncle George.

Sebie Tussie came to spend the night with us and brought his wife and two youngins. He was Grandpa's first cousin Abe Tussie's second boy. He took a room on the first floor where he could be close to Grandpa and Grandma. He seemed to think that it was their money that was a-runnin the big house. He wanted to get "next" to them. This pleased Grandpa that he was noticed more by one of our visitors than anyone else. Sebie followed Grandpa and Grandma about the place. Often he stood lookin at Uncle George's new clothes, admirin them.

Two days after Sebie came with his family, Sebie's father, Abe, and his wife, Thursday, came. Abe Tussie was Grandpa's first cousin and they had lived close to one another when they were boys on Lost Creek and had played together. Now they talked over old times, except on dance night, which was every night. Abe and Thursday Tussie was one of the fastest couples on the floor. Then Abe's brother Felix came and brought his wife, Claradore. They took a room on the second floor. Uncle George and I were glad because they didn't have no youngins to play in the bathroom and run up and down the hall. Uncle Mort Higgins, who had married Grandpa's youngest sister, Belle, came to live with us and they took a small room on the second floor. And since the rooms would be filled, I was glad we had another couple up our way that didn't have youngins. I was glad, too, that the house was about full. There was only one empty room in the house.

"One thing about it," Grandpa told Grandma and Aunt Vittie, "we haint a-goin to have anybody a-livin in the dance hall. That room aint to be occupied. That's a pleasure room! It's our exercise room!"

"We'll haf to turn 'em away then," Grandma said. "More will be here and there's only one empty room! Ye'll haf to larn to say no when they come, Press!"

"I can do it, Arimithy," Grandpa said, shakin his head. "B-gad, I can say no when it comes to a-fillin up that dance hall."

Dave Tussie came with his wife and three youngins to occupy the last room. But it was on the floor below us. Grandpa and Dave Tussie sat for hours and they couldn't figure where they were akin. Dave Tussie was only a distant cousin—sixth, seventh or eighth cousin, the way they figured it. He was descended from Ezekiel Tussie, a brother to Grandpa's father. But he said that he felt closer kinship with us now than he had ever felt before. And he apologized to Grandpa for all the things he had said against Grandpa.

"The house is full, Press," Grandma said. "There ain't room to put another soul unless we put somebody in the rooms with Vittie, George, Mott and Sid."

"We won't stand for that," Uncle George said.

"I don't want to be crowded, Ma," Uncle Mott said.

"I won't be crowded," Aunt Vittie said. "I think we have

enough. Haf to set three tables and have a second sittin at two of 'em. It's too much already."

"I don't want anybody with me," I said.

"Then we won't take nobody else," Grandpa said. "I think we've got about all we can take care of. It's never been my nature to turn people out on the road. I've never had much before and I've always let everybody share with me. You know that, Arimithy."

"But you've shared more from the other feller than he has shared with you," Grandma said.

"Don't think so," Grandpa said.

"Think it over and see," Grandma told 'im.

"Guess you are right," Grandpa said with a cacklin laugh. "Guess I've got the best bargin after all."

"Remember we are a-sharin right now," Grandma said.

"You are right," Grandpa said. "I just hadn't thought about it in that light."

Pert Tussie came that night with his wife and four youngins. He knocked on the door. Grandpa went to the door and he asked Grandpa to spend the night with us.

"House is full up," Grandpa told 'im. "You've come too late!"

"But I'm closer akin to you than a lot you've got in there," he said to Grandpa.

"First come is the first served," Grandpa told 'im. "You'll haf to go away. Can't take any more. Aint got bed room!"

"But we can sleep on the floor," Pert said. "We've walked a long way and we're tired and hungry."

"Can't help that," Grandpa said. "Can't take another person."

"When you get to be rich," Pert said, "you forget your poor kinfolks; but damned if I ever forget you, Uncle Press! This is the second time you've cornswaggled me. Now I'll cornswaggle you!"

Pert Tussie went down the road a-cussin Grandpa every

breath. Several of the Tussies wanted to flog him but Grandpa stopped them.

"Let 'im begone," Grandpa said. "I told Arimithy that I could say no. I could say no when it comes to puttin somebody in the dance hall."

Cletus Tussie came and brought his wife and four youngins; Grandpa turned them away. Both Cletus and his wife, Zelpha, went away a-cussin Grandpa and all the Tussies who were his friends. Nando Tussie, who was a little off in the head, so Grandpa said, came a-carryin his few belongins in a turkey across his shoulder. Grandpa told him there wasn't any more room in the house, that he had come too late, and Nando went away satisfied. But when Grandpa turned away Elden Tussie and his wife, Lecta, and their four youngins, I thought we would have to fight Elden for Grandpa. He threatened Grandpa with his knife. "I feel like a-cuttin yer damned throat," he told Grandpa. "You kept me offen relief; now you won't let me spend a night in your mansion."

Grandpa's sixth and seventh cousins came and brought their families. His first cousins, nephews, nieces, a brother Tim, his sisters' youngins—great crowds came to stay with us. But Grandpa told them the house was full, that it wouldn't hold another person. Many of them quarreled with Grandpa and called him bad names; many wanted to fight him right in our yard, while many were very nice about it. Grandma had said the locusts would come and devour. The locusts had come, if you wanted to call Tussies "locusts," and they were devourin. The delivery truck made two loads a day now—one in the mornin and one in the afternoon. Relief grub didn't go very far with forty-six mouths to feed and all big eaters.

The Tussie wimmen kept their rooms cleaned; they helped Grandma and Aunt Vittie with the cookin. They helped prepare the meals and put them on the table. Most of the work fell to the women; there wasn't much for the men to do but get kindlin and carry relief grub from town. Soon strange men came to our back yard and the Tussie men met them. They were a few of the twenty-eight men that sold bootleg whiskey in town on Saturdays, hoss-sale days, relief days and holidays. When Toodle Powell came, he drove up the lane in a rattletrap car. And when we had our dances, many of the Tussie men swayed over the floor. I've never seen anything like the dances we had, as many as four sets a-dancing at the time. Watt Tussie was a guitar picker, Sebie played the jew's-harp and Dave Tussie played the french harp. Many nights we danced all night. Life went on in the George Rayburn house as it had never gone before. All we did was eat, dance and be merry. And there was plenty of lovin a-goin on.

Once when I went to my room alone and locked the door to keep the Tussie youngins from a-drivin me crazy, I thought, what if Uncle Kim could come back to this earth a livin man! What if he could see all that was a-goin on in the big Rayburn house! What would he think? Would he be proud that he had made so many people happy or would he have wanted Aunt Vittie to have taken the money she got at his death and have gone away from his people? Would he have wanted her to have lived alone the rest of her days or would he have had her to marry again? What would he say if he could come back and see Uncle George a-takin a walk with Aunt Vittie one day and Uncle Mott a-takin a walk with her the next day? Uncle Mott, his brother; Uncle George, his uncle—would he say anything to Aunt Vittie or would he pull one of his two pistols or both of them and start a-shootin?

I don't believe Uncle Kim would know Aunt Vittie now, I thought, the way she has changed. She talks a lot more than she has ever talked; she laughs a lot more than she had ever laughed when she lived with Uncle Kim. I had been around their shack enough to know. I remember when Aunt Vittie was afraid to open her mouth. And now she was a queen; a queen she would be for a while—as long as her money lasted. Uncle Kim wouldn't know her in all her new clothes, with her cheeks rouged, her lips rouged, her fingernails polished, her toenails polished, and her hair curled. He wouldn't know her a-wearin a watch on her wrist, rings on her fingers, rings in her ears and beads around her neck. Aunt Vittie had lost the ways of the hills; she looked and acted like a girl from town. She was dressed more like the women that I had seen in Greenwood.

But there was no use to have these thoughts, for I knew Uncle Kim could not come back for he was planted on the mountain top with mountain clay and mountain rocks above him. Uncle Kim was planted there to stay. His dreams of Aunt Vittie and his life with her and the days that he had lived with her, the things he had remembered about her, the touch of her lips, their nights of love together, the words she had spoken to him and he had remembered, the joys, sorrows and the happenins of the little life they had known were all planted with Uncle Kim. And the shack where Uncle Kim had lived, the furniture he had used, the color of the hills in spring, and the shape of these hills, their colors in autumn and their ugly shapes in winter were planted there with Uncle Kim. It was not a mansion Uncle Kim knew. But it was the handle of a pistol, the good feel of destruction in his hand, the squeeze of the trigger, the crack-crackin of his pistols and the smell of burnt powder—were things that Uncle Kim loved and took to his grave with him.

Men a-comin to collect debts from him, the words they had said to him, their threats and good clothes they wore and how he got away from them—I wondered if Uncle Kim wouldn't remember, if he could remember anything, such happenins as these. And the killin of wild game the year around, the places where he had killed game in fresh spring weather, hot summer weather, cool autumn weather and cold winter weather, I wondered if he wouldn't remember if he could remember anything. And nights when the rain poured from an autumn sky when he went to hunt the coon and possum in the deep wooded valleys and came home with wood scent, the scent of pine and wild ferns on his big rough brown body, I wondered if he didn't remember if he could remember anything. And I wondered if Aunt Vittie didn't remember a few of these things while we frolicked in the dance hall until the mornin hours.

Though Uncle Kim didn't like me and I knew that he didn't like me, I thought these things about him. I knew that Uncle Kim passed through my brain more than he did any other brain in the George Rayburn house. I had often wondered why Uncle Kim didn't like me from the time I could remember and why he'd pinch me every time he got the chance; it was something I never could understand. He was a huntin man, a rough-and-tumble fightin man that I wanted to grow up and be like. I wanted to be like him when I grew to be a man.

Now I didn't want to be like Uncle Kim when I thought about him a-sleepin on the mountain top; not so much that I still didn't want to be like Uncle Kim as the thoughts about marryin a woman like Aunt Vittie, who would, at my death, take the money that had been given to her for my life lost a-fightin for my country and have a good time with it. Not that I wouldn't have cared to have married a woman pretty as Aunt Vittie but I wouldn't have wanted her to have been sparkin my brother less than two months after I was brought home and buried, sparkin both my brother and my uncle and a-havin them mad at each other over her. And this was one reason why I hoped that dead men couldn't remember anything when they couldn't do anything about all that was a-goin on. If Uncle Kim could remember, and if it were in his power to do anything about it and if he had been buried with a pick and shovel beside 'im, he would have dug himself out and he would have done something about it if powder would have still burned.

It's wrong for me to have sicha thoughts, I thought, but these thoughts come to me and I can't help their comin. And even Uncle Kim's funeral day came back to me. I remembered the long walk to the top of the mountain, the hard climb that nearly winded all of us, and the songs we sang—but one thing I remembered most of all was that Grandpa and Grandma didn't shed a tear. He was their son and I wondered why they didn't shed a tear. Now I knew why they didn't shed a tear. It was because they knew that Aunt Vittie would get all this money and that she would stay with them, that they wouldn't live in a schoolhouse or a rock cliff as long as the money lasted, but they would live gloriously while it lasted; yet I couldn't understand why Grandma hadn't shed a tear when she had given Uncle Kim birth and had raised him.

Then I wondered what Aunt Vittie, Grandpa, Grandma, Uncle George, Uncle Mott, all the Tussies a-livin with us, and I would do when all the money was spent. I wondered who would take care of Grandpa and Grandma. I wondered if Uncle George and Uncle Mott would want to spark Aunt Vittie then! I wondered what Grandpa would do if he lost his old-age pension and his relief! What would he do for something to eat, a bed to sleep on and a roof to sleep under? What would he do for terbacker to chew? He wouldn't work to raise it. He never had. He'd been able to get along but he was much younger then than he was now; he was a-gettin older day by day. I wondered what would become of me, if I would leave the Tussies and if anybody would keep me. To think these thoughts bothered me more than to hear wild screams of the Tussie youngins as they climbed over Aunt Vittie's and Grandma's new furniture with their dirty feet and hands. I opened the door and walked out among them to be refreshed by their wild screams.

CHAPTER X

❧

J<small>ULY</small> and August passed. September had come. Uncle
George sat in a chair under a locust shade in our back yard
while the September sun slanted its rays down upon the thin-
leafed locust, allowin little squares and circles and lines of sunlight to filter through the leaves, onto the wilted grass, where
Tussies were sprawled, a-sittin and a-layin flat of their backs
on the grass with hands over their eyes to keep out the
little squares, circles and lines of sunlight that filtered among
the leaves. Everybody was quiet for once; even the Tussie
youngins stopped fightin and squallin. Uncle George was
sittin on a long-legged chair with his fiddle a-restin on his
broad shoulder and against his beardy cheek. He was a-playin
one of his tunes for us. It was the tune of the dyin grass, the
leaves and the flowers and the chirrupy notes of the grasshoppers, the September wind in the dyin grass and fodder blades,
the wailin notes of the cicadas. It was a tune that would almost
make you cry when Uncle George snapped the scissory notes
of the grasshoppers.

It's the way you play your fiddle, Uncle George, I thought,
is the reason I love you. I've never heard anything like it in
this world. If you never work a lick, Uncle George, I would
still love you. I can't help it if you have been married to many
women in the West and planted your sons there. I wonder if
you have a son anywhere in the West whose hands are like
your hands, long hands and long fingers to touch the fiddle
strings and pull the bow as smoothly and make the sounds of
a drowsy summer 'r a dyin autumn. I'm not the only one that
loves your fiddle, Uncle George, I thought, even these little
Tussies, middle-aged Tussies and the old Tussies love your
fiddle. You've earned your keeps and your good clothes. And

if one of you are to marry Aunt Vittie, I thought, I hope it is you, Uncle George, instead of Uncle Mott.

But before Uncle George had finished with his song of September, a well-dressed man walked around our house. Before he reached me, I watched him as he stopped, looked the house over; then he frowned like one does when one bites into a green persimmon. He was a tall man, wearin a blue suit, a white shirt and blue necktie, a soft blue-gray felt hat with the front brim slightly turned down. Uncle George kept on playin his fiddle and we listened to Uncle George, none of us speakin to the man while he stood before us and acted like he wanted to speak to one of us. We waited and he waited until Uncle George was through. All the time, his face was deeply lined with persimmon frowns.

"Is this where Press Tussie lives?" he asked with a stern voice.

"Yes, it is," Grandpa said.

"I'd like to see 'im," the stranger said.

"You're a-talkin to Press Tussie right now," Grandpa said proudly as he braced his hands on the grass to help himself up. Grandpa groaned a few times as if he were too stiff to rise. But I knew he didn't act that way in our dance hall. If he were stiff and sore it was from dancin all night.

"Would you mind walkin somewhere with me so we could talk business?" he asked Grandpa.

"We could talk it right here," Grandpa said. "No use to wear our legs out a-walkin away from here. A man has to take care of his legs when he gets as old as I am. He can't get a new pair of legs!"

Grandpa laughed a wild cracklin laugh as the September wind played with his light milkweed-furze whiskers, lifted them out and up and down, showin where the roots of his beard went into his chalk-white flesh.

"No use to be funny about it," the stranger said.

"Say, you don't happen to be another Tussie that's a-comin

here a-wantin to claim kin to me and stay overnight, do you?"
Grandpa asked him with a chuckle.

"No, thank God," he said, "I'm not a Tussie. If I were I
wouldn't want to come here and stay with all this mob. Looks
like you have enough company without wantin more."

Grandpa looked at us; then he looked at the stranger.

"Thank God you're not a Tussie," Grandpa said. "They've
been a-comin right sharply here lately."

"Let us get down to business," the stranger said. "I'm a
relief investigator, Mr. Tussie. I've had several reports about
what was goin on here. I have checked at the local office and
found out that you are still gettin your relief. Is that true?"

"It's the God Almighty's truth," Grandpa told him.

"A man that lives in a fine house as this one," he said, "is
not entitled to relief."

"But, mister," Grandpa said, "I'm just a boarder at this
Tussie Hotel. I don't own it; I don't furnish the grub!"

"You furnish part of it," he said.

"Just the relief grub," Grandpa said. "Look at the mouths
we feed here. You know the little dab of relief I get won't
keep all these people. My daughter-in-law, Vittie Tussie, who
got the money for her dead husband, who was my son, is
a-doin it!"

"But she's keepin you," the man told him.

"That's right," Grandpa said.

"You are wearin good clothes," he said, lookin Grandpa
over. "Did she buy them for you?"

"She did."

"You're not entitled to any more relief," he said. "I shall
leave instructions at the office that you are not to get any
more."

There was a lot of talkin among the Tussies, sittin, sprawled
and a-layin on the grass. There was so much talk, some curses,
so much commotion, I couldn't hear the last words he said
to Grandpa before he turned to walk away.

"Somebody, maybe more than one, has reported me," Grandpa said. "That feller was riled."

"It's been more than one," Grandma said. "You turned away too many Tussies, Press. I could've told you that something was a-goin to happen. I've been a-feelin this was bound to come."

"B-gad," Grandpa snorted, "I didn't know it would happen so soon."

Grandpa and Grandma talked that night about the ones they thought had reported Grandpa. They talked about the relief investigator. He was a man that none of us had seen before. He wasn't from our county or some of the Tussies would have known him, since they had lived all over the county and knew practically everyone in it and could call them by name. Grandpa asked all the Tussie men if they had ever seen this man. None of them had. Then Grandpa thought he'd been sent by the govern-mint. He thought he might have come from the state capital. It was a puzzle to Grandpa.

"Just come to think about it, Arimithy," Grandpa said, "I don't think the Tussies I've sent away had time to report me and get this feller here. I think somebody must've reported me sooner."

I guess none of us will ever know who reported Grandpa. But I remember, when Grandpa asked young Ben Tussie and Dee Tussie to help him carry sacks of relief grub from town, they didn't like it. They were mad as hornets because they had to help carry the grub from town that went into their mouths, their wives' mouths and their youngins' mouths. I know that when the stranger started talkin to Grandpa that I happened to be lookin at young Ben Tussie, who was lyin on his side on the grass with his legs drawn up like a frog's legs and his beardy face was a-restin on his hand, and I saw him wink at Dee Tussie, who was a-sittin on the grass near him. And when the relief investigator told Grandpa his relief would be stopped, Dee Tussie smiled at young Ben. I'd say they were the men that reported Grandpa; these men who were a-sleepin in our beds and a-eatin our grub, whose families were a-sleepin in our beds and a-eatin our grub, were the very ones to report the hands that were feedin them.

"I guess every man must have his Judas," Grandpa said with a laugh.

But Grandpa's laugh was a forced laugh. He left the dance early and went downstairs. I went downstairs, snapped on the light and found Grandpa a-sittin with his beardy jaw a-restin in his cupped hand, which was supported by his elbow on the rocker's leather arm. Grandpa was a-thinkin; he was worried. I knew that it hurt Grandpa to take his relief away from him. He had had it many years; it was something that seemed to him would go on forever and forever. Now it was gone; and that was the only thing that I had ever seen that had stopped him from dancin when a dance was a-goin on to fast and furious music upstairs.

We had just finished breakfast that September mornin when a man walked up to our front door. He didn't wait for us to ask him in; he walked inside our house as if he owned the place. By the way he was dressed, I thought he was another Tussie. I thought he was a-comin to stay with us. He wore pants that were threadbare at the knees; but the seat of his pants wasn't wore slick like Grandpa's, Uncle Mott's and Uncle George's. The seat of his pants looked new. I should have known by the knees of his pants he wasn't a Tussie. I'd never seen a Tussie's pants worn out at the knees. They wore out on the seat first; often the seat of a Tussie's pants got too slick for a fly to alight on and stick there.

"Is Press Tussie here?" the man asked.

"He's just finished breakfast," I said. "Have a seat and wait a minute for 'im."

"I don't have time," the man said. "I've got a lot of work to do."

I looked at his faded blue work shirt. It was split around the collar. His brogan shoes looked crumpled and worn. His big hands were gnarled like the roots of old trees.

"I'll tell Grandpa you want to see 'im," I said.

As I got up from my chair to go to the kitchen, I looked around and every chair was filled with Tussies. Many of the men and women had youngins on their laps. I had asked this stranger to have a seat and there wasn't a seat for 'im to have. But I didn't think it mattered anyway; although I did wonder why he had come to our house and just walked in. It could be that he was a Tussie with the knees of his work pants worn out.

"Howdy, Mr. Tussie," the man said to Grandpa soon as he entered the front room.

"Howdy, George," Grandpa said.

Then Grandpa looked around over the front room at everybody huggin to their chairs to sit the mornin hours away.

"It wouldn't have hurt one of you," Grandpa said, "if you'd a-got up offen your lazy end and offered Mr. Rayburn a chair. After all, he owns the house!"

"No, no, Mr. Tussie," George Rayburn said. "Don't have anybody to do that. I'm not a man who does much sittin in a chair. I never had the time! I've come over to see you on business."

"All right," Grandpa said, a-lookin at George Rayburn.

"Might as well state my business here," George Rayburn said. "I don't see a spot of privacy in the house."

"No, it's full up," Grandpa said.

"That's just it, Mr. Tussie," George Rayburn said. "It's too full. I rented this house to you, your wife, son and grandson. Now you've made a hotel outten it! Reports have been reachin me about how you all are a-carryin on over here. I've had several reports from my neighbors. Said there was so much noise at night they couldn't sleep."

"We've just had a few square dances," Grandpa said.

"You've had a dance here every night for the past three

weeks, Sunday nights included," George Rayburn said, "and you've danced until daylight many mornings."

Grandpa didn't deny the truth. He looked at us; then he looked at George Rayburn.

"I want to look over this house," George Rayburn said.

"All right," Grandpa said.

George Rayburn knew every room in the house since he had helped build it with his own hands. He led the way over the house, inspectin the walls and the floors, and Grandpa followed. He went into every room that he could get into. When he came out of Dee Tussie's room, I heard Grandpa tell 'im, "I didn't know that Dee's youngins had busted the winder glasses; honest I didn't, George."

"Looks like one took a hammer and busted 'em out to hear the glass shatter," George Rayburn said. "I've never seen floors treated like these. I had these floors varnished and waxed. Now they look worse than the floors in my granary and smokehouse."

George Rayburn and Grandpa walked through the halls. George Rayburn would stop and look at the wallpaper.

"Had new wallpaper put on these walls," George Rayburn said. "Now it looks like it's been on these walls ten years! Must have a lot of pencils in this house 'r it is charcoal smeared on this wallpaper!"

"I didn't even know the paper was marked, George," Grandpa said.

"It's awful the way this house has been treated," George Rayburn said, a-shakin his head.

They walked down the hall toward the bathroom, where there was a long line a-waitin to get in.

"If I'd a-known this house would've been used for a hotel," George Rayburn said, "I would have put a bath in every room."

"It would've been a lot better if you had," Grandpa said. "That place is so crowded any more that I never try to use it. Most of us on the first floor go outside the house!"

"I don't want you to do that," George Rayburn said in a mean voice. "It's not sanitary. I don't want anything like that goin on around this house!"

"But aint we a-payin you big for this house?" Grandpa asked him.

"Not big rent for this house," George Rayburn said.

"We didn't have it in the contract how many people would live in this house," Grandpa told him. "I know that I told you there'd only be five of us."

"Do you think the Law would let you get by with this?" George Rayburn asked Grandpa.

"You aint a-goin to report it to the Law?" Grandpa asked him.

"That's what I'm a-goin to do if you don't get these lazy people out of this buildin, stop these dances, and take care of my property. You've damaged it ten times as much as the rent you've paid me."

They stood waitin for somebody to come out of the bathroom so they could go inside.

"How many people do you have in my house, Mr. Tussie?" George Rayburn asked.

"Forty-six," Grandpa said.

"Forty-one more than you rented this house for," George Rayburn said with a quick nod of his head.

Effie Tussie came out of the bathroom; Starkie Tussie was next in line. He started in.

"Just a minute, fellow," George Rayburn said. "I want to look that place over."

Starkie waited until Grandpa and George Rayburn went inside. They did a lot of loud talkin inside the bathroom; then they came out and Starkie Tussie shot like a bullet a-past them through the door.

"I didn't know it, George," Grandpa said. "I told you that I never went inside the bathroom any more. I've been whipped out!"

"Press Tussie, you know such work as that is uncalled for,"

George Rayburn said. "They've made a playhouse out of that bathroom. They even smeared the white walls with charcoal—marked long black tongues for the fish that I had painted on the walls. Made little nests around the swans and put eggs in 'em, and they've even made bumblebees and birds above the flowers. It will cost me something to put this house in order."

"Then you want us to get out?" Grandpa asked.

"That's it," George Rayburn said. "Get the hell out of here and quit makin a hotel and pleasure resort out of my house. I'm bringin a suit for damages over what you've already done! I won't bring the suit if you'll clear out now!"

Before George Rayburn left the place he walked out over the back yard where we'd done a lot of wallowin on the grass.

"You surely don't have anything to do around here," George Rayburn said, pointin toward the grass. "Even the blue grass that I sodded here has been wallowed out by the roots."

George Rayburn went away like a puff of wind. He was mad as a hornet. He didn't see the fence posts that we'd taken up for kindlin; he didn't see that the door of the coalhouse and a few of the planks were gone. Grandpa called us together in the dance hall, because there wasn't another room in the house big enough to hold all of us, and he told us what George Rayburn had said. Grandpa told the Tussie youngins not to go around a-markin the walls. He told them that they found winderpanes busted outten five of the winder sashes. He told us that due to bad treatment of the house George Rayburn was a-goin to sue him for damages if we didn't clear out.

"Who do you mean?" young Ben Tussie asked Grandpa.

"I mean everybody that's come here to live with us," Grandpa said. "I rented this house for five people."

"We aint a-clearin out, Uncle Press," Dee Tussie said.

"I say we aint a-clearin out," young Ben Tussie said.

"But you come to spend a night with us," Grandpa said, "and you are still with us."

"And we'll be here long as anybody else stays," Starkie Tussie said.

"We aint a-leavin," men and women spoke from the crowded room.

"Then I'll be sued," Grandpa said.

"You'll haf to be sued," Dee Tussie said.

"Then we'll have to move out and leave you," Grandpa said. "We can't go on like this. George Rayburn is a man that means what he tells you."

There was a lot of cussin among the Tussie men. They were good to Grandpa as long as he fed them; but the very minute he told them that he couldn't keep them any longer, they turned on Grandpa and started cussin 'im. And it was their faults and the faults of their youngins why he wasn't a-keepin 'em longer. He would've kept them as long as the money held out.

"Not one step will we go, Uncle Press," Dee Tussie said. "We aim to stay in this playhouse long as the others stay. We are entitled to as much as they are."

"And we aint got as much as they got," young Ben Tussie said. "Look at the fine clothes that you are wearin, that Uncle George, Cousin Mott and Sid are a-wearin. We aint even been treated fair; yet you are askin us to leave. We aint a-doin it!"

Young Ben Tussie looked wild outten his eyes when he talked. He never batted his eyes once. He looked at all of us and looked hard like a snake looks at a dog with its lidless eyes. Big drops of sweat stood over his beardy face.

CHAPTER XI

🜍

I thought something was a-goin to happen. It couldn't go on like this. It would soon haf to end. How could Aunt Vittie pay the house rent and have a grocery truck come twice a day bringing bigger loads than ever since Grandpa had lost his sacks of relief grub every week? Relief grub was a lot of help when it come to feedin forty-six mouths. How could Aunt Vittie buy clothes for us, buy jewelry for herself and have money very long? Since something had to happen it had just as well happen now, I thought. The break must come sooner or later.

There was much confusion among us. I saw Aunt Vittie talkin to Uncle George. They were off to one side. I saw the Tussies who had come to spend one night with us a-gettin together, all tryin to talk at once and all layin the words that they spoke with their mouths off with their hands. Grandma, Grandpa, Uncle Mott, Uncle George, Aunt Vittie and I went downstairs together and left them upstairs. I thought they may get riled more than they were and try to wreck the house if they had to leave it. They felt the same way about leavin the house, the once-clean soft beds, the good store-bought grub and the bathroom, just like Grandpa felt when he lost his relief. Grandpa acted like he could go on livin without it; they were actin like they didn't think that they could go back to their old lives after the taste of this good life.

"Come in our room," Grandma said soon as we reached the first floor.

We followed Grandma and Grandpa inside their room. They closed the door so we could hear one another talk. There was so much confusion of talk, cusses and threats a-comin from the dance hall upstairs that we couldn't hear one another talk until we had closed the door.

"Let's don't get 'em riled any more than we haf to," Grandma warned us. "If we do they're liable to tear up our new furniture and wreck the house before they leave. Feed 'em just like we have fed them until we can do something about it. Just tell 'em they can stay and share with us as long as we stay in this house. Tell 'em we'll all share what we have together and be thankful to the Lord we have it!"

"I think you are right, Arimithy." Grandpa spoke with a tremblin voice.

"I think that's all we can do," Uncle George said.

I wondered why Uncle George had come over to our side. He was once the leader of the Tussies upstairs. He led them when he had first come from the West. Now Uncle George was on our side and I was glad that we had 'im.

"What do you think about it, honey?" Grandma asked Aunt Vittie.

"I guess ye are a-doin right," Aunt Vittie said. "But we can't go on much longer like we're a-goin. My money won't hold out."

"We want to get rid of that pack of wolves soon as we can," Uncle Mott said without anyone askin him for his advice. "I can't help it if they are our kinfolks. They don't appreciate what we give 'em. They're an unthankful pack of wolves!"

"I'll go upstairs and tell 'em that they can share long as we live in this house," Grandma said.

That afternoon, Sheriff Whiteapple came to see us again. He brought one deputy with him and parked the car at the gate. We knew his car soon as we saw 'im a-drivin out the spur of road that led to our house from the turnpike.

"That's Sheriff Whiteapple's car," Grandpa said. "I'd know it in the next world, I've seen it so many times."

"Wonder what he's a-comin for?" Grandma said.

"More trouble," Uncle Mott said.

That's one time that everybody in the house was as quiet

as a mouse when a cat is near. I thought that the reason every Tussie was afraid of the Sheriff was that the Sheriff was always an enemy to the Tussies, whether he'd ever had to arrest one or not. Just as soon as a friend of theirs was elected Sheriff, a man that they had voted for, soon as he wore the Sheriff's badge, he was their enemy. The reason was, the Tussies never liked the laws. They never liked to be told what to do. They wanted to do as they pleased and get all they could without havin to work for it. I hate to say this about my people but it was the truth. Grandpa and Sheriff Whiteapple were once good friends; Grandpa had helped elect him high sheriff of our county. From the day he wore his badge Grandpa didn't have any more use for him. Most of the Tussies knew his car since he'd had to visit 'em one time or another. So when some of them had seen his car rollin up the spur of road toward the house, the news spread and everybody went to his own room. They might have thought that Grandpa had sent for the Sheriff to have them put out of the house.

When Sheriff Whiteapple knocked at our door, Grandpa was a-standin by to open it.

"Good afternoon, Sheriff," Grandpa said friendly like. "Won't you come in?"

"No, I aint got the time, Press," Sheriff Whiteapple said. "Guess you think I'm a bother since I used to visit you at the schoolhouse so much!"

"What is it now, Sheriff?" Grandpa asked with a tremblin voice.

"I'm a-servin an order on you to leave these premises," Sheriff Whiteapple said. "You know, Press, that I haf to do it. George Rayburn wants you to vacate this house in a hurry!"

"Oh, that's it," Grandpa said, takin the piece of paper in his tremblin hand. "I've always thought if I had enough money I could live in any house I wanted. I think the best thing in the world to own is a little piece of land with a shack or a good rock cliff on it."

Soon as Sheriff Whiteapple left, the Tussie men came out of their rooms. Many of the men were a-tremblin until you could hear their teeth chatter, those that had enough teeth to chatter. Grandma went among them and told them that the Sheriff had come to serve a paper on Grandpa to make him leave the house. They seemed to feel better now since they knew that they would have to leave; they felt that we would all be a-leavin together. Grandma must have told them she was sorry over what had happened in the mornin, for everybody was friendly again, except there was a split among us. Uncle George had come over to our side; all the other Tussies had held together.

After we'd finished the last sittin at the dinner tables, Grandpa and Grandma took a walk out the spur of the road toward the turnpike. Grandma was a-smokin her pipe; Grandpa was a-chewin his burley leaf. I could see them stop and talk. I could see Grandpa hold to his beard when the September wind fanned it; I could see him spit. I could see Grandma puff a small cloud of smoke from her long-stemmed pipe and the wind carry it away until it faded to nothingness on the September wind. I wondered why they were out together; I thought they must be a-layin their plans. They never got out together unless they were. They were talkin about what they would do when we were forced to leave the Rayburn house.

I sat under a front-yard maple tree and listened to Uncle Mott twang sad songs on his banjer. Uncle Mott's face was red; his blue eyes looked watery. I didn't haf to think to know what was wrong with him. I saw Uncle George and Aunt Vittie a-walkin out the path hand in hand. Uncle George was so tall that Aunt Vittie didn't come to his shoulder. In one hand Uncle George carried his fiddle. They walked among the little scrubby black sumacs that grew on Mr. Rayburn's pasture field. Since so many of the leaves had started turning

I thought that Uncle George was a-goin out to play songs
about the dead leaves to Aunt Vittie.

Soon as Aunt Vittie and Uncle George got back to the
house and Grandpa and Grandma came back, Grandpa called
Aunt Vittie down where they were a-standin by the gate.
They had a long talk together; but it was so quiet that no one
could hear what they were talkin about. Dee, young Ben,
Starkie and Uncle Ben Tussie walked around through the
front yard several times pretendin they were a-takin exercise
by walkin around the house, so they could hear what
Grandma, Grandpa, and Aunt Vittie were a-talkin about. But
I don't think they heard anything. When they walked near
where Grandpa, Grandma and Aunt Vittie were a-standin,
their talkin stopped until these men walked past. Then they
started talkin again just above a whisper.

After supper we had our dance. But Grandpa didn't dance.
He went to bed early. Next mornin I knew the reason why.
Grandpa left the house soon as he had finished breakfast at
the first sittin. The September sun was a-risin over the dew-
covered black sumac leaves and Grandpa walked toward
the sunrise, a red agate of fire a-rollin over a ridge. His long
arms swung like pistons as he hurried down the spur of the
road toward the turnpike. I knew that there was somethin in
the wind.

"George Rayburn can make us pay for damages we have
done to this house," Grandma told Aunt Vittie after Grandpa
was outten sight.

"I don't know enough about the Law," Aunt Vittie said. "I
know the Law has often been twisted here among these hills.
Some people can get relief; others can't get relief. You know
that, Ma Tussie!"

"Honey, you are right," Grandma said.

I knew that Aunt Vittie was right. I knew that she had seen
Grandpa's relief sacks filled fuller than other men's relief sacks
in the relief storeroom. Aunt Vittie knew when she had to

tote one of the sacks. I knew that Aunt Vittie was right; I had helped carry too many sacks of relief grub from town. I have carried more sacks of relief grub, I thought, than I will ever carry again. And I knew that Grandpa had carried more sacks of relief grub than he would ever carry again.

All day long the Tussies talked to one another secretly. They walked under the locust trees in the back yard and talked; they grouped in one another's rooms upstairs and downstairs and talked. I never could get close enough to hear what they were sayin for they quit talkin when I got near them. And when I passed them they talked in whispers. But I could hear the words "Press," "Uncle Press" and "Grandpa." I knew they were a-talkin about Grandpa. They were wonderin where he had gone, I thought.

Grandpa was gone someplace all day. Before the sun had gone down over the black sumacs, Grandpa walked up the spur of road, shufflin his big feet along the dusty automobile tracks like he was tired. Grandma and Aunt Vittie went down the road to meet him. And when they met, I saw Grandpa a-talkin. I could see him shake his white head and move his hands to help with the words he was a-sayin. The Tussies peeped through the winders at Grandpa, Grandma and Aunt Vittie. I knew that they were wonderin what was a-goin on.

While Grandpa, Grandma and Aunt Vittie stood on the spur of road a-talkin, I saw Toodle Powell's car whip up the dusty road spur. He left swirls of soup-bean-colored dust behind him as he moved toward our house. He passed Grandpa and waved his hand to him. I knew that he was bringin us a supply of rotgut to pep the Tussies before the dance. Toodle drove up to the gate and Uncle Mott and Ben Tussie met him. They carried two coffee-sack loads of moonshine over their backs for I heard the jugs a-rattlin as they passed me a-goin toward the house. Toodle didn't waste any time a-turnin his car and a-gettin back down the road, leavin a long low cloud of dust behind him.

I stood beneath a front-yard locust tree watchin the sun,

a round reddish new ground pumpkin, go over the hill where
the sumac leaves were turnin red—not pumpkin red, the color
of the sun ball, but a rusty copperish red. I waited to see
Grandpa. I loved Grandpa more than anybody I had ever
known—and when he went away for even a day I wanted to
go with him. When I was smaller I cried when I couldn't go
with him. And I was always the first to meet him when he
came home, that was if he didn't have something he wanted
to talk over with Grandma. And when I heard the Tussies
call Grandpa an "old fox" it made me mad. I wanted to fight
them. They didn't call Grandpa "fox" to his face; they waited
until his back was turned.

"We can git it, Arimithy," Grandpa said. "I know we can."

"We'll haf to do somethin soon, Pa Tussie," Aunt Vittie
said.

I tried to hear more of what they were a-sayin but when
they walked near where I was a-waitin to see Grandpa they
hushed talkin. I think the reason they hushed talkin was, Tussies were everywhere around the house—just a-walkin around
listenin to hear somethin. When it come to lettin the Tussies
know what he was a-goin to do, Grandpa was as sly as a red
fox. He talked about everything to the Tussies but his business. Soon as Grandpa reached the yard he started talkin about
the weather.

We didn't have as many good things to eat that night for
supper as we had been havin. But we had plenty for everybody to eat. I heard Grandma say that we had the last of five
hundred pounds of soup beans on the table. She said that our
supply of grub was a-dwindlin. She named over a lot of things
that we wouldn't have again on our tables, but the Tussies
didn't mind. No one seemed to care. Everybody ate, talked,
laughed, joked just like it was a picnic and we'd keep on
a-havin good meals forever. Everybody seemed happy. Many
of the Tussie men were more than happy. And I knew why.

They'd swigged Toodle Powell's rotgut moonshine to give 'em an appetite. I could smell it on Ben Tussie's breath. Uncle Mott's breath smelled like a moonshine mash barrel.

After supper all the men lit their pipes, cigarettes and cigars and smoked in the house and out in the front and back yard while the women washed the dishes. Uncle Mott and Uncle George went over the dance tunes they were to play for the dance. They sat in the front room and tuned the fiddle and banjer. And soon as the women had washed the dishes, Grandpa called everybody to the dance hall.

"Dance tonight, children," Grandpa told them. "Dance and be merry. That's what the Word tells us. Dance and be merry for tomorrow you may die. Be happy tonight. I want everybody to have a good time while he is in this house."

I don't know what made it. Maybe Toodle Powell had brought a better kind of moonshine. It must have been his dancin kind. I'd never seen them dance like this before. I'd never heard Uncle Mott pick his banjer and Uncle George bear down on his fiddle like they did on this night. The dust flew up from the floor and the dust dropped down from the ceilin. They made the big house rock from their hard-hittin brogan shoes. Sweat poured from the beardy faces of the men, and the women danced like sparrows hop around their nests in spring. Their small feet hit lightly on the floor while the men's heavy brogan shoes roared like low thunder. The men swung their wives until you could see the color of their petticoats. They lifted them from the floor and swung them high in the air, their feet a-stickin straight out toward the walls, barely a-missin the next couple.

Everybody must have thought something was a-goin to happen and they would have a good time together on this night before they parted. They would have a good time while Aunt Vittie's money lasted, while we lived in the big house together. Maybe they were a-thinkin about the words that Grandpa had told them when he called everybody to the

dance hall, that to dance and be merry on this night for tomorrow they may die. But the way everybody danced it didn't
look like anybody was near death. Everybody clapped their
hands when they weren't a-swingin their partners on the floor.
And when they swung their partners, they clapped their heels
on the hardwood floor until there wasn't a speck of varnish
left. There were heelprints and maybe toeprints left on the
hardwood floor.

Grandpa danced with Grandma. They went over the floor
like two light ghosts, Grandpa's white beard flyin up and
down on his chin, fanned by the fast breaths of hot air that
swirled in the dance hall. He didn't lift Grandma high as
some of the Tussies lifted their wives but he lifted her from
the floor. When I walked along the highway with Grandpa,
I'd a-never thought he could have danced like he did. I don't
think anybody else ever thought that he was as active as he
was for an old man. He could jump up and crack his heels
together three times. Not many of the young men could do
this. They could only crack their heels together twice. But
Grandpa didn't dance on into the mornin hours with the
other Tussies. Grandpa and Grandma only danced until one
o'clock in the mornin and then they slipped out and went
downstairs to bed while the dance went on. I danced with
Watt Tussie's oldest girl, Effie. I didn't know how much akin
she was to me; it didn't matter. Uncle Mott and Uncle George
took a time about dancin with Aunt Vittie; I thought it was
all right for me to dance with my kinfolks since everybody
in the house was some akin.

I'd never seen Aunt Vittie look prettier than she did when
Uncle George laid down his fiddle to dance with her. Uncle
George held her close and as I watched Uncle George I tried
to hold Effie like Uncle George held Aunt Vittie. I tried to
swing Effie like Uncle George swung Aunt Vittie but I didn't
have the strength. Uncle George was a big man and he was
powerful with his big arms and his long legs when it come to

dancin and playin the fiddle. I tried to look at Effie's brown eyes like Uncle George looked into Aunt Vittie's blue eyes but I couldn't do it. I couldn't make love to my girl like Uncle George was a-makin love to Aunt Vittie and a-dancin at the same time.

Before the dance ended in the late mornin hours everybody was a-lovin one another. They were a-lovin one another like brothers. I knew it must be Toodle Powell's magic moonshine in 'em that caused so much lovin. Men even tried to love the wrong wives. They got their wives mixed up or somethin; they hardly knew their wives and some of their wives hardly knew them. It was some night—a night I'll always remember. When I went to my room, I saw Tussies a-goin down the hall a-lovin their wives—with their arms around them and their wives' arms were around them. They'd stop and kiss and take another step and stop and kiss again. They were a-talkin like I'd never heard 'em before. I'd never seen as much kissin before. I saw Uncle George a-kissin Aunt Vittie one time and Uncle Mott a-kissin her another time. But Aunt Vittie was a-tryin to get away from Uncle Mott all the time he was a-kissin her.

CHAPTER XII

W HEN I got in bed I couldn't go to sleep for the noise in the house. They were still a-lovin and a-talkin. I heard them a-goin to the bathroom—and I heard them a-wantin to go to the bathroom. I heard them make threats if they didn't get to the bathroom. I heard them say what they would do to the house if the one in the bathroom didn't hurry and get out. I laid in bed and listened. I was wet with sweat for I'd never danced before like I had danced this night.

It's all because Uncle Kim got killed, I thought as I lay restin on my bed. What if Uncle Kim could have come back tonight and danced with us. He would have enjoyed this night. He would have lifted Aunt Vittie high and swung her around until her head was dizzy. I tried not to think of Uncle Kim. I had thought so much about him—the hot day in July that we had carried him up on the mountain, and how fast things had happened since he had died. I thought about how Aunt Vittie cried and how she had kissed his coffin and how she danced now. I thought about how Uncle Kim's brother, Uncle Mott, loved Aunt Vittie and how Uncle George, Uncle Kim's uncle, had loved her too. I wondered what Uncle Kim would have done to the men he caught a-kissin his wife. I wondered what he would have done to his brother and his uncle. I thought he would have done a-plenty for Uncle Kim loved to fight as much as he loved to hunt. But Uncle Kim was dead, I thought, and I shouldn't be a-thinkin about him since Aunt Vittie's tears had dried on his coffin and he was mountain dust anyway. And now he didn't matter a lot to his livin kin. It shouldn't matter a lot to me the way he treated me, I thought, but I think more about him than any of his kinfolks. There was hardly a day passed and scarcely a night went over my head I didn't think of Uncle Kim.

And I thought about Uncle George and Uncle Mott. I had heard Grandpa a-talkin to them. I thought he was talkin to them about Aunt Vittie. I heard 'im a-tellin 'em that he didn't want any trouble in his house and that he wanted them to play music together. But they told Grandpa that they didn't like one another. And I knew the reason why. It was because of Aunt Vittie. Before Uncle George had come to live with us and long before Aunt Vittie got her pension money, I'd heard Uncle Mott talk about Uncle George. He'd wish that Uncle George would come to visit us and bring his fiddle. Now when he passed Uncle George in the yard or in the house, Uncle Mott didn't speak. And when they played music for the dances they didn't speak. One would start a tune one time and the other would follow and the next time the other would start the tune. I wondered what would happen to them. I knew that the Tussies would fight at the drop of a hat and they would drop it themselves to start the fight. I knew the Tussies would shoot to kill and they would knife to kill. I knew that trouble had come between Uncle George and Uncle Mott.

When I got out of bed the sun was a-shinin and the sparrows were a-chirrupin in the locust trees behind the house. I went downstairs and Claradore Tussie fixed my breakfast. I asked her where Grandma and Aunt Vittie were. She told me that they had gone to town with Grandpa. She said that they had left early and that she was left in care of the cookin. She said that it was just nine o'clock and I was up early, for only a few had gotten up for breakfast. She asked me why I'd got up so early and I told her the sparrows had awakened me with their singin. Claradore laughed while she fixed my breakfast.

Before I had finished my breakfast George Rayburn and Sheriff Whiteapple walked into the dinin room.

"You could have knocked, Sheriff, before you come in," Claradore said.

"Didn't haf to knock," George Rayburn said, archin his

shaggy black eyebrows over his mean black eyes. "This is still my property—what's left of it."

"Remember Aunt Vittie's payin rent here," I said.

"Shet up, you little knot on a log," he said. "You'd better have your hair cut and be in a schoolroom instead of dancin all night."

"Where's Press and Arimithy?" Sheriff Whiteapple said.

"Gone to town," I said before Claradore could answer.

"A-tryin to get away, huh?" George Rayburn asked.

"Not that I know of," Claradore said.

"Well, I got wind of it," George Rayburn said. "Can't leave me a-holdin the bag. I'll see that they don't. They won't make their gitaway with all this fine furniture."

"What are you a-talkin about?" Claradore asked.

"You know what I'm a-talkin about," George Rayburn hissed like a viper.

"I do not," Claradore said as she poured me a cup of coffee.

"Let's don't argue with them, George," Sheriff Whiteapple said as he fondled his pistol butt that was stickin above his hip holster. "Let's wait until Press and Arimithy get here."

"But I want you to go over my house with me, Sheriff," George Rayburn said. "I want to show you how they've treated this house!"

"But you'll wake everybody up," Claradore said.

"Wake everybody," George Rayburn repeated. "That's what I've been tellin you, Sheriff! They dance all night and sleep all day."

"It's time to wake 'em," Sheriff Whiteapple said. "We've come to look over this house and we're a-goin in every room!"

I guess I caused the panic in the house, for I went to every room and pounded on the door and told them the Sheriff was here. I never heard sich a yawnin and groanin—and a-rollin outten bed. And in some of the rooms I heard the women scream when I told them the Sheriff was here. Since Uncle George's Tussies had voted against Sheriff Whiteapple, they were scared to death of him. Soon the halls were filled with half-dressed men, women and youngins. They were a-whisperin and yawnin; their eyes were bloodshot and drool was a-stringin from the corners of their mouths. It was a terrible sight to see them scamperin around a-fallin over one another like they were tryin to find a hidin place while Sheriff Whiteapple and George Rayburn went into the rooms.

They had come at the worst time, for the beds weren't made; the house was dirty and everything looked worse than it really was. I could hear George Rayburn cuss and then I could hear him talk to the Sheriff like he was a-cryin. While Sheriff Whiteapple and George Rayburn went over the rooms upstairs, all the Tussies hurried downstairs. Some of the men took to the brush and stayed while they were at the house. And when Sheriff Whiteapple and George Rayburn came downstairs, many of the men, all the women and their youngins went back upstairs. I didn't know how many of them ate breakfast. I knew they all wanted coffee but this was one mornin when many of them drank water instead.

After the Sheriff and George Rayburn had inspected the house, I thought they would leave. But they went into the back yard and inspected the coalhouse. They found we'd split the fence posts for kindlin. Then they went into the front room and sat down and waited for Grandpa and Grandma and Aunt Vittie. And while they waited, many of the Tussie women packed what few belongings they had to be ready to leave. They were sure that something was a-goin to happen.

While they waited in the front room, we went into the dinin room and got somethin to eat. We were glad to get what we could to eat and eat quietly. We didn't sit around the table and laugh and talk as we had done when Grandpa, Grandma and Aunt Vittie were here. Everybody was scared to death. Tussie men slipped back from the bushes, grabbed somethin to eat and hurried back to their hidin places again. I think they were the Tussies that had made moonshine and had been given suspended sentences. Soon as they were caught in another unlawful act they were to be "railroaded." They didn't know a lot about the Law and they were afraid to take any chances. Soon as the Sheriff got out of the house, I thought, they'd be leavin.

I never was as glad to see Grandpa get back as I was this time. I stood under the front-yard maple trees and watched down the road for him. It was about two o'clock in the afternoon when I saw him, Grandma and Aunt Vittie a-walkin up the spur of the road. I hurried down the dusty road to meet them.

"George Rayburn and Sheriff Whiteapple's up at the house a-waitin on you," I told them. "They've been a-goin over the house. They've looked into every room!"

"I told you, Press," Grandma said.

"Wonder what's up now?" Aunt Vittie said.

"I don't know," Grandpa said. "But I can guess."

"Damage for the house, Vittie," Grandma said.

"Do you reckon that's it, Ma Tussie?" she asked.

"That's it," Grandma said.

"They'll take my furniture," Aunt Vittie wailed.

"Never mind, Vittie," Grandma said. "Take it easy. No use to cry, honey, over spilt milk. Wait until we see."

Grandpa didn't say anything more but I could tell he was worried the way he moved his terbacker from one side of his mouth to the other. He felt of his long beard with his big hand the way he did the day Uncle Kim's coffin was in the coalhouse. He shuffled his tired feet low on the ground and kicked up more dust as we got closer to the house.

Aunt Vittie was a-cryin when we reached the house. Sheriff Whiteapple and George Rayburn met us at the door.

"Well, we meet again, Press," Sheriff Whiteapple said, raisin his big arms above his shoulders and yawnin.

"I see we have," Grandpa said softly.

"What is it this time, Sheriff?" Grandma asked with tremblin lips.

"You ought to know what it is," George Rayburn said. His voice sounded like a man a-tryin to cry. "Anybody ought to know why we're here. A little child ought to know if it would go through my house!"

"Here's a present for you, Press," Sheriff Whiteapple said.

"But you just gave me one yesterday," Grandpa said.

"This present is a little different from the one yesterday," Sheriff Whiteapple said.

He pulled a paper from his pocket and gave it to Grandpa.

"What is this present?" Grandpa asked, holdin the paper in his tremblin hand.

"Read it and see," George Rayburn said.

"Read it for me, Sheriff," Grandpa said.

"It's an attachment on your furniture," Sheriff Whiteapple said. "It means you can't move your furniture outten this house until you've settled the damages!"

"What damages?" Aunt Vittie asked.

"My God, woman," George Rayburn said, liftin his hands above his head. "You ask what damages! Can't you see? Don't you have eyes?"

"I told you, Arimithy, this house was too good for us," Grandpa said, turnin to Grandma. "We aint the people that belongs in a big house like this."

"We aint hurt this durned old house that bad," Grandma said.

"Hurt my house!" George Rayburn said. "The varnish is gone from my hardwood floors. There's ambeer spittle all over my wallpaper. Everybody in this house, even to the women and youngins, must chaw terbacker and squirt the juice like grasshoppers. They don't care where they squirt it either! And everybody must have hobnails in their shoes from the looks of my floors. My dance hall will have to be refloored. The bathroom, with all its wall decorations, is ruint. Who marked out the swans and fish over the wall? Can you repaint them?"

"I didn't see no business with all that foolishness on the privy walls no how," Grandpa said.

"It will cost me money to get that bathroom fixed up," George Rayburn moaned. "You've burned most of my coalhouse for kindlin. You've even burned my fence posts and cut down one of my locust shade trees and burnt it."

"We found a whiskey jug in about every room, Press," Sheriff Whiteapple said. "Maybe you could tell us where you got these jugs! They are good evidence in court, you know!"

"I helped elect you, Sheriff," Grandpa said. "And you've been after me since you first wore your badge. I'll help beat you next time."

"Haha," Sheriff Whiteapple laughed. "There'll be no more runnin for me. You ought to know, Press, that the High Sheriff can't succeed himself. I can't run again!"

"Too bad you can't," Grandpa said. "I'd like to help beat you!"

"Let's don't talk about that now, Press," Sheriff Whiteapple said with his mouth spread in a smile. "George Rayburn has you foul. You'd just better let 'im have this furniture to sell to fix his house! He'll haf to build a new coalhouse and put new posts in his fence."

"But my furniture," Aunt Vittie wept.

"Don't cry, honey," Grandma said, pattin Aunt Vittie on the shoulder.

Then Grandma turned around to Sheriff Whiteapple, looked him in the eye and said, "I'll never shed a tear to please you. You rotten piece of Law. You've come to steal this furniture. You've got the Law on your side and you'll take it!"

"Fix my house then," George Rayburn said.

"What will it cost to fix this house?" Grandma asked him.

"More than this furniture is worth," he told Grandma.

"Where will we go, Grandma?" I asked.

"Don't worry, Sid," Grandma said. "We've got a place to go!"

"Then you'd better get goin," Sheriff Whiteapple said. "Give this man his house. He's notified you to vacate!"

"But you watched and listened to find out when we's a-goin," Grandpa said. "You waited like a bunch of buzzards over a dead carcass to get our furniture! Somebody told you that we planned to move!"

"We have our friends all over the county, Press," Sheriff Whiteapple said.

"Then we had better be a-goin, Arimithy," Grandpa said.

"Just what can we take, Sheriff?" Grandma asked.

"Your clothes," Sheriff Whiteapple said. "This attachment includes all your furniture. Take what grub you have in the house."

"You'd better clean all the hoodlums outten this house, Sheriff," George Rayburn said.

"Okay, George," Sheriff Whiteapple said.

"We'd better get our family together," Grandpa said.

"All right," Grandma whispered, takin her long-stemmed pipe from her apron pocket and fillin it with bright burley ter-backer crumbs as she walked toward the dinin room.

Sheriff Whiteapple and George Rayburn went through the house, opened each door and poked their heads into every room and told the Tussies to clear out. And when Sheriff Whiteapple warned a Tussie, the Tussie took the Sheriff at his word. He got away fast as he could. Now the Tussies knew that their good times, good things to eat, plenty of rotgut to drink, dancin, lovin and frolickin had come to an end.

I saw Watt Tussie, his wife and five youngins run outten the house like it was on fire. Watt had a turkey of clothes across his shoulder. He made for the gate, then down the dusty road with his wife a-holdin to his arm and his youngins a-runnin to keep up with 'em. I watched Effie Tussie from the front door until she reached the turnpike and turn to her left toward the schoolhouse. Sebie Tussie, his wife and two youngins were just behind Watt Tussie and his family. Abe and Thursday, a-carryin their packs; Felix and Claradore followed a-cryin because they had to leave the big house.

Not one of the Tussies came near Grandpa and Grandma and Aunt Vittie and thanked 'em for the good times they'd had. Maybe it was because Sheriff Whiteapple was in the house a-roundin them up like he would a bunch of cattle and hurryin them outten the house. But I don't think it was that— I think it was because they were so ungrateful to Grandpa. They got all they could and didn't thank anybody for it.

Then Mort Higgins and his wife Belle took down the road in a hurry. Dave Tussie, his wife and three youngins took out after Mort and Belle. The spur of the road that led from the main highway to the house was filled with fleein Tussies. Young Ben Tussie and Dee Tussie, after they'd whispered something to Sheriff Whiteapple, took off with their families and youngins. The youngins were all a-screamin as they left the house. It didn't bother me to hear them cry for I thought they'd caused Grandpa most of the trouble. I couldn't be sorry for young Ben and Dee if they never found a rooftree to shelter 'em.

I did feel sorry for Uncle Ben and Aunt Vie as they hobbled down the road; yet when I thought about the brogan-shoe prints that Uncle Ben had left in the hardwood floor of the dance hall, I couldn't feel sorry for 'im. He danced like a young man in the dance hall and walked like an old man on the highway. He walked that way to make people feel sorry for 'im but I couldn't feel that way when I thought about the way he could dance. Starkie Tussie, his wife and three youngins were the last to leave.

"Thanks a lot, Uncle Press, for the good time," Starkie said, wavin his hand to Grandpa as he pulled out in a hurry.

"You're welcome, Starkie," Grandpa said in a soft voice. I know what Starkie said had touched Grandpa, for he was the only one of the Tussies to thank 'im! Now that all the Tussies were outten the house but our family, Uncle Mott

and Uncle George came downstairs and Sheriff Whiteapple and George Rayburn were behind them. Uncle George had his fiddle, his turkey of clothes, and Uncle Mott had his banjer and all his clothes.

"Pap, I guess we're on the move again," Uncle Mott said to Grandpa.

"That's right, Mott," Grandpa said.

"Where am I to go?" Uncle George asked Grandpa.

"You're to go with us, Uncle George," Aunt Vittie said.

Uncle Mott looked with sad eyes at Aunt Vittie.

"Come with us and bring your fiddle, George," Grandpa said. "We'll need music now more than we've ever needed it."

Uncle George seemed pleased.

"Now get your things and clear outten here," Sheriff Whiteapple ordered us.

We gathered our clothes, guns and grub together. Grandma tried to take a few of her dishes but Sheriff Whiteapple stopped her.

"This attachment reads 'chinaware' too," Sheriff White-apple said. "I think that means dishes. It says 'all pots and pans.' So you'll haf to clear out without 'em. It's time you's on the road."

"You're a-hurryin us so fast we may forget somethin," Grandma said.

"That's all right if you do," George Rayburn said.

"It won't be all right with us, Mr. Rayburn," Grandma said. "We could come back here and bust a winder out and go inside and get it."

"We'd better guard this house, Sheriff," George Rayburn said. "Hear that threat!"

"I hear it," Sheriff Whiteapple said. "If this house is broken into, we'll know who's done it!"

"You bet we will," George Rayburn said.

Grandpa was tremblin while he stood lookin at Sheriff Whiteapple and George Rayburn. Grandma and Aunt Vittie gathered what grub they could find, hunted up all of our clothes. Uncle Mott put our few belongins into coffee sacks so we could carry them to our new home. I wondered where that would be. I'd never heard Grandpa say. But I knew that he had a place to go for us. Sheriff Whiteapple and George Rayburn waited to lock the winders and doors. Grandma and Aunt Vittie took their time. Grandma quarreled all the time she was lookin for our belongins. She was as mad as a wet hornet. Grandpa was mad too. He was mad enough to fight George Rayburn and Sheriff Whiteapple. While Uncle Mott put our guns together, Sheriff Whiteapple stood with his hand on his pistol butt a-watchin Uncle Mott. I know that he was afraid Uncle Mott might use one of our guns on 'im. Sheriff White-apple had been shot at before. He guarded Uncle Mott long as he was near our guns.

Soon as Grandma and Aunt Vittie gathered the few belongins we were allowed to take, Uncle Mott sacked them. There was a sack for each of us and a few things to carry in our hands, such as a gun or a bundle of clothes.

"One thing that we're fergettin that we'll need in our new house," Grandpa said. "It's the ax. Sid, run to the coalhouse and fetch it."

"All right, Grandpa," I said.

"Hurry it up," Sheriff Whiteapple said to me. "We want you to get outten here so we can lock up!"

I hurried to the coalhouse and came back with the ax. Our sacks were filled to the tops—they were so full that they bulged around the middles.

"I hope you got every crumb of grub there was in the house," Grandpa said.

"We got it," Grandma told 'im.

"We'll need it," Grandpa said.

Grandpa was worried since he couldn't get relief anymore. But he still had his old-age pension. That was something to have. We could get along. Now we loaded the sacks on our shoulders, the first load that I had had to carry in many weeks. Uncle George carried a big long white-meal sack stuffed full over his shoulder, and under his arm he carried a bundle of new clothes that Aunt Vittie had bought for 'im and in his hand he carried his magic fiddle. He was the first to leave the house with his load. We followed him one by one down the front doorsteps with sacks across our shoulders, bundles stuck under our armpits so they couldn't fall, and a bundle, ax or gun in our hand.

"I hate to leave," Grandma said as she turned to look at the house for the last time. "It's the best house I ever lived in. I'll never forget a-livin in this mansion."

"It's the worst thing that ever happen to us, a-comin to a house like this," Grandpa said. "We aint the kind of people to live here! We aint been used to sich a house. Look what happened! Didn't know how to take care of it!"

"My furniture," Aunt Vittie wept as she looked back at the house and quickly turned her head, faced the dusty road and the ball of sun that was a-sinkin over the mountain.

When I looked back at the house I saw George Rayburn and Sheriff Whiteapple standin by the front door. George Rayburn was turnin a key in the front door. I looked a minute; then I turned my head and faced the road ahead.

CHAPTER XIII

To look at Grandma, one wouldn't think she could carry a sackload heavy as Uncle Mott's load. Grandma's wrinkled face, her pipe between her wrinkled lips, held in her mouth by dark snaggled teeth, her long thin arms and long bony fingers with big jints, covered with soft, wrinkled saggin skin, her long thin body on her pipestem legs that were lumped with broken veins—one wouldn't think that she could carry a loaded coffee sack for miles. But that was where one was fooled. Grandma could carry her big load and never take it from her shoulder except when she wanted to knock the ashes from her pipe and refill and light it again.

Uncle Mott, Uncle George and Grandpa got hot beneath their loads. I knew one thing that caused it—so much beard on their faces. If they had shaved their faces, they would have kept much cooler. I knew, when the time come for me to shave, I wouldn't have a lot of beard on my face to keep me hot. I made up my mind to do this when we'd carried heavy loads along the highway and would haf to stop for Grandpa to wipe his sweaty face with his big bandanna. I knew if he'd shave his beard that he wouldn't haf to wipe so much sweat.

As we walked along the highway Uncle Mott often laid his load down beside the road, rolled him a cigarette. Uncle George didn't haf to use but one hand to get to his poke of chewin terbacker. All he had to do was lay down his fiddle, put his hand into his pocket and bring out a chew. That's all Grandpa had to do. And he only had to do this once for Grandpa just laid the chew of terbacker behind his beardy jaw and held it there. Aunt Vittie had a package of cigarettes and she had to lay down her load to light one.

As we trudged along the turnpike cars passed us—but not

one stopped to pick us up. Most everybody in the county knew about us and the money we'd got for Uncle Kim's death and I suppose they thought we were still rich. They didn't know that we had been robbed of our furniture and that we'd fed a lot of hungry people that the govern-mint would haf to feed if we didn't. Somebody would haf to feed 'em. We had just saved the govern-mint a big feed bill. People didn't know what had happened to us and they must have wondered as they passed us in their automobiles and left us behind 'em in their clouds of dust. Grandpa and Uncle Mott spit dust from their mouths and cussed the automobiles. Grandma wished we owned an automobile so we could haul our loads and feed other people some of the yellow road dust.

"How much further do we haf to go?" I asked Grandpa since my load was a-gettin heavier every step I took.

"Never mind, Sid," he said, "you are young and on your first legs. You needn't worry."

I thought we were on our way back to the schoolhouse where we had once lived. We were a-goin in that direction. Now the sun was down; twilight was settlin over the land. Fodder shocks looked like pictures of Indian wigwams I'd once seen in a picture book. And we could only see the dim outline of houses that sat a distance back from the turnpike.

"Look," Grandpa said, stoppin in the middle of the road and noddin to Grandma.

I looked in the direction that Grandpa nodded. I saw a fire built near the roadside and a lot of people gathered around it. It was built at the place where the gypsies used to camp, where the horse traders camped before they went to town on stock-sale days.

"Tussies," Grandma said. "For God's sakes, keep still so they won't know who we are!"

"If we do," Uncle Mott said, "they'll be a-followin us to eat us outten our next home!"

"I blame them for what's happened to us," Aunt Vittie said.

"Just to think of that old George Rayburn a-gettin all my furniture!"

"Honey, don't think about your furniture," Grandma said.

"It's better not to think of water that's already run down the creek," Uncle George said. "It's better to think of the water that's yet to run down the creek."

The Tussies gathered around the fire waved to us; but we didn't wave to them. They couldn't tell who we were in the dim twilight; they thought we were wayfarin people like they were. They didn't know we had a little home somewhere—a little shack somewhere in the woods a-waitin for us. They didn't have any a-waitin for them. And it was best to leave them beside the road. If they found us again, they'd come and fill the house long as one could stay in it. We passed them by. And as we walked along, we saw more campfires near the highway.

"Notice every fire we've seen is near a cornfield," Grandpa said. "I guess they'll eat parched corn tonight."

"It won't be as good as the grub they had at our house," Grandma said. "The fare will be a little harder."

"But a Tussie can stand anything when he has to," Uncle Mott said.

"He can stand anything before he'll work to make it better," Grandma said.

I was a-gettin so tired I could hardly take a step when we came to the mouth of Higgins Hollow. It was the first creek that emptied into Little Sandy just below the schoolhouse where we used to live.

"Here's where we start for our new home," Grandpa said. "We had to buy what we could get. It won't be a-livin in a mansion. But it will be a place where Sheriff Whiteapple can't run us out!"

"It will be near the river where we can fish," Uncle George said.

"It will be in the woods where there'll be plenty of wild game to hunt," Uncle Mott said.

"It will be a lonesome place," Grandma said as we started up the hollow with only the moonlight and starlight to light our way up the narrow wagon road with a rut on each side.

Grandpa and Grandma stumbled along. They couldn't see as well as the rest of us. I guess when you get old it does something to your eyes. But if old age had done anything to Uncle George's eyes, he didn't let on. Maybe he wanted Aunt Vittie to think he was young. Maybe he didn't want her to know if his eyesight was a-failin him. He didn't want her to know if he was tired. He didn't say anything about bein tired. He walked along with his load, never grumblin.

We walked along the narrow road until I thought we'd gone two miles. Maybe it wasn't that far; maybe I was just tired and thought it was farther than it was. Uncle George led the way; Aunt Vittie stepped in his tracks and Uncle Mott stepped in Aunt Vittie's tracks; Grandpa stepped in Uncle Mott's tracks and Grandma stepped in Grandpa's tracks and I followed Grandma. We walked to a pine grove.

"Turn to your right, Brother George," Grandpa said. "There's a path that leads to the shack. It's the old Jim Turner place!"

"It's awful dark beneath these pines," Uncle George said.

"But you'll soon get outten the pines," Grandpa said, "then the moonlight can fall on our path again."

We moved slowly under the dark pine trees, almost touchin one another, until we came to an old field where corn had once been tended and now the deserted field had grown up with brush and briers. The moonlight fell onto our path again. We were welcomed by the hoot-hoots of an owl. I thought the owl may be warnin us not to come into this forsaken land—but we'd lived in worse places. It will hurt us, I thought, after we've lived in one of the best houses in the county. I didn't know of a better house in the county than the George Rayburn house.

"It's good to get back to the woods again," Grandpa said

as he stood long enough to listen to the hoots of many owls that seemed to be a-talkin with one another.

"This doesn't sound good to me," Grandma said.

"Wonder if we can get enough people back here to have a square dance?" Uncle Mott asked.

"People will go anywhere to a good dance," Grandpa said. "If you got good music, people will climb mountains to dance."

I thought we would never get there. I was afraid to ask Grandpa how much farther we had to go. I just swayed beneath my load and thought I could carry my load and not grumble if Grandma could. I listened to the hoot-hoots of the owls and the wind among the autumn leaves. These were lone-some sounds to hear as we walked along the narrow path under the starlight and moonlight.

"Yander's the new home," Grandpa said. "I'll be glad to reach it and lay my burden down!"

I looked ahead of us where there was a little clearin in the middle of the woods. I couldn't tell much about the shack but it looked small to me. Maybe it was because we'd been a-livin in sich a big house. I could see a chimney top above the shack—and now our steps got faster so we could lay down our loads.

"Our land, our home," Grandpa said as he laid his sack down on the front porch. "Good water, land and timber. And we own it! Glory!"

Grandpa seemed real happy. Grandma was glad to get her load down. I don't know whether she was glad to come to this shack or not.

"We don't even have a lamp," Aunt Vittie said.

"We can make a fire in the fireplace," Grandpa said. "That will give us light enough until we can do better."

"When can we do better?" Grandma asked.

"When I get my old-age pension check," Grandpa said.

I wondered if Aunt Vittie had spent all of her money. Only Grandpa and Grandma knew about it, for they had gone with

her when she bought furniture to furnish a sixteen-roomed house and when she had bought our clothes; they had gone with her when she bought this farm. She had fed forty-five Tussies. And I don't know who had bought the rotgut moonshine from Toodle Powell and the other bootleggers unless Aunt Vittie had. Maybe it had been "charged" and had never been paid for. I didn't know. But I knew that Aunt Vittie had spent a lot of money on herself. She had made herself pretty again. She had her face, fingernails, toenails and hair worked on. She had bought new clothes, jewelry and beads for herself. But her money must have been gone 'r Grandpa wouldn't have said that we wouldn't have lamps in our new home until he got his old-age pension.

"It's too dark to find kindlin," Uncle Mott said.

"But look," Grandpa said, pointin to some loose boards on the front porch floor. Grandpa pulled them up, broke them and pushed the door open and went inside. He put the boards in the fireplace, pulled some saggin newspapers from the once-papered walls, struck a match to the paper and the flames leaped up and started the boards to burnin.

"That will make enough light," Grandpa said.

It made enough light for us to see the dirty front room.

"I'm ready to eat something," I said.

"We'll have a snack to eat in a few minutes," Grandma said.

We sat the sacks around the walls.

"Not even a bed," Aunt Vittie said.

"Wish we hadn't a-busted up that old furniture and burnt it in the schoolhouse," Grandma said. "We have a use for it now."

"Not even a dish," Aunt Vittie said.

"But we can get along if we'll only have patience," Grandpa said.

"That's it," Grandma said. "I've had too much patience all my life."

As I looked around the wall plate I saw a long house snakeskin a-hangin over a nail. I saw mud daubers' nests all over the walls. I saw wasp nests hangin from every corner, spider-webs strung all over the walls with dead flies in them. I saw a bird's nest upon the wall plate. It looked like a peewee's nest.

"We'll get adjusted all right," Grandpa said. "The thing that's wrong with you all is you've had too much; now you can't bear to go along with a little!"

"We'd better be glad to have a roof above us," Uncle George said. "Winter is a-comin on."

Uncle George stood before the blazin fire a-playin his fiddle while Aunt Vittie and Grandma went into our grub sack and found some cold bread, meat and taters for supper. Never did grub look better to me. My mouth watered as I looked at it. And while Uncle George played his fiddle, a mouse ran from behind the loose paper on the wall, stopped in the middle of the floor until Uncle Mott ran at it a-stompin to kill it—but he missed the mouse. It ran back behind the paper. I wondered if it had heard the fiddle 'r had just come out to look over its new neighbors.

"Three hundred dollars aint half bad for fifty acres of land covered with good timber, with a good well and this shack on it," Grandpa said.

"Good timber?" Uncle Mott asked.

"Good pine saw logs, plenty of oak crosstie timber and locust fence posts," Grandpa said.

"That means money," Uncle Mott said.

Uncle George had soothed us with his fiddle music. Now the food was handed to us. We had to eat from our hands since we didn't have dishes, spoons and forks. Though it was cold, grub never tasted better to me in my life. It was good to sit on the dirty floor before a warm blazin fire and eat again.

Soon as we had finished eatin, Grandma took a bundle of sheets and quilts from the sack that Uncle Mott had carried.

"George Rayburn didn't see me get these," Grandma said, "and I got some pillows too."

She laid a quilt down on the dirty floor; then she spread a sheet over the quilt and another quilt over the sheet. She fixed a bed in each corner of the room and one near the hearth. Then she took six pillows from the sack Grandpa carried and put two down on each pallet.

That was why Grandpa carried his load so much easier than the rest of us, I thought. He had his big sack stuffed with pillows. But Grandpa watched every little thing and took advantage of it. He would even take the advantage of Grandma when it come to carryin a load.

"Sid, you and Mott can sleep together in that corner," Grandma said, pointin to the corner where I'd seen the mouse. "George, you can sleep over in this corner with Press. Vittie, honey, you can sleep with me before the fire."

"It's not like a-havin a room all of your own like we had in the big house," Uncle Mott said.

"No, it aint," Grandpa said. "But I feel more at home here."

"I don't feel more at home here," Grandma said as she filled her pipe, dipped it into the embers to light it.

And soon as Grandma raised from before the fire and wheezed on her pipe, she said, "I'll always tell people that come to visit us that we once lived in the George Rayburn house and that I had every room filled with fine furniture."

"I'll remember Sheriff Whiteapple to my dyin day," Grandpa said. "If he ever runs again, I'll beat 'im. There's enough Tussies akin to me and my friends to beat 'im. I've got the power right in my hands to beat 'im and I have a feelin that he's a-goin to run for county jedge."

Grandpa pulled nervously at his whiskers when he mentioned Sheriff Whiteapple's name. I could tell that Grandpa was riled at the County Sheriff for we hadn't been able to live anywhere without his comin to our house to serve some kind of papers on us.

"Let's don't talk about that polecat, Press," Grandma said. "Every time you mention his name, I start gettin riled. I feel a warm glow come all over me from my toes to my head."

"Play the fiddle some more, Uncle George," I said.

Uncle George never refused an invitation to play his fiddle. He stood with his back to the fire while we sat on the floor before the fire, facin Uncle George. He put his scarred fiddle against his shoulder and whipped his bow across it.

"I'll play you the tune of our weary march from the mansion to the shack," Uncle George said. "I'll start it with Press and Arimithy's argu-mint with Sheriff Whiteapple and George Rayburn and I'll end it with our rest beneath a rooftree before a blazin fire—restin with our stummicks full of grub."

Uncle George made music on his fiddle that would make you mad. You could almost hear the Sheriff's words and Grandpa's answers. And you could almost hear George Rayburn a-cryin about his house. Then you could hear 'im a-sayin that he would take our furniture. Uncle George almost closed his eyes as he made his fiddle tell the story. And you could hear the gate click as we left everything behind us and closed the gate. You could even hear George Rayburn a-turnin the key to lock the front door. And you could hear our steps as we marched away. They were fast steps except once or twice he had us stop to look back. And then you could hear tramp, tramp, tramp, on the dusty road and our groans beneath our loads as we walked along the highway. You could hear us a-talkin to one another only you couldn't tell the words we were a-sayin. And then you could tell, as we marched and marched along the highway beneath our loads, that we were a-gettin tired. You could hear our steps—slower than they were when we left the house. And you could tell when we left the highway on the dark rutty moonlit road. When we reached the path beneath the pines Uncle George fiddled the moan of the wind in the pine boughs above us and the rustle of the pine needles beneath our feet. He fiddled our talkin just above a whisper, we were so tired beneath our loads. And you could even hear the hoot-hoots of the hoot owls. Then his fiddle got slower and finally there was a loud happy music. We had reached the shack. And then Uncle George fiddled happy music as we sat before the fire eatin our suppers. He ended with soft music—sleep music—as the fire was burnin low and the room was a-gettin dark. Now we could pull off our clothes, since the room was gettin dark, and go to bed.

"It's wonderful, Uncle George," I said.

"It's pint-blank right," Grandma said.

"You nearly made me cry, George," Grandpa said.

"You've made me cry, George," Aunt Vittie sobbed, wipin her eyes with her hand.

Uncle Mott looked silently into the dyin embers.

Uncle Mott soon fell asleep. I got a little cold just under one quilt and I hugged close to him to keep warm. But I couldn't go to sleep for the snorin. I didn't hear Aunt Vittie snorin. I think she must have been awake. I knew the kind of snores Grandma snored; I remembered them from summer nights when we lived in the schoolhouse.

I was half asleep when I thought I heard a hundred mice a-cuttin the newspapers on the walls. Once I thought I heard somethin like a snake lumber across the upstairs loft. I thought it was after the mice. And then I thought early October was late for house snakes. I thought one of the logs was hollow and the snake lived in the hollow log in a last year's mouse nest to keep 'im warm. And when he wanted somethin to eat that he crawled out over the loft and behind the paper on the walls until he found a mouse. Then he went back into his hollow log and slept in his warm nest. I thought a snake could live in October in a shack like this one. I heard the hoot owls a-laughin and a-talkin among the dark pine trees.

I couldn't go to sleep. Maybe it's the hard bed beneath me, I thought. I could feel the hard floor beneath my back. I wasn't sleepin on a good set of springs now with a sheet beneath me and one over me and a bathroom near me. I'm back at the old life, I thought—back the way we ust to live. And it seemed to me like a dream. I couldn't believe that all this had happened. I wondered if it was a dream. I couldn't believe that we had once lived in a mansion and that in less than three months we had spent ten thousand dollars and that we had at last moved to a shack—miles back into the dark woods. I couldn't believe that we had once had the finest furniture of anybody in the county and now we didn't have any furniture.

And then I thought: Maybe it's a sin that God has sent upon us. Maybe it's a sin to take the money that Aunt Vittie got for Uncle Kim and spend it for fine furniture to fill sixteen rooms, to take his money and buy fine clothes for Uncle Kim's kinfolks and then Uncle Kim's wife go to town and have her toenails and fingernails polished and her face worked over and her hair curled and buy herself cigarettes and kiss Uncle Kim's brother, Uncle Mott, and kiss Uncle Kim's father's brother, Uncle George. And I wondered if it was right for all of Uncle Kim's kinfolks to come in and drink, feast, love and dance on Uncle Kim's money. And as I lay hugged up close to Uncle Mott's warm body I wondered if he was a-dreamin of Aunt Vittie, who slept with Grandma just a few feet from us. And I wondered what dreams were a-goin through Uncle George's head. He was sleepin just a few feet from Aunt Vittie over in the other corner.

And I went to sleep wonderin what we would do for beds, dishes and a few pieces of furniture. I wondered if we'd play the game on dark winter nights when one left the house with a lantern for the bushes like we used to play at the schoolhouse. I didn't see anything funny about it then and now more than ever I wouldn't see anything funny about it. New furniture, a-livin in a big house and a-wearin good clothes had changed me.

CHAPTER XIV

W̲ₑ ᴡᴇʀᴇ awakened by the singin birds. And I was one of the first to awake. I pulled my clothes under the quilt, all but my shoes, and put them on. Then I saw Grandma a-rubbin her eyes. She pulled her clothes under the quilt—just like we used to do at the schoolhouse. Uncle George, Uncle Mott and Grandpa started yawnin and a-rubbin their eyes and pullin their clothes under the quilts. It was broad daylight, and the sun rays slanted through the big holes in the front window sash where all the panes had been knocked out.

"We'd better all roll out and look the place over," Grandpa said. "I didn't get to see all of it the other day when I was here with Jim Turner."

"I'll hate to see it in daytime," Grandma said, "if it looks any worse than it does at night."

"Don't get above your raisin, Arimithy," Grandpa said. Grandpa walked barefooted into the kitchen.

"Lucky," Grandpa said. "We've got a stove in here."

"What kind of a stove?" Aunt Vittie asked.

"A cook stove," he answered.

"Is it a good'n?" Grandma asked.

"Not as good as the one we left in the big house," Grandpa said, "but it will do until we can do better."

"We'll never do better," Grandma said.

Then Grandma and Aunt Vittie went into the kitchen.

"You'd better get your shoes on, Press," Grandma said. "You are liable to get a piece of glass in your foot."

I saw slivers of glass a-shinin where rays of sunlight slanted through the window across the floor.

"Stove," Grandma said, laughin. "Has rocks for legs. Door is wired on. Oh, it's a makeshift."

"It'll haf to do when we can't do no better," Grandpa said.

"Here's enough dry sticks of stove wood under the stove to get breakfast with. We're lucky."

"But we have nothin to cook in," Grandma said.

"We need dishes, pots and pans," Grandpa said.

Dishes, pots and pans, I thought.

"What about water?" Uncle Mott said.

I looked out at a hole sawed for a winder in the kitchen.

"Yonder's a bucket on the well sweep," I said.

"Lucky," Grandpa said.

"But we can't bring it in here," Grandma said.

"Unfasten it from the sweep," Grandpa said.

I went to the well, pulled the sweep down with the pole, sank in the wooden bucket into the clear blue water. I pulled it along the rock wall and lifted it from the well box. Then I unfastened the wooden bucket from the pole by unwindin a rusted wire from around the mule shoe that was fastened to the pole. I carried the water to the house.

"Ma Tussie, we can warm our grub in this oven," Aunt Vittie said.

"But I've been used to sich a good stove and so much to cook," Grandma said.

"But we don't have it now, Ma," Uncle Mott said. "There's no ust to keep on gripin about what we have had; we've just got to make the best of what we have."

"Thank God we've got enough grub to last us nearly two weeks," Aunt Vittie said.

"Enough until I get my pension check," Grandpa said.

"Just so we have coffee," Uncle George said.

"We can make that in a can, Uncle George," Aunt Vittie said softly. "I'll see that you have your coffee."

While Aunt Vittie and Grandma warmed breakfast and made coffee, and Grandpa tore more planks from the porch and made a fire in the fireplace, I walked around the house. The dead grass, the greenbrier stools and the leafless trees were white with frost. The cool frosty air was good to breathe and it was good to see little clouds of mist where the sun had melted the frost a-risin toward the sun. As I walked around the house I found a tumbled-in cellar in the bluff above the house; I found a smokehouse with a leaky board roof and I found a place where a barn used to be. There were foundation rocks, sills and a few pieces of the framework still left. And I found clumps of rose vines still clingin to parts of a palin fence. This had once been all the way around the yard.

Dishes, pots and pans, I thought as I walked around the shack a-lookin our new home over.

Then I looked at the shack where we were to live. There were two rooms downstairs and a big room upstairs. It was covered with boards that curled up at the ends. Grandpa said they were nailed on the house in the dark of the moon was the reason they had curled. We could tell the house leaked by the circled newspapers on the wall and on the ceilin. But by lookin at the roof, I couldn't see why it hadn't leaked more. And then I looked at the woods all around the house. I saw dead locust, persimmon, pine, sourwood and sassafras poles. These poles will make good stove wood, I thought.

"Grandpa, we got plenty of good poles for stove wood around this shack," I said. "Every way you look, there's timber. And among the green timber are these small dead poles—small trees that have been smothered by the big ones!"

"There's wood closer than that," Uncle Mott said. "I've got my eyes on panels of palins, framework of an old barn and an old smokehouse that's about to fall in!"

"We can use that smokehouse if we rive some boards to patch the roof," I said.

"It's good for wood," Grandpa said.

"And we can rive a few more palins and finish palin the yard," I said.

"We don't want to be fenced in," Uncle Mott said, laughin. "Palins are easy to cut for wood. You don't even haf to use an ax. You can just break 'em across your knee into the right stove-wood lengths."

"Burn all that old stuff," Grandpa said, "just so we get some-

thin to eat outten. It's hard for everybody to haf to drink
coffee from the same tin can."

"Maybe we'll have somethin by dinnertime to eat outten,"
I said.

"I don't know where it'll come from," Grandma snarled.

But Grandma doesn't remember, I thought.

Soon as we had finished breakfast, Grandpa walked out into
the yard and with his brogan shoe he kicked up a frozen
clump of leaves. Beneath the leaves there was a black rot-leaf
loam that wasn't frozen; it was soft and Grandpa stooped over
and lifted a handful of the rot-leaf loam from the ground,
looked at it with his soft blue eyes, played with it in his hand,
lettin it run between his fingers back to the earth, while the
mornin October wind played with his beard, liftin it up and
lettin it down until it looked like a dead clump of fine crabgrass ruffled by a winter wind.

"It's wonderful to know that this land is mine," Grandpa
said. "It's the first time in my life I've ever had a deed fer
land. This land is mine. I raised Kim, and Vittie married 'im.
Now he's dead and for his death Vittie bought this land with
her last money and give it to me. I'm a proud man to own
land!"

I thought I could see a light a-comin from Grandpa's face
as he spoke of ownin land and looked up toward the blue sky
where the white cloud mists were a-floatin toward the sun.
Maybe it wasn't light I saw a-comin from Grandpa's face—
maybe it was the mist—but I know that he was happier than
I had ever seen him.

"I need me a plug mule," Grandpa said, "and a little clearin.
I'd try farmin in my old days. I'd farm corn and terbacker.
Take my time. Live here happy as a coon in a holler log the
rest of my days."

Uncle Mott laughed at Grandpa and there was a smile on
Uncle George's face. I know that they thought that Grandpa

was just a-talkin. I didn't know, but the words he said sounded good to me. And I was glad to see Grandpa so happy. Maybe he had found a new kind of life. Maybe, that was why he was so happy.

I'll fool Grandma, I thought as I carried a sack from the house. Uncle George and Grandpa were a-sittin before the fire; Aunt Vittie and Grandma were a-cleanin the kitchen. Uncle Mott was a-gatherin broom sage and wrapping it around a sassafras handle with thongs of hickory bark. He was a-makin Grandma a broom. I passed Uncle Mott while he was bent over a-breakin broom sage from its cluster for the broom. I followed the path the way we had come. I crossed the old field, soon came to the big pine grove. And as I tramped on the pine needles I thought of Uncle George's fiddle. I hurried down Higgins Hollow road, reached the turnpike and turned to my left—only a few steps to the schoolhouse.

When I reached the schoolhouse I was almost afraid to go on the school ground. I didn't see anybody a-stirrin around the schoolhouse but I saw a lot of faces pressed against the winderpanes a-peepin out toward the bright autumn trees where the sun had dried the frost from the tough-butted white-oak leaves. I wondered how it looked inside this schoolhouse now. But I knew that I wasn't a-goin inside to see how it looked. And I wondered what a school was like inside where you sat at a desk and studied a book. But there was no use to think about that, for I had never been to school. I had come to find somethin for Grandma. I made straight for the gulley where Uncle Mott and I had thrown Grandma's old stained dishes, cracked dishes, good dishes, pots and pans, teacups and saucers.

The gulley was down under the hill from the schoolhouse and the faces at the winders, a-watchin the jaybirds a-carryin hickory nuts and acorns and fillin a hollow-topped tree, couldn't see me. I wondered what they'd do if they did see me. I remembered that we had moved away and left the school-house in a mess and the stove was mighty dirty. I had often wondered who had cleaned the stove. I wondered if the teacher cleaned it or if the boys and girls that went to the school cleaned it for the teacher.

I found a few saucers, teacups and a pot and pan in the gulley where I raked among the leaves. But I couldn't find near all the things that Uncle Mott and I had carried outten the schoolhouse and had thrown into this gulley that night. I wondered if the school boys and girls had carried them home. But I raked around until I found an old coffeepot that Grandma had us carry out and throw away. It was good to find a coffeepot; I knew if I didn't find anything more than what I had already found she would be pleased.

Then I heard a bell sound and the boys and girls came out of the schoolhouse a-runnin, a-laughin and a-talkin. They had their dinner buckets in their hands and they made for the gnarled roots of the hickory trees. I laid flat on the ground with my eyes barely up to the level of the school yard where I could watch them eat, listen to them talk. And I wanted to watch them play.

Soon as one had finished eatin, he hurried to the school-house with his dinner bucket, dumpin what few pieces of bread he had left upon the ground. The bread looked good to me; it made me hungry. I wanted to pick it up soon as the bell rang for books. Grandpa and Grandma would be pleased with this, too, for we didn't have enough to last us until Grandpa got his pension check. I wondered what we'd do for somethin to eat. But I couldn't think about what we'd do for somethin to eat when I saw everybody a-gatherin under a big oak at the edge of the school yard near the coalhouse. I was close to them. I thought every minute that someone would see me but no one ventured over the bank.

I almost yelled when I saw Grandma's dishes. The girls were a-playin "home." The boys were their husbands and they carried things to the house and the girls pretended that they were a-settin the tables. I could see the dishes washed clean and sittin on tables made of planks and rocks and covered with wood moss. All I had to do was keep quiet and hug against the ground until the bell rang and then I could climb around the side of the bluff and take the dishes from the tables without anyone's seein me. I waited for my chance.

Soon as the bell rang, they walked slowly to the schoolhouse. I climbed around the steep bluff, lifted dishes, pots, pans, teacups and saucers from the moss-covered rocks and planks. I put them down into my sack and put pieces of wood moss around them to keep them from breakin. I didn't think that Uncle Mott and I had ever carried this many dishes, pots, pans, glasses, even spoons, knives and forks to the gulley. My sack was over half full. Now I wanted the bread that had been thrown under the hickory tree and I saw a dog a-comin to get it. He was a thin, hungry-lookin hound.

"Git," I yelled.

The hound took to the bushes.

I shouldered my sack, walked slowly around the steep bluff and walked upon the school ground at the hickory tree. I laid my sack off my shoulder carefully and loaded the slices of light bread, biscuits and pieces of corn bread into my sack fast as I could. I saw faces squirmin at the winderpanes as I worked. Boys and girls inside the schoolhouse acted like they were a-tryin to get out. And then I saw more dishes at another playhouse under a hickory tree. I guess it was a mistake but I got them—and then I shouldered my sack and took over the bank in a run. I was a-tryin to go through the woods and reach Higgins Hollow road instead of a-goin down the turnpike. And I didn't more than reach the Higgins Hollow until I heard voices a-screamin at me.

"Lay down that sack," one shouted. "You've robbed our playhouses!"

Another shouted, "Our teacher said for you to throw down that sack!"

"Make me if you can," I yelled as I ran faster than ever.

I heard them a-comin after me like a pack of hounds and I had a good lead on them. I sidestepped into a thick pine grove, hurried under the dark woods, goin around this tree and that one, until I reached a gulley. I laid down in the gulley and tried to hold my breath so they couldn't hear my breathin. I was a-gittin my breath hard. I held my face up where I could see the Higgins Hollow road from the gulley. I saw a crowd of boys run up the road like a pack of hounds after a fox. Then I heard them stop when they were out of sight.

"He's got away," one said.

"Who was that boy?" another asked.

"I don't know," another answered.

I lay perfectly still now that I wasn't a-gittin my breath so hard. I listened to everything they said.

"What do you think o' that?" one said. "A thief a-comin on the school ground and a-gettin the girls' dishes!"

"Wonder where he went?" one asked.

"You tell me," another said.

"That's what we'd all like to know," they all agreed.

I saw them a-walkin slowly down the Higgins Hollow road toward the schoolhouse. But one talked about goin home and bringin his dog to school and puttin the dog on my track.

"Old Bowser'll find 'im all right," the boy said.

"Teacher won't let you do that," a tall boy told him.

They stopped talkin about the dog before they got from my sight. I watched them walk to the turnpike, turn to their left around the high bank outten sight. I crawled from my hidin place, walked down under the pine trees to the road, then to the path under the pine grove and hurried along this path for home.

CHAPTER XV

"COME, honey," Grandma called to Aunt Vittie. "Look what Sid's brought home!"

Grandma hugged and kissed me. That was the first time in her life that she had ever kissed me.

"My old dishes," Grandma said. "My old coffeepot! I'd a-knowed 'em anywhere. I had 'em so long! And now I've got 'em again. Sid, honey, I'm so glad that you found 'em! I thought we put 'em in the big fire at the schoolhouse!"

"It's wonderful, Ma Tussie," Aunt Vittie said as she watched Grandma wipe the tears from her eyes with the corner of her apron. Even Grandpa and Uncle George walked inside the kitchen. And they were tickled to death.

"You couldn't've fetched dishes in a better time," Grandpa said. "Where did you find 'em?"

"Grandma's old dishes that Uncle Mott and I carried to the gulley when we left the schoolhouse," I said. "That's when Grandma and Aunt Vittie were a-buyin new things and they didn't think they'd need the old things again!"

"You're a smart boy, Sid," Uncle George said. "I'll play you a lot of tunes on my fiddle for this. I won't haf to drink my coffee from a tin can now!"

"Not if you can get the coffee," Grandma said.

"Where'd the bread come from, Sid?" Aunt Vittie asked.

"Youngins dumped it from their dinner buckets under a hickory tree," I said.

"Don't think you ought to've brought it," Grandma said.

"We won't need that," Grandpa said.

"What if your pension check is late?" I said.

"Guess we'd better save it," Grandma said. "Might need it."

"It's best to save when we don't know where the next meal's a-comin from," Uncle George said.

"Oh, if you could only've brought my old cord beds and my big three-cornered cupboard back to me," Grandma wailed. "Now we need them."

Grandma and Aunt Vittie took the bread, dishes, pots, pans, coffeepot, plates, teacups and saucers from the sack.

"Enough dishes here for a family," Grandma said.

"Enough for us to make out on," Aunt Vittie said.

"Now we have brooms and dishes," Grandpa said.

"I've been a-thinkin about beds," Uncle George said. "If Mott can make brooms, I can make beds!"

"But I can find some secondhand beds," Grandpa said, "when I get my pension check this month."

"That won't more than buy grub," Uncle George said.

"God, I wish I's back on relief," Grandpa said. "I'd like to know who reported me."

"No use to wish that," Grandma said.

"But I'll get it back on 'em when election time rolls around again," Grandpa said. "I'll help beat a slew of 'em."

That afternoon Uncle George went into the woods with an ax. He came back to the yard a-carryin a dead chestnut pole. I knew why he'd cut dead chestnut—because it was easy to chop and light to carry. But I watched him as he worked a-makin beds. He set a post in the corner of the front room and nailed a slab to it and stuck it through a crack in the wall. Then he put another slat to the post and stuck it through a crack in the wall. Then he put another slat to the post and stuck it through a crack in the other wall. He found some rusty spike nails at the barn and pulled them from a half-rotted barn sleeper. He drove the nails through the chestnut slab and fastened them to the post. Then he split bed slats, carried them from the woods and put them across the bed from the long slab to the crack in the wall and nailed them to the slab. Aunt Vittie sewed sheets together to make a bed tick while Grandma and I gathered broom sage and filled the bed tick soon as Aunt Vittie had it made. Grandma put the bed tick on the chestnut bed slats; then she spread a sheet over the bed tick and then she put pillows and quilts over the sheet. It wasn't a bad-lookin bed and it was a lot better than sleepin on the floor.

"Tomorrow we'll put two more beds in this house," Uncle George said. "If Mott can use his head enough to make a broom I can use my head enough to make a bed!"

Aunt Vittie was pleased to hear Uncle George talk like this. She looked at him with her soft blue eyes.

"I'll hep you, Uncle George," she said. "I'll make the bed ticks."

Since Grandma had hung a sheet over the winder for a windbreak, I had to pull the sheet to one side so I could see the sun go down over the timbered hill like a big ripe pumpkin. I watched the sunset while Uncle George played his fiddle. Grandpa sat with the toes of his brogan shoes almost in the ashes a-listenin to Uncle George's fiddle while he moved his terbacker from one jaw to the other. And Grandpa would sit and play with his beard first with one hand and then with the other. Then he would spit into the fire to hear the ambeer sizzle on the embers. Some of the ambeer would hold to Grandpa's lips and get tangled in his beard and Grandpa would lift it from his beard with his hand and sling it into the fire. Some of his ambeer would fall on the hearth rock—but that was all right, since he could rub it out with his shoe sole until only the stain of it was left.

Uncle George would often take a chew with Grandpa; often Uncle George would smoke a home-rolled cigar 'r make a home-rolled cigarette outten burley terbacker crumbs and brown sugar poke. But when Uncle George played the fiddle, he never smoked. Maybe he was afraid that the cigar ashes would fall from the end of his cigar when he swayed with his fiddle, fall down among his beard and catch it on fire. Uncle

George always chewed terbacker when he played his fiddle. He would sit and play his fiddle for hours with a chaw behind his jaw. And we hardly ever saw 'im spit ambeer into the fire. I often wondered what he did with it. Grandpa told 'im once that if he swallowed ambeer it would give 'im the night sweats.

While Uncle George played his fiddle, Uncle Mott opened the door and brought inside the house seven rabbits, six quails and two fox squirrels.

"Plenty of game here," Uncle Mott said. "I've had myself a time. Shot sixteen times and brought back fifteen pieces of game."

"Good shootin," Grandpa said.

"Who made the bed?" Uncle Mott asked soon as he looked over in the corner and saw it.

"Uncle George made it," I said.

"It's an ugly thing," Uncle Mott said.

Uncle George kept on playin his fiddle as if he didn't hear what Uncle Mott had said. But Grandpa looked at Uncle George and then he looked at Uncle Mott.

"God, I wished old Kim'd been alive and a-been with me," Uncle Mott said. "He liked good shootin. So many men off at war that the woods are full of game again! Jump a rabbit anyplace among the greenbrier stools and in the broom-sage clusters! If I'd a had a good rabbit dog I could've killed all the rabbits I could've carried. How Kim would've loved to have been with me this afternoon."

Uncle George didn't pay Uncle Mott any minds. He started playin a tune on his fiddle sad as the October wind among the pine needles at night. I wondered if he played the tune when Uncle Mott spoke of Uncle Kim. That was the first time I had ever heard Uncle Mott mention Uncle Kim's name since he had been dead. I wondered if Uncle Mott mentioned his name to hurt Uncle George, since he thought Aunt Vittie loved Uncle George more than she did him. And I wondered what would have happened if Uncle Kim had been back a-rabbit-huntin with Uncle Mott and if he had found out that Uncle

Mott and Uncle George were both in love with Aunt Vittie. It wouldn't have been very good for either one and Uncle Kim with a gun in his hand. I knew that Uncle Mott had said these words to hurt Uncle George for Uncle Mott wouldn't have felt safe around Uncle Kim.

"Rabbits, birds, squirrels," Grandma said, as she opened the kitchen door and looked in the front room. "We're a-goin to have plenty of wild meat!"

"Oh, look at the rabbits," Aunt Vittie said when she walked into the front room. "Where did you get 'em, Mott?"

"In the woods," Uncle Mott said sourly.

"Do you want me to hold the rabbits while you skin 'em?" I asked Uncle Mott.

"Yep, come and hep me, Sid," he said.

"Better than any store meat you can buy," Grandpa said as he pulled the cooked meat from a rabbit's hind leg at supper. "Better than any relief grub a man can get."

We stood around in the kitchen eatin since we didn't have a table and chairs. But we had dishes to eat from.

"Where did you get all these dishes?" Uncle Mott asked.

"While you killed wild game, Uncle Mott," I said, "I went back to the schoolhouse and got the dishes that we dumped into the gulley. Remember when we carried 'em there?"

"Sure do," Uncle Mott said. "Why didn't I think about 'em? They'd slipped my mind."

"You had huntin on your mind, Mott," Grandpa said. "When you live in woods like these, huntin's the first thing that pops into your mind!"

"About the first thing that pops into my mind right now," Uncle Mott said, "is a table. If Uncle George can make a bed, I know that I can make a table! I don't like to stand up and eat hot grub. I like to sit reared back with my feet stuck under the table. Then I can loosen my belt and put the grub away."

"Mott, honey," Grandma said, "I do wish you could make us a table. We sure do need one."

Next day Uncle Mott cut a post and put it in the corner of
the kitchen; then he knocked planks from the smokehouse loft
and carried them into the kitchen. He put the end of a plank
into a crack and let one end rest on the post. Then he put
another plank from the post to the end logs and covered them
with planks—the same way that Uncle George had made the
bed. I thought that the bed Uncle George had made had given
Uncle Mott his idea for the table. Grandma covered the rough
planks with papers. And now we had a table.

Uncle Mott must have thought the table wouldn't be much
good unless we had something to sit on. He went into the
woods and cut a saplin. He scored and hewed one side until
it was as smooth as if it had been sawed. Then Uncle Mott
chiseled holes into the unhewed side with the double-bitted ax
and cut four legs from a smaller saplin and wedged them into
the grooves. Grandpa and I helped him carry the bench into
the kitchen and put it beside the table. Then Uncle Mott
made a smaller bench to be placed at the end of the table.

"If things are a-goin to be made around here," Uncle Mott
said, soon as he had finished with the table and benches, "I'll
show you that I can make my part."

"Mott, honey," Grandma said, as she wheezed on her pipe,
"that's a wonderful job. I'm pleased with them, Mott. It aint
as much as we've been used to but it will do us until we can
do better."

"I'm proud of you, Mott," Grandpa said. "I didn't know
that you was so handy with an ax. Soon as dinner is put on
the table today we can put our feet under the table and eat
from dishes agin. We can use spoons, knives and forks instead
of eatin with our fingers."

"And we can drink our coffee from teacups and saucers
agin," Uncle George said.

"It's more like livin," Aunt Vittie said.

"I'm a-livin just the way I like to live," Grandpa said.

CHAPTER XVI

AUNT VITTIE wouldn't stay in the kitchen to help Grandma with the dishes. Just as soon as Uncle George got the ax on his shoulder and started to the woods, Aunt Vittie went with him. She walked beside Uncle George under the tall leafless trees. Uncle George had the ax across his right shoulder and he gripped the ax handle with his right hand. He had his left arm around Aunt Vittie and his left hand held both of Aunt Vittie's hands. Grandma watched them through the kitchen winder. Uncle Mott saw them from the front yard. And Grandpa sat before the fire; he didn't bother to go look when Grandma called to him.

"Let 'im spark," Grandpa said. "Sparkin's a natural thing."

Then Grandpa laughed a wild laugh, slapped his long thin thighs with his big hands and spit ambeer into the fire.

"Nothin funny about seein Brother George with a woman," Grandpa said. "He's not a geldin. Look at the wives George has had! He's had more than his part. Guess George is lonesome without a wife!"

I didn't try to follow Uncle George and Aunt Vittie to the woods. I knew they wouldn't want me along. I would've gone with 'em to've helped carry the chestnut poles but something inside me told me not to go along and be in the way when Aunt Vittie was a-sparkin Uncle George. I went down to the old barn and pulled nails from the half-rotted planks and sleepers. I knew that Uncle George would need them when he started makin beds. He'd need them to nail the slabs to the post and to nail the slats to the slabs. I hunted for nails while Uncle George and Aunt Vittie hunted for dead chestnut saplins.

While they were gone to the woods, Uncle Mott took his double-barrel shotgun to the woods. He didn't go the way they went; he took to the woods in the opposite direction. Uncle George and Aunt Vittie weren't gone an hour until they came back. Uncle George was a-carryin a long chestnut saplin on his right shoulder and his ax in the left hand; Aunt Vittie followed 'im with a tiny pole across her shoulder. They walked from under the dark pine woods into a leafless oak grove and then they walked into the little clearin where our shack stood.

That afternoon Uncle George made a small bed in the front-room corner across from Grandpa and Grandma's bed. He took a lot of pains with the bed for he knew that Aunt Vittie would sleep on it. And he made two beds in the long room upstairs. He put one bed, big enough for two people, in one corner of the room and in the far corner he put another bed that was just big enough for one. And while Aunt Vittie and Uncle George used the rusty nails that I had gathered to make the beds, Grandma and I gathered broom sage to fill the bed ticks.

"Four beds in our house," Grandma said. "Not the best beds in the world but they are good beds to sleep on. They aint as hard to sleep on as the floor."

It didn't bother Grandpa a lot whether he slept on the floor or on one of the beds. He complained that the bed was too high and that he had trouble of gettin into the bed. But I couldn't understand that when I'd seen Grandpa jump up and crack his heels together three times before he came down on the floor at the square dances. He said that Uncle George was sich a tall man that he had built the beds for a tall man. He said that the bed would have been about right if Uncle George had used the crack below to put the ends of the slabs on. But Grandma told him that the bed wasn't too high for her, said she could climb into the bed all right.

Aunt Vittie thought the table had been put in a crack too high. When she sat down at the table her chin was barely above the table. She could hardly see across the table.

Uncle Mott returned at sundown with sixteen rabbits and fourteen steel traps.

"Where did you get the traps, Mott?" Grandpa asked.

"Found 'em, Pap," Uncle Mott said.

"B-gad, you're a good finder, Mott," Grandpa said, laughin. "We can use the traps this winter."

"Thought I'd give 'em to Sid," Uncle Mott said.

"But I never set a trap," I said.

"I'll show you how to set 'em," Uncle Mott said. "You can set your traps and catch you some fur-bearin animals. You can make yourself some money!"

"Thank you, Uncle Mott," I said. "That's wonderful!"

"You brought Ma's dishes back," Uncle Mott said. "You're good to work. I think you'd make a good trapper."

"I'll make me some money," I said. "I may need money."

"Another ugly bed in the house," Uncle Mott said, pointin to the bed that Uncle George had built.

Uncle George didn't speak to Uncle Mott. He sat before the fire a-tunin his fiddle after he'd worked all afternoon on the beds. Aunt Vittie helped Grandma get supper.

"I'll help you skin the rabbits, Uncle Mott," I said.

"We're a-havin plenty of wild game now," Grandpa said. "We won't starve for meat."

"Sixteen shells and sixteen rabbits," Uncle Mott said.

After supper we carried the benches from the kitchen and placed 'em before the fire while Aunt Vittie and Grandma washed the dishes. And while they washed the dishes, Uncle Mott tuned his banjer and Uncle George tuned his fiddle. Uncle Mott sat on one side the fireplace and Uncle George sat on the other. They faced each other and looked with mean eyes. They never spoke to each other but it was understood that on the October evenins Uncle Mott would pick one tune and then Uncle George would play a tune. And while they rested Grandpa would talk.

Grandma led the way from the kitchen, a-smokin her pipe. Aunt Vittie followed Grandma, a-carryin a pine torch. When Aunt Vittie blew out the pine torch, she put the resined stick of rich pine against the wall. Aunt Vittie sat down on the small bench beside Uncle George and me. I sat on one side of Uncle George and Aunt Vittie sat on the other. Grandma sat down beside Uncle Mott. Grandpa was a-sittin on the other side of Uncle Mott.

"Let's have a good banjer piece, Mott," Grandpa said.

"I'm a-goin to play and sing 'Careless Love,' " Uncle Mott said.

> Love, oh, love, oh, careless love,
> Love, oh, love, how can it be,
> Love, oh, love, oh, careless love,
> To love somebody that don't love me.

Uncle George seemed pleased when Uncle Mott sang "to love somebody that don't love me."

I'd never seen Uncle Mott play his banjer better or sing prettier than he did. He thinks he's a-losin Aunt Vittie, I thought. He thinks Uncle George is a-goin to get her. And I thought that Grandma and Grandpa thought the same thing. They would look at Aunt Vittie and then they'd look at Uncle Mott. And I don't think they wanted Uncle Mott to marry her since she'd already been a wife to Uncle Kim. While Uncle Mott played and sang, he would look at Aunt Vittie to see if she was a-watchin 'im.

Just as soon as Uncle Mott had finished his song, Uncle George started a mournful song on his fiddle. He sang the words as his long arm moved gently with his fiddle bow.

> Oh, carry me back to the mountains,
> Beneath the southern skies;
> Oh, carry me back to the mountains,
> There's where my sweetheart lies.

I get so lonesome without her.
Why did I ever roam?
Oh, carry me back to the mountains,
Back to my home, sweet home.

While Uncle George played his fiddle and sang, I saw Aunt Vittie wipe the tears from her eyes. And I saw Grandma wipe the tears from her eyes with the corner of her apron. Even Grandpa was deeply moved the way he twisted on the bench and pulled at his whiskers. Uncle Mott was touched by the song the way he dropped his head and looked at the floor. Uncle Mott might be better with a double-bitted ax a-makin things than Uncle George but he couldn't bring the music from his banjer that Uncle George could bring from his fiddle. I don't know why I cried; maybe it was because of the mountains around our shack with little creeks of runnin water I loved to hear a-spillin over the rocks. Uncle George's fiddle playin made me think of the rock cliff, schoolhouse and mansion that we'd lived in. His music made me think of the Tussies that used to live with us, and I wondered where they were now and what they were doin. I thought of Effie Tussie while Uncle George played that song.

"Gee, Uncle George," Aunt Vittie said, "I don't know what to tell you!"

"Sure was a pretty song," Grandpa said. "Made me think o' my young days."

"Brought back memories of the past to me," Grandma said.

Uncle Mott didn't say anything and I didn't say anything but I wondered if Uncle Mott didn't want to say something to Uncle George. I wondered if he didn't want to tell him that he liked the song, but he couldn't do it.

"Now it's your time to tell us somethin, Press," Grandma said.

"I've just been a-sittin here a-thinkin about Michigan all afternoon," Grandpa said. "When I look out at this winder and see these dark hills, I think of the dark hills in Michigan. When I lift up a handful of this dark dirt and let it slide between my fingers, I think of the good land in Michigan."

"Tell us about Michigan," I said.

"You'll hardly believe me when I tell you about some of the things I saw in Michigan," Grandpa said. "You won't believe me when I tell you about the things I've done up there. They grow big corn in Michigan."

"Tell us about it, Grandpa," I said.

"When I was there fifty years ago, I saw corn grow high as that scrubby pine out there in the yard," Grandpa said. "Each stalk had a ear of corn behind every blade."

"Tell Sid about your train ride in Michigan, Press," Grandma said, wheezin on her long pipestem.

"I got on the train in Michigan," Grandpa said. "I traveled two days and nights through timber. Never saw a town. Never saw anybody but the people on the train. We only stopped for water and coal. We passed through timber tracts where the trees were big around the butts as sixty-gallon mash barrels."

"Didn't they know the champean lassie maker in Kentucky?" Uncle Mott asked.

"When I was in Saginaw I met a man," Grandpa told us, "who came to me and said: 'Say, you are that champean lassie maker in Kentucky, aint ye?' 'I'm the best that ever biled cane juice in a pan,' I said. Then he said: 'I thought you were that feller.' Then he pulled out a little book that had my name and picture in it. He showed me a picture of myself a-stirrin a pan of sorghum. They knew me in the state of Michigan before I got there."

"What about that sand hill, Pap?" Uncle Mott said. "You ought to tell Sid about it."

"That was a big hill of white sand among the timber," Grandpa said. "There was a lot of people on this hill. I said to a feller there, 'Can you tell me why there's so many people out here?' And he said: 'Didn't you know there is a prize of five thousand dollars offered to any man or woman who can walk in this sand without gettin it in his shoes?' I'll win that prize, I thought to myself since I had on lumber artics that would turn water. When I pulled my shoes off, they were full of sand."

"What about the big fishes you caught up there, Press?" Grandma said.

"The fishes come through a hole in the mountain," Grandpa said, throwin his cud of chawed terbacker in the fire. "Men killed 'em with clubs as they come out. They came through a hole no bigger than a nail keg. Some weighed thirty pounds."

"Pa Tussie, didn't you used to drive oxen when you were in Michigan?" Aunt Vittie asked Grandpa.

"I was given up to be the best ox driver in Michigan," Grandpa said. "I drove forty yoke of oxen."

"All in the same team?" I asked.

"All in the same team," Grandpa said. "When I drove my team across a holler with a big tree, I've seen ten yoke of oxen a-hangin in the air. Cattle would drag 'em right over the bank till they could get their feet down."

"How big was the log, Pap?" Uncle Mott asked.

"Big enough that they could run four sets of a square dance on its stump," Grandpa said. "Then there would be room on the stump for the fiddler, banjer picker and two guitar pickers."

"Michigan is some place, Grandpa," I said.

"It sure is, Sid," Grandpa said.

And when I went to my bed upstairs in the corner to sleep with Uncle Mott, I thought about Michigan. I thought about Michigan while Uncle George snored in his bed on the far corner of the long room. I wondered why we didn't have big trees in Kentucky like they had in Michigan.

CHAPTER XVII

✗

U NCLE MOTT cut wood for the fireplace in the mornins
and rabbit-hunted in the afternoons. I often went with
Uncle Mott to carry his rabbits. And one afternoon Uncle
Mott took me along the ridge top not far from where Uncle
Kim was buried. We could look down upon the schoolhouse
from the tops of the jagged cliffs. There were holes under
these rocks that were worn slick.

"Here's the best place to trap in this county, Sid," Uncle
Mott said. "I've trapped all over this county and I know."

Uncle Mott showed me how to set a steel trap and how to
hide it so a coon, fox, possum, mink or a polecat would walk
into it. He told me to use gloves on my hands when I set the
traps so the wild animals wouldn't smell my hands.

"I'm a good hunter, Sid" Uncle Mott said. "I'm a good
trapper. But I'm not a good lover."

I didn't say anything, for that didn't bother me.

"And my banjer won't come up to Uncle George's fiddle,"
he said. "I can't get as much music from it as Uncle George
can get from his fiddle. Take that fiddle away from 'im and
I'd stand a chance with the woman we love. And neither one
of us is a good-lookin man but I think I'm as good a lookin man
as Uncle George. I'm a damn sight younger. It's that fiddle of
Uncle George's that's opened up the hearts of women to 'im."

In the afternoons while we hunted Uncle George chopped
stove wood for the cook stove. Aunt Vittie dragged the little
dead poles down from the woods to the chop block while
Uncle George chopped them into short sticks. And Grandpa
sat before the fire and told Grandma the great things that he
had done while they were a-waitin for the fifteenth of October so they could go to town together and git his pension
check.

On the fourteenth of October a well-dressed man walked around the path toward our house. I thought he was a lawyer a-comin after us, that we had done something and the Law was after us again. That's what Uncle Mott thought, too, for he trembled like a white-oak leaf in the winter wind. Uncle George was a-choppin stove wood when he saw the stranger. He dropped his ax at the chop block and made for the house. I ran to the winder, stuck my head through a paneless square and yelled to Grandpa that a strange man was a-comin.

"Aint Sheriff Whiteapple, is it?" Grandpa asked.

"Nope, it aint 'im," I said.

By the time the stranger reached our shack Grandpa was out in the yard beside me. I saw Aunt Vittie and Grandma a-standin by the kitchen winder to listen to what the stranger wanted.

"Does Press Tussie live here?" the stranger asked.

"Yep, he does," Grandpa said. "I'm Press Tussie."

"I'm Eddie McConnell," the stranger said, a-shakin Grandpa's hand. "I'm the county attendance officer."

"What's that?" Grandpa asked. "Is it one of them A.B.C. letter offices?"

"No, it's not that kind of an office," Eddie McConnell said. "I'm to see that children in this county go to school. It's been reported to me that you have a boy here of school age that is not enrolled in this county and has never gone to school a day in his life."

"Who reported that?" Grandpa asked.

"I'm not to tell you that, Mr. Tussie," Eddie McConnell said. "I just want to know if this is a fact. How old is your boy?"

"Don't know exactly," Grandpa said. "'Spect he's in the neighborhood of thirteen, fourteen, maybe fifteen."

"And he's never gone to school a day in his life?"

"Nope."

"Is this the boy?" he asked Grandpa, pointin to me.

"Yep, that's Sid."

"Now, Mr. Tussie, it's not for the want of clothes you haven't sent him, is it?" Eddie McConnell asked. "He's wearin good clothes and good shoes."

"Nope, it's not that," Grandpa said. "I never went to school a day in my life and I'm still a-livin. I've reached my three score year and ten."

"But there's a law in Kentucky that now compels you to send your children to school," Eddie McConnell said. "If you don't send your children to school you can be brought before the county judge and fined!"

"A law," Grandpa said. "Shucks, I didn't know that."

"You'll find out about this law if you don't have this boy in school by Monday," Eddie McConnell told Grandpa.

"I'll have 'im there before Monday if that's the law," Grandpa said. "I'll have 'im there day after tomorrow."

"He's in the Six Hickories School," Eddie McConnell said. "Do you know where that schoolhouse is?"

"Yep—yep, I do," Grandpa said with a tremblin voice.

I heard Grandma cough at the kitchen winder. I thought I heard Aunt Vittie laugh.

"Do you know where it is, young man?" he asked me.

"Yes, I know where it's at," I said.

"Then this will be all," Eddie McConnell said. "I'll expect 'im in school by Monday. If he's not there, you can see the county judge."

"He'll be there," Grandpa said.

"Good day, Mr. Tussie," Mr. McConnell said as he turned to go away.

"Ssslon-long," Grandpa said with a weak tremblin voice.

We stood in the yard and watched him walk outten sight around the path. Grandma and Aunt Vittie watched 'im from the kitchen winder.

"Gee, Grandpa," I said, "I hate to go to school. I can't bear to go back to that schoolhouse again."

"But you'll haf to go, Sid," Grandpa said. "It's the law. I didn't know it was the law. I didn't know the law could make you send a boy to school. Things have changed since I was a boy."

"Somebody's a-doin a lot of reportin," Grandma said, stickin her head outten the kitchen winder. "I think it's some of your kinfolks, Press."

"It's that young Ben Tussie and Dee Tussie, Ma," Uncle Mott said.

"The Law is a dangerous thing," Grandpa said.

Next mornin Grandpa dressed in his best suit that Aunt Vittie had bought him. He combed his beard and the hair on his head. He was as spry as a bird when it's first let out of a cage. Uncle Mott dressed in his best suit. He put on a white shirt and tied a red necktie around his neck. Grandma wore the best dress she had, a long gingham dress that came to the tops of her black shoes. All the time Grandma was a-gittin dressed Grandpa was a-hurryin her.

"Let's hurry and get to town and get the bacon," Grandpa would say. "It's a-waitin for us in the post office."

Uncle Mott was in a big way too. I knew why Uncle Mott wanted to go to town. Uncle Mott hadn't had a drink for a long time. He had drowned his worries in the woods with his gun. Now he wanted to get on a big toot. I knew he didn't have any business in town. That's the only reason he was a-goin. He'd make Grandpa give him two dollars. He could buy enough rotgut from Toodle Powell with two dollars to get on a toot.

"Sid, you be a good boy," Grandpa said. "We'll fetch you somethin from town."

"All right, Grandpa," I said.

Grandpa was the first to leave the house. Uncle Mott and Grandma followed.

"We'll be back, Vittie," Grandma said, "soon as we can get back."

"No use to rush, Ma Tussie," Aunt Vittie said. "It's a fur piece to walk."

"I know it," Grandma said.

Aunt Vittie and Uncle George wanted them to get away, I thought as I stood beside the kitchen a-watchin Grandpa, Uncle Mott and Grandma followin the windin path outten sight. They want 'em to get away so they can have the house to themselves. They want to do some sparkin.

"Don't you want to take your Uncle Mott's gun and go a-huntin?" Uncle George asked me soon as I went into the house.

"I'd be afraid," I said.

"Aint you never hunted with a gun?" he asked me.

"Nope," I said.

"It's time you's a-larnin," he said.

"I'm afraid Uncle Mott will care," I said.

"He'd be proud of you if you'd kill five or six rabbits," Uncle George said.

"Then I will take his gun and go into the woods," I said.

I wanted to take a gun into the woods. I'd always wanted to take a gun into the woods since I could remember but Uncle Mott and Grandpa wouldn't let me. They said that my takin a gun into the woods would be a waste of shells and that I had better wait until I got older before I hunted with a gun; yet Grandpa and Uncle Mott would sit before the fire and brag about how young they were when they went into the woods with a gun. Uncle Mott said that he was so small that he couldn't hold the shotgun to his shoulder and Grandpa said he was so young and small that he couldn't cock the trigger; yet he said that he killed rabbits.

Uncle George lifted Uncle Mott's double-barrel twelve-gauge from the front-room joist where the trigger guard was hooked over a nail and the barrels rested over a big spike driven into the joist for a gun rest. He showed me how to break it down, to reload it, and how to use the safety. And he found enough of Uncle Mott's shells to fill both of my pockets. Now I was a hunter off to the woods. I hadn't got outten sight of the house until a rabbit jumped from a brier cluster; I aimed and fired both barrels. The rabbit went end over end. I was glad that Uncle George had told me to take Uncle Mott's gun into the woods. Never did I enjoy anything more than this. The sun had melted the frost on the leaves and dead grass and had made them damp. And I could slip up on a rabbit, find him asleep, scare 'im out and shoot at 'im runnin. I didn't haf to shoot at 'im a-runnin; I could shoot his head off while he was asleep. I knew why Uncle Mott brought so many headless rabbits to our shack now. He had found them asleep and killed them. But I hated to kill the rabbits that way; I liked to scare them out and give 'em a chance for their lives. I liked to see what I could do with a gun.

Before noon the last mist clouds of melted frost had gone up toward the blue skies and the leaves and grass got crispy dry beneath my feet until I scared the rabbits out before I got near them. I had shot twelve times and I had killed ten rabbits. I watched after my first shot not to git too excited and pull both triggers at the same time. Now I knew that I was a hunter and that I loved the woods. I went through the dark pine woods toward the shack with my rabbits tied to my belt. When I went into the house, Uncle George laughed and called Aunt Vittie from the kitchen.

"Look at the young hunter," Uncle George said. "He'll make a better hunter than his Uncle Mott."

"Skin a couple now, Uncle George," Aunt Vittie said. "We need meat to go with our bread."

I held the rabbits' legs while Uncle George skinned them. Aunt Vittie cooked two rabbits for our dinner and all we had was rabbit and bread. And the bread was what I'd picked up from the school yard.

"No use to keep the rest of that bread," Aunt Vittie said. "Pa Tussie will get his check today and he'll bring back a sack of meal and a sack of flour."

"Don't throw bread away, Vittie," Uncle George said. "Keep it until they get back anyway. I never could stand to see bread wasted."

The bread was a little dry but it was good with rabbit. Aunt Vittie warmed the bread in the oven. And she cooked the rabbits tender. I'd never tasted anything better—not even at the big Rayburn house—than the bread that I had found and the rabbits that I had killed. Uncle George could almost eat a piece of rabbit at one bite. All he had to do was run the rabbit leg through his mouth and he'd pull the bone stripped clean as a peeled pawpaw stick from his mouth.

"I've always liked good rabbit," Uncle George said. "I've always liked any kind of wild meat."

After we'd eaten until we were stuffed, Uncle George said, "Since you've killed the rabbits, Sid, and carried the bread to this house, now I think it's time for you to go in the front room and rest before the good fire that I've made for you while I help Vittie wash the dishes."

"All right, Uncle George," I said.

I heard them a-talkin in the kitchen while I laid on the floor flat of my back before the fire. I heard Uncle George a-callin Aunt Vittie his "wild pigeon" and his "pretty little percoon blossom" and his little "shoot of sweet annias." I heard 'im a-callin her all the names of wild flowers and birds and I'd hear 'em kiss. I knew that they didn't want me in the kitchen a-botherin 'em. And I'd hear the dishes stop rattlin for a long spell. I knew that they were a-huggin and a-kissin. I just laid before the fire and wondered about Uncle Mott, Uncle George and Uncle Kim. What if they were all in this shack, I thought, I wonder which man that Aunt Vittie would choose?

I must've gone to sleep before the fire for Uncle George woke me a-pullin at my coat collar.

"Sid, Sid," he said. "Somethin you fergot."

"What did I forget?" I asked, sittin on the floor and a-rubbin my eyes.

"Your traps," he said.

"That's right," I said.

I jumped up and hurried outten the shack, leavin Aunt Vittie and Uncle George a-sittin on the little bench before the fire. They want to git rid of me again, I thought. They want to be by themselves so they can spark when there's not anybody around to bother 'em. I hurried to the line of traps that Uncle Mott had helped me set. I got two possums outten my traps and I reset the traps the way that Uncle Mott had showed me. I carried my possums with a tail in each hand. I hurried back to the shack to show Aunt Vittie and Uncle George.

"Two hides and a change of meat," Uncle George said.

"Do you like possum, Uncle George?" Aunt Vittie asked.

"I sure do," Uncle George said.

"What must I do with 'em?" I asked.

"Put 'em in a sack until Press and Mott get back," Uncle George said. "I never liked to kill a possum. They are too hard to kill. I don't want to kill anything right now, do I, honey?"

Uncle George looked at Aunt Vittie when he spoke.

"No, you don't, Uncle George," she said.

I went into the kitchen, got a sack and put my possums in it.

"Sid, have you seen any wild flowers on your rambles through the woods?" Uncle George yelled to me while I was a-tyin the possum sack.

"Some farewell-to-summers up there under the pines," I said.

"Let's go get 'em, honey," Uncle George said to Aunt Vittie.

I hadn't seen any farewell-to-summers there but I knew if they hunted for some that they'd find them under the pines where the frost hadn't blighted all the wild flowers. And I knew that it was my time to stay in the shack a little while and let them get out. I didn't know why two people old as they were wanted to get out and hunt wild flowers and carry on with a lot of soft words and call one another "honey" and the names of wild flowers and wild birds. Aunt Vittie had been married once and Uncle George had been married five times. But I had heard about love and I'd seen one little girl that I hadn't forgot. I couldn't forget the nights at the "big house" when I had danced with Effie Tussie.

When I had finished a-tyin my possum sack, I went into the front room and Uncle George and Aunt Vittie had gone. I looked out at the winder and I saw Uncle George and Aunt Vittie a-goin up the hill under the leafless oaks toward the pine grove. Uncle George's arm was around her and her arm was around Uncle George and they were a-walkin so close together that they could've both walked side by side of a little narrow path. I watched them walk slowly, Uncle George a-mashin down the greenbriers with his big feet and a-holdin them so they wouldn't catch Aunt Vittie's dress tail. I watched them until they'd disappeared among the dark pines.

I watched the path that led toward the turnpike. I watched for Grandma and Grandpa. I didn't expect to see Uncle Mott with 'em because I knew that, soon as Grandpa gave 'im a dollar or two, he wouldn't be back until tomorrow. I knew that Uncle Mott would get on his toot and that Grandpa and Grandma would haf to tote the load of grub from town. While I stood inside the kitchen and looked from the winder at the long windin path, I got homesick to see Grandpa. It seemed that when he was away I felt lonely to see 'im. Grandpa had always taken me with 'im, and I loved 'im. And it was hard for me to stay away from 'im. When I'd heard anybody say anything about Grandpa's bein lazy, I wanted to fight that person. I thought Grandpa was the best man in the world. He'd been the best man to me that I had ever known.

I watched for Grandpa from the kitchen winder; then I went into the yard and once I walked out the path a piece and then back to the house. While I watched for them, I looked up on the hill and Uncle George and Aunt Vittie walked from beneath the pines with their arms around one another and Aunt Vittie had a cluster of farewell-to-summer blossoms wreathed in her hair. Uncle George was a-wearin a cluster of farewell-to-summer blossoms in his coat lapel. And when they got nearer I could see that Aunt Vittie had wild violets stuck here and there in her soft fluffy broom-sage-colored hair. I knew where they'd got the violets; they had had to rake away the fallen leaves to find them.

"Have they come yet?" Uncle George asked.

"Nope," I said.

"It's about time for 'em, aint it?" he asked.

"Yes," I said.

Uncle George and Aunt Vittie hadn't more'n got into the house when I saw Grandpa's head pop up far out the path. And then I saw Uncle Mott's head and then Grandma's big hat with a plume in it. I saw them a-comin and I wondered why Uncle Mott had come back with them. I stood waitin for them to reach the shack.

"Grandpa," I said.

"Sid," he asked nervously, "are you glad to see yer Grandpa?"

"Sure am," I said.

"I couldn't fetch you anything, Sid," he said as he hurried into the house. He didn't have any load and Uncle Mott wasn't a-carryin anything. Grandma was a-puffin her pipe like she was riled. I'm glad Aunt Vittie saved the bread, ran through my head.

"I'm ruint, George," Grandpa said soon as he entered the front room. "Somebody's turned me up for ownin land."

"Tussies," Grandma snorted. "It takes your kinfolks to ruin you!"

"Who killed these rabbits?" Uncle Mott asked.

"I did," I said.

"Whose gun did you use?" he asked. "And whose shells did you shoot?"

"Yours," I said.

"Who told you to?"

"Told myself to," I said. "We just had bread and no meat."

"Wonderful," Uncle Mott said. "How many shells did you use and how many rabbits did you kill?"

"Twelve shells and ten rabbits," I said.

"You'll make a great hunter," Uncle Mott said. "You'll be as good a shot someday as your Uncle Kim."

Uncle Mott had seen the farewell-to-summers in Uncle George's coat lapel and he had seen the farewell-to-summers and the violets wreathed in Aunt Vittie's hair and that had made 'im mad. I thought he was already mad because he had gone to town to get drunk and Grandpa hadn't got his check.

"When I got my letter outten the post office," Grandpa said, "I told Arimithy something was wrong for I opened it and there wasn't a check in it. We went straight to Lawyer Landgraves' office and he read the letter to us. The letter explained that when you owned land you couldn't get old-age pension. Said if I were able to buy a farm, as it had been reported to them, then I wasn't entitled to a pension. I tell you, I'm ruint and winter is a-comin on. I went down to the relief office and the people, who used to be so friendly and wanted to fill my sacks, looked at me with mean eyes. I tried to get relief again and everybody thought I was a rich man. A-movin in that big house and a-carryin on like we did has damned nigh finished us!"

"Don't mention that house any more, Press," Grandma said. "I love to sit before the fire and think about a-livin there. And when we walked along the turnpike a-goin and a-comin today, I had to stop and look at the house. I'll always remember it and love it to my dyin day."

"Taters are the nearest thing to bread, aint they, Pap?" Uncle Mott asked.

"Yes, they are, Mott," Grandpa said.

"Taters and wild game will tide us over," Uncle Mott said.

"We can't manage on 'em until spring, Mott," Grandpa said. "Bread is the staff of life; we must have bread. Lord, I wish I's back on relief!"

"Give the farm to Vittie," Uncle George said. "Then you won't own land. You can get your relief back."

"No, we won't give the farm back to Vittie," Grandma said, a-wheezin on her pipe. "Kim was our boy. We worked and raised 'im. Vittie just married 'im."

I knew that Uncle George had said the wrong thing to Grandma. And I knew why that Uncle George had said it. He was in love with Aunt Vittie and he wanted her to have the farm. He wanted her to have the best grub and the best bed; he wanted her to have everything. And now I wondered if Grandma would go around a-callin Aunt Vittie "honey." I wondered if it would be "honey this" and "honey that" after Grandpa and Grandma had spent her money and she was a-courtin Uncle George.

"First time I ever had a deed for land in my life," Grandpa said. "I'm not a-givin it away when I've got dirt black as the dirt in Michigan. Hold the dirt in your hand and let it run between your fingers. Feel of the dirt and you wouldn't want to give it away either."

"We aint a-givin it away, Press," Grandma said. "The deed's in your name and we'll hold it. If you die first I'll hold it. If I die first I want you to hold it."

"That's exactly what I'll do," Grandpa said.

"But I thought you wanted relief," Uncle George said.

"I do want relief," Grandpa said, "but I want to keep my land."

"Ye can't have both," Uncle George said.

"I'll keep the land," Grandpa said.

Aunt Vittie looked at Uncle George and then she looked at Grandpa and Grandma. I looked at Uncle Mott and he looked mad as a wet hornet to me. I thought trouble was a-brewin now. But it was the first time real trouble had started in our shack. We never had had any trouble long as we had plenty of grub on the table but when the table was bare it meant trouble. But I'd seen dogs get along as long as there was plenty of bread but when the bread got scarce every dog made a grab for what was left and it ended in a fight.

"It was my money that went into this land," Aunt Vittie said.

"It was my boy," Grandma said.

"No trouble now," Grandpa said. "Let's have peace."

"Let's have peace," Uncle George said.

"Peace be damned," Uncle Mott said.

CHAPTER XVIII

%

M Y HAIR was nearly long as Grandpa's beard but I combed
it back over my head. And my hair wasn't corn-silk
yellow like most of the Tussies' hair; my hair was black as a
crow's wing. I put on a white shirt and a necktie and my best
suit of clothes. Grandma fixed my dinner; she put the last
pieces of bread that I'd picked up on the school ground with
a few pieces of rabbit and wrapped them in a newspaper.

"First boy I ever sent to school," Grandpa said. "I want you
to be a good boy and larn a lot."

"You aint a-sendin 'im, Press," Uncle George said. "The
Law's a-sendin 'im."

"Don't git into fights and ruin your clothes," Grandma said.

"Be a good boy, Sid," Aunt Vittie said.

"When you leave school this afternoon," Uncle Mott said,
"see about your traps. I'll kill and skin your possums today
and stretch the hides for you. You'll be needin money to buy
paper and pencils."

"All right," I said as I left the shack for Six Hickories
School.

I'd been a-dreadin this day. And now I dreaded it more than
ever. I was scared to death to go back to this schoolhouse. I
wondered if anyone would remember me as the one that
robbed the playhouse and picked up the bread on the school
yard. I hoped they wouldn't but there was a lot of faces up
against the winderpanes. I walked along the path not a-thinkin
about my steel traps. I wanted to think about 'em so I could
quit thinkin about school. And when I went down the path
and the Higgins Hollow road and reached the turnpike, I
heard the school bell ring. Everything was quiet when I
reached the schoolhouse.

I opened the door and walked up the aisle toward the table

we used to eat offen. A well-dressed woman sat there; she wore glasses and she looked straight at me. The boys looked at me from their side of the house but I just glanced at them once and turned my head. Many of them was a-tryin to laugh and the girls looked at me from their side of the house. They looked at me as if I were a ghost. I walked up to the teacher's desk and stood before her. I didn't know what to do. I thought she was to speak first. And she did.

"What do you want?" she asked me.

"I've come to school," I said.

"Where did you go to school last?" she asked.

"Never went to school," I said.

"Never went to school?" she asked.

All the boys and girls in the schoolhouse laughed and hit their desks with their hands.

"Nope, I never went to school," I said.

"No more of that laughin, children," the teacher said, hittin the desk with a small peeled stick. "This isn't anything to laugh about."

Then she turned to me and said, "What is your father's name?"

"Grandpa," I said.

Everybody started laughin again. The teacher hit the desk louder than ever with the little peeled stick.

"Your Grandpa is not your father," she said.

"He's mine," I said.

"Grandpa who?" she asked me.

"Grandpa Tussie," I said.

"Oh, Tussie," she said.

"Press Tussie," I said.

"Who's your mother?" she asked.

"Grandma Tussie," I said. "Arimithy Tussie."

Now the boys whispered to one another about me and the girls whispered to one another. I knew they were a-whisperin about me for they looked right at me when they whispered.

The teacher wrote something on a piece of paper.

"How old are you?" she asked me.

"I don't know," I said.

"Find out when you go home and tell me tomorrow," she said.

The teacher put me on a front seat by myself. I was glad she did because I couldn't see the boys and girls a-lookin at me. And while I sat on the front seat, I looked at the stove. It had been cleaned since we left this schoolhouse. I was a-sittin near the corner of the schoolhouse where I ust to sleep and I thought of the many nights that I had slept in this schoolhouse and I wondered if any of the girls and boys knew that I had once lived here, had slept in the corner and had eaten many meals offen the teacher's desk. I remembered the many good dances that we had had in this schoolhouse and how we'd torn the seats up from the floor and put them in a pile. Now they had been nailed back to the floor. I was a-sitting here a-thinkin these thoughts and a-lookin the schoolhouse over when the teacher called for the "Primer Class."

"You come up with this class, Sid," she said to me.

They were little boys and girls and I was big as three of 'em put together. And when I went up with them everybody laughed. I saw a smile spread over the teacher's face.

"Miss Clark, let me count first," a little girl said.

"Let Sid count first," Miss Clark said.

Then she turned to me and said, "Stand up and see if you can count to ten for us, Sid."

"I can count more than to ten," I said.

I stood up beside the long bench and counted a hundred.

"Who taught you to count, Sid?" Miss Clark asked me.

"Aunt Vittie larned me," I said.

"Can you write your name, Sid?" she asked.

"Nope," I said.

"Can you make figures with chalk on the blackboard?" she asked.

"I can make them up to ten," I said. I almost told her that Aunt Vittie showed me how to make a few figures on the blackboard when we lived at this schoolhouse.

"Go to the blackboard and make figures up to ten," she said.

Miss Clark didn't believe me but I showed her.

"That's fine," she said.

Then she turned to a chart in the corner. I had seen it before for it had the corners torn off where Uncle Mott used to tear 'em off and stick 'em in the stove to light his cigarettes. She turned to the A.B.C.'s and she couldn't show me one I didn't know. Then she had me to read. I read everything there was on the chart.

"You say you've never been to school before?" she asked me.

"Not until today," I said.

"You're doin well," she said. "You won't stay with this class very long."

The boys and girls had stopped laughin at me now.

"Let's see if you can read in this first reader," Miss Clark said, showin me how to hold the book.

I didn't know that I could read in a book but I could.

"That will do," Miss Clark said, after I'd read the first page. It was fun to read and I liked it.

A little old book that tiny, I thought, I'll soon read everything in it.

At recess the boys wouldn't come near me. The girls looked at me and laughed. I stood around and watched them play and I saw them have some more of Grandma's dishes on the moss-covered planks under a big oak tree. I'll haf to get 'em for Grandma, I thought. Grandma needs 'em.

I went back into the schoolhouse and I sat on my seat and listened to the boys and girls come up to the long benches in front when their classes were called. I heard them read— a-stumblin over the words and a-havin a time. And I listened to 'em count; I saw 'em make figures above ten on the blackboard and I watched them carefully. I wanted to larn more than what was in my class. Just as well larn it all while I'm here, I thought.

At noon I slipped away from the boys and girls to eat my dry bread and rabbit under a hickory tree on the far side of the schoolhouse. I was afraid that some of them would know the bread that they had dumped from their dinner buckets. And then they'd know that I was the one who had robbed their playhouses. Before I'd finished my dinner I saw six big boys a-comin toward me. Somethin inside of me told me that they were a-goin to do somethin to me. They were a-whisperin to one another. When they got near me they broke in a run and piled on me, a-holdin my hands and legs, and the girls came a-runnin and brought ribbons and tied on my hair. They even plaited my hair. And when they let me up, the bell started ringin. I didn't know what to do—I hated to go inside the schoolhouse with the ribbons on my hair and my hair plaited; but I was afraid to go home. I was afraid of the Law. I went inside the schoolhouse.

"Sid," Miss Clark said, "come here!"

I walked up the aisle to her desk.

"Did you do that to your hair?"

"You know I wouldn't put ribbons on my hair," I said.

"Who did that?" she asked.

"I don't know their names," I said.

"Show them to me," she said.

I pointed to the boys and the girls.

"You will stay after school," she told them.

When school was over, boys waited for me at the turnpike, but I took over the bank and climbed the mountain to my traps. I fooled them. I guess they waited a long time. As I climbed the mountain, I thought about my first day in school. I didn't think it was a bad place and that I would soon like it. I'd like to be able to know how to read books and to write my name and to write letters. I could read and write for Grandpa,

Grandma, Uncle Mott and Uncle George. And I could help Aunt Vittie, for she could read only the little words and she could barely write her name.

Soon as I'd reached our shack with two possums, I went to the kitchen.

"Come, Mott," Grandma called. "Sid's got two more possums."

"Did you get a whoppin today, Sid?" Grandpa asked me.

"Nope," I said.

"Did you like school?" Aunt Vittie asked me.

"Yep, I did," I said.

"Did you larn anything?" Grandma asked me.

"Yep," I said.

They seemed real proud of me. Even Uncle George stopped playin his fiddle and walked into the kitchen. He looked at me and smiled. I knew that it took somethin to make Uncle George stop playin his fiddle.

"School's not as bad as I thought it was," I told 'em. "I don't think any of them knows that I ust to live in the schoolhouse. They don't know that I slipped back to the school yard and got Grandma's dishes either."

Then Grandpa laughed like he thought it was funny.

"Some boy," Grandpa said.

"Where did you get all these taters?" I asked, lookin at a full sack of taters leaned against the kitchen wall.

"Your Uncle Mott found 'em in a patch where they weren't dug," Grandpa said.

I started to say that the taters were dry, that they hadn't come otten the ground, but I didn't. I had heard Grandpa say many times that Uncle Mott was a good finder and I knew that we had to have bread. And I could take baked taters and rabbit to school.

CHAPTER XIX

I N our shack trouble had started. Grandma had got so she wouldn't speak to Aunt Vittie. And Uncle Mott didn't like Uncle George, but I was like Grandpa; I loved everybody. Grandpa laughed and talked with Aunt Vittie and Uncle George same as he did with Uncle Mott, Grandma and me. And when I went to school a-carryin my baked taters and rabbit, I wondered what would happen when rabbit season was over and Uncle Mott couldn't find any more taters. I wondered if there would be any more trouble at our house.

Then I would look at the thick timber on the place that Grandpa owned that bordered my path. I thought the tall gray limbless poplar trees looked like frozen-stiff possums' tails a-standin in the frosty air; the gray, bushy hazelnut bushes looked like gray squirrels' tails when they ran away from me, a-barkin, to the tall oak trees with hollow knots upon them, where they ran to hide; the red sumacs with their pods of berries looked like roosters' red combs. And the dark bushy pine tops, after the sun had gone down, looked like the black bushy polecats' tails. The greenbrier clusters looked like piles of little green snakes wrapped around one another and the brown saw briers looked like piles of little brown ground snakes. And I could see dogs, mules, schoolhouses, trees and big mountains with deep gulleys streaked down their sides among the white clouds that rolled across the sky over these mountains. When I saw these things I'd forget the trouble at our shack. And I was larnin to read so that I could read many books.

After eight days Miss Clark put me in the Second Reader. And when I went home to tell everybody about it, I could tell that something had happened at our shack. I talked to everybody and everybody talked to me but they didn't talk to one another, except Aunt Vittie sat on Uncle George's knee. I'd never seen her do this before and she had her arms around him a-kissin his beardy face and Uncle George was a-kissin her and a-callin her his "littel violet," his "little daisy," his "little wren bird" and his "buttercup." I couldn't stand all the little soft names he was a-callin her.

Grandma didn't speak to Uncle George and Aunt Vittie at the supper table. And after we'd finished supper, we went inside the front room before the fire.

"Ma Tussie, we have the right to stay here," Aunt Vittie said. "I've spent all the money I had here and we have no place to go now. Uncle George aint any more able to work than Pa Tussie."

"You mean you spent my money," Grandma said.

"No, I mean just what I said," Aunt Vittie told Grandma. "I mean that you spent my money. It was the money for my dead husband. If he wasn't mine, whose was he?"

"Mine," Grandma said. "My boy. That's whose he was."

"Let's stop quarrelin on Vittie's weddin night," Grandpa said.

"Weddin night?" I asked.

"Yep, Brother George and Vittie got married today," Grandpa said.

Aunt Vittie pulled Uncle George close to her and kissed his face.

"Yes, we got married, didn't we, Uncle George?" Aunt Vittie said softly, fondlin Uncle George's beardy face with her little hands.

"Yes, my little buttercup," Uncle George said. "But you mustn't call me Uncle George now; you must call me George."

"But I forget," Aunt Vittie cackled like a hen.

"Mott, you'll haf to sleep down here tonight," Grandma said. "You'll haf to let the lovebirds have your bed."

"All right, Ma," Mott said, never lookin up from the hearth.

"Where'll I sleep, Grandma?" I asked.

"You'll haf to sleep in your Uncle George's bed upstairs," Grandma said. "It's just big enough for one. Give the lovebirds the bed you and Mott slept in."

Uncle George and Aunt Vittie got up from the bench with their arms around each other. They went into the kitchen, feelin their way through the dark to the stairs. And we heard 'em a-laughin as they went up the creaky stairs a-feelin their way with footsteps.

"Old men are fools when they take a notion to marry again," Grandma said.

"But Vittie's comb was a-gettin red, Arimithy," Grandpa said, laughin so hard that he shook all over.

"It's not funny, Press," Grandma snarled.

"I think it's funny," Grandpa said.

"He's too old to marry a young woman," Grandma snorted. "How can he make 'er a livin a-sittin around a-playin lonesome winter tunes on his fiddle?"

"They can live on love," Grandpa said.

"When starvation comes in at the front door," Grandma said, "love goes out at the back winder."

"Uncle George and Aunt Vittie'll hear you a-talkin," I said.

"Don't care if they do hear me," Grandma said. "I'd say to their faces what I'm a-sayin here."

Uncle Mott still looked down at the hearth. He looked to me like that he was hurt. He was a-thinkin about something. I didn't know whether he was a-thinkin about Aunt Vittie or not. I wondered how he'd feel to be a-sleepin in her bed—the good little bed that Uncle George had made for her; I wondered if he'd lay there a-thinkin about her a-sleepin upstairs in his bed. And I wondered how I'd feel to be a-sleepin in Uncle George's bed. But I couldn't sleep with Uncle Mott downstairs on the little halfbed that Uncle George had built for Aunt Vittie.

"No use to be so sad about Vittie, Mott," Grandpa said. "If she loved George more than she did you, you'd better be glad she married George."

Uncle Mott didn't say anything; he didn't move. He watched the glow of dyin embers, never battin his eyes.

"I'm glad Mott didn't marry 'er," Grandma said.

"I don't want to go upstairs and sleep," I said.

"But you'll haf to sleep up there," Grandpa said.

"I know I ain't a-goin up there," Uncle Mott said.

"I know you aint a-goin," Grandma said. "I don't want trouble in this house."

"Ain't no ust to be blue about 'er, Mott," Grandpa said.

"I aint a-thinkin about 'er, Pap," Uncle Mott said. "I'm a-thinkin about somethin. You know I didn't want to marry my dead brother's wife. But I did love Vittie."

"If you aint a-thinkin about 'er, what are you so blue about then?" Grandma asked him as she filled her pipe to smoke.

"Ma, I need money," Uncle Mott said. "I need to go to town."

"To get drunk and drown your troubles?" Grandma asked.

"If we had money you could have some, Mott," Grandpa said.

"I've been a-thinkin of a way to get money," Uncle Mott said.

"You can have my possum hides, Uncle Mott," I said.

"I don't want 'em, Sid," he said. "You'll need that money to get your hair cut at the barbershop in town."

"How'll you get money, Mott?" Grandma asked.

"Kim was my brother," Uncle Mott said. "You've got this land; I aint got anything. I've lost everything."

"But I can't give you my land," Grandpa said.

"But what about the timber?" Uncle Mott said.

"I aint thought about that," Grandpa said.

"Then be a-thinkin about it," Uncle Mott said.

"Just so I keep my good black loamy land," Grandpa said.

"If I don't get something there'll be trouble," Uncle Mott said. "Kim was my brother and the money you got for 'im paid for this land and that makes me entitled to some of it."

"We'll think it over, Mott," Grandpa said.

I don't know whether Uncle Mott was entitled to something because Uncle Kim was his brother or whether Grandpa and Grandma thought it best to give Uncle Mott the timber because he had always stayed with them and hadn't married. But they gave Uncle Mott the timber and the day he sold it to Ben Hinton I went to town with 'im and took seven possum hides, three polecat hides, two coon hides and a mink hide. And Uncle Mott had sold his timber but he hadn't got his first down payment and all he asked me for was two dollars. I gave Uncle Mott the two dollars. I thought more than that belonged to 'im for he'd skinned my game and stretched the hides. And he took me to the man in town that bought hides. And that day he took me to a barbershop and had the barber to cut my hair. Then I told Uncle Mott what they had done to me my first day in school and that was the first time that I had seen 'im laugh in a long time.

With seventeen dollars in my pocket, I stood on the street corner where Uncle Mott told me to wait for 'im. I waited until the moon was up and Uncle Mott hadn't come, so I struck out over the snow-covered turnpike for home with a poke of meal and a poke of flour. I couldn't stand baked taters three times a day any longer. I wanted a change of grub and I knew that Grandma, Grandpa, Aunt Vittie and Uncle George would be pleased.

And when I got home Uncle George and Aunt Vittie had gone to bed and Grandpa and Grandma were a-sittin on the bench before the fire a-talkin. First thing I did was to show 'em the meal and flour and Grandma was pleased as much as when I found her dishes. She wiped tears from her eyes and I think the reason she cried was she was tired of baked taters three times a day. But it didn't hurt Grandpa's feelins any more than it pleased 'im.

"You're a up and a-comin young man, Sid," Grandpa said. "I'm proud of you."

Then Grandma asked me, "Where's Mott?"

"He left me on the street corner and told me to wait for 'im until he got back," I said. "I waited until the moon was up and he didn't get back. I shouldered my meal and flour and beat it for home."

"Did he get his money for the timber?" Grandpa asked.

"Not yet," I said.

"Did you give 'im any money?" Grandma asked.

"Two dollars," I said.

"That's it," Grandma said.

"It's a bad time for Mott to have money and a winter freeze on like this," Grandpa said, a-shakin his head.

"Vittie's caused it all," Grandma said. "Just to think, Kim's own wife upstairs in the bed with old George a-slobberin 'im with 'sugar.' "

Uncle Mott has got on big toots ever since I could remember, I thought. Vittie didn't cause 'im to do it then. The only thing that keeps Mott from a-gettin on a toot is the money. If he's got the money, he drinks. And Grandma and Grandpa ought to know that. Grandma is just mad at Aunt Vittie because she married Uncle George. And Uncle George and Aunt Vittie are a-stayin in the house with us and a-eatin with us and Grandma doesn't like that now. When Aunt Vittie had the money, even from the day Uncle Kim was buried until the day grub got scarce in our shack, Grandma called Aunt Vittie "honey."

"But Mott ought to feel satisfied now," Grandpa said. "He'll get a big slice of money for the timber. I 'spect he sold it for five or six hundred dollars. I don't know how much he got, for Mott aint a man to tell everybody his business."

"I wanted 'im to have it," Grandma said.

Then she bent over and whispered to Grandpa. "Who knows but what Vittie and George will try to give us trouble."

"I'm expectin it," Grandpa said. "I don't know what we'll give 'em if they try."

"Give 'em the wind," Grandma said. "That is what they've sown, and the wind's what they'll reap—a cold winter wind."

Grandma and Grandpa sat up a-waitin for Mott to come home until midnight. If Mott didn't come home, I wanted to sleep in his bed. I stayed up with them and every few minutes Grandpa would go to the kitchen winder and pull the quilt back and stick his head out into the winter wind. He would look out the moonlit snow-covered path. But Mott didn't come home.

"Let me sleep in Mott's bed tonight," I said.

"Can't do that, Sid," Grandpa said. "If Mott would come home drunk and catch you in his bed and he'd be a-thinkin about Brother George he'd likely use a knife on you. Go back to your bed upstairs."

Since Grandma was mad at Uncle George and Aunt Vittie I couldn't tell her why I didn't want to sleep upstairs. And I wouldn't tell Grandpa. I'd think that I'd tell 'im the first time I got a chance but when I'd start to tell 'im I couldn't. I'd turn from what I started to tell him and tell 'im somethin about the school, how well I liked to go and how I was a-gettin along. That would please Grandpa. And I'd tell 'im about takin a possum 'r a coon from a steel trap and Grandpa would laugh and tell me about the way he used to trap coons in Michigan. He had always had so much better luck than I'd had. He'd caught as many as fifty coons in one day in his traps, he told me. Said he didn't fool much with little game. Said he hunted deer and bears. He told me about the fight he had with a bear and how he killed it without his gun. Said he beat its brains out with a club. I knew that sometime I would haf to tell Grandpa why I didn't want to sleep upstairs.

CHAPTER XX

THE sawmill moved onto our farm in December. Ben Hinton tried to get Uncle George to cut roads for the oxen so they could snake the logs.

"Can't do it," Uncle George said.

"But it's not hard work," Ben Hinton said.

"Just can't do it," Uncle George said.

"How about you, Mr. Tussie?" he asked Grandpa. "I'm short of men and this would be a good easy job for you."

"Don't need the work," Grandpa told 'im. "You'll haf to get somebody else."

I hated to see them slaughter my possum-tailed poplars and knock the red berry seed from my red rooster-combed sumacs. I hated to see 'em cut my polecat-tailed pines. Pine logs lay so close on the ground that you could jump from log to log. And the big cattle, six yokes of them, snaked the big logs down to the sawmill. They even cut the black and yellow locusts for fence posts. And the little trees that managed to stand were skinned from tops to roots. And nearly all that Uncle Mott got from the timber went down his neck. He would go to town and stay a week at the time. He would stay drunk from the time he got a payment on his timber until it was gone. And he'd ask Ben Hinton for another monthly payment before it was due. Sometimes Grandma would get a little money from him to buy meal, lard and flour. Once Uncle Mott sent a box of groceries to Grandpa and Grandma on one of the lumber wagons a-comin back from town. He did buy Grandma a set of chears and a table. And he bought her some winderpanes for the winders.

I'd never seen Uncle Mott go on a toot like this one. Grandpa and Grandma said that he'd never tipped the jug like this before. Grandma said that Aunt Vittie was the cause

of it. "She led Mott on," Grandma told Grandpa one evenin after Uncle George and Aunt Vittie had gone to bed. "Vittie jilted Mott is why he drinks to drown his worries."

"If he didn't have the money he wouldn't drink," Grandpa said.

"But poor Mott is entitled to somethin," Grandma said.

In January I could write my name until anybody could read it. I could write letters. Miss Clark had promoted me to the third grade.

"I've taught many Tussies in my day," Miss Clark told me, "but I've never taught a Tussie that could learn as fast as you can."

This was the first thing I told Grandpa soon as I got home from school.

"Wonderful," Grandpa said. "You'll make a county jedge 'r a county high sheriff when you grow up to be a man."

"Just don't tell your Aunt Vittie about how fast you larn," Grandma said.

I'd show Grandpa and Grandma how I could add numbers. And then I told them I larned how to substract them and multiply them. I showed them how I'd larned to divide numbers. Grandpa and Grandma thought it was wonderful. And it made me wonder why I hadn't gone to school before. Now I was mad that I hadn't—just to think that I'd larned faster than any of the Tussies. That pleased me.

I'd stop at the sawmill and Ben Hinton would show me how he measured lumber. He'd show me how to measure it to get square feet. I'd take my little arithmetic book along with me and I'd sit on a sawed block by the firebox of the steam boiler. And Ben would help me get my arithmetic. I didn't tell the boys and girls in my class and I didn't tell Miss Clark. Now I was glad that the attendance officer, Eddie McConnell, had come to our shack that day; I was glad that somebody had reported Grandpa for not sendin me to school. I was glad there was a law to make me go to school. I loved the school, my teacher and the boys and girls. And I was glad that the boys didn't know that I was the boy they chased last October with a sack of dishes and bread across my shoulder. The boy that wanted to go home and get his dog to run me down was my seatmate in school now and I liked him.

The January sun warmed the winter earth. Meltin snow slid from the schoolhouse roof; little creeks filled with melted snow water hurried down the rugged valleys to Little Sandy River. I climbed the mountain to my traps; then I crossed a high ridge down into the valley below our house. I had a path made this way past the traps, past the sawmill home. The winter leaves, soaked with melted snow water, were soggy against the earth and smelled like smartweeds in July.

When I reached the sawmill I saw Grandpa a-standin there a-talkin to Ben Hinton. Grandpa had come from the shack to feel the warmth of the sun again on his pale face; maybe he wanted the warm January wind to lift his beard up and down like the August wind lifted the dyin corn silks. Grandpa liked to let the wind hit his face and seep to the roots of his whiskers to cool his warm face. The wind lifted his whiskers up and down and blew them against his face. Grandpa was a-laughin while he talked to Ben. He was glad to be out again since the weather had warmed. He wouldn't leave the house to get wood for the fire when the weather was cold. Grandma and Aunt Vittie would haf to carry wood from the chimney corner to build the fires. Uncle George said that he wasn't able and Aunt Vittie would carry wood for 'im. Grandpa said that he wasn't feelin well and that the weather was too cold for 'im. It was good to see Grandpa out again.

"I've just been holed up in the shack like a groundhog," Grandpa told Ben Hinton, then he laughed and slapped his long lean thighs with his skinny hands. "I'm glad to get out again to get a breath of fresh air."

"I'm glad to see you out, Grandpa," I said as I walked down the little path to the sawmill.

"Scare me to death, Sid," Grandpa said, laughin. "I didn't know you come this way from school."

"This is the way I come," I said. "Are you about ready to go home?"

"Ready any time," Grandpa said. "I've got my airin out."

Grandpa walked in front and I walked behind him.

"Grandpa," I said, "I——"

"What did you start to say, Sid?" Grandpa asked.

"I love school, Grandpa," I said.

"You'll be jedge of this county someday, Sid," he said.

"Grandpa, I——"

"What did you start to say, Sid?"

"I want to sleep downstairs in Uncle Mott's bed."

"Oh, that won't do, Sid," Grandpa said. "Your Uncle Mott's been a-comin home here lately and he goes to bed with his knife open. He puts it under his piller. He cusses and cavorts all night somethin awful. Believe he's drunk so much of Toodle Powell's rotgut he's a-gittin snakes in his boots. Your Grandma and me's might' nigh afraid of Mott. I'll bet he's put a thousand saw logs down his gullet already."

"But, Grandpa, I can't sleep upstairs," I said.

"Why can't you sleep?"

"Too much noise," I said.

"What kind of noise?"

"Uncle George and Aunt Vittie keep me awake all night," I said.

"Ha, ha, ha." Grandpa laughed a wild laugh like the wind among the oak tops. Grandpa stopped on the path, bent over and slapped his knees and laughed until he started coughin. "That's funny. Tell me what they say. Tell me everything you've heard!"

"I don't want to do that," I said. "I could start talkin now and tell you until in the mornin and I couldn't tell you all I've heard 'im say. I've heard Uncle George call 'er every wild flower in the woods and every sort of a honey bee, wild bird and every sort of a pet name!"

"Must be real love," Grandpa said, laughin.

"I'm a-needin sleep," I said. "I fall asleep at my desk."

"But you can't have Mott's bed," Grandpa said. "And you know we can't put Mott upstairs. You can sleep with your Grandma and me."

"I don't want to do that," I said.

"Brother George has been a great lover," Grandpa said, "but I thought he's old enough to be through with love. I'm glad George is still a lover. Tell me more about it!"

"You come upstairs and sleep in my bed one night and let me sleep in Uncle Mott's bed and then ye'll know," I said.

"Your Grandma wouldn't let me do that," Grandpa said. "But I'd like to."

"I can't stand to sleep up there any longer, Grandpa," I said.

"I'll fix everything," Grandpa said. "I'll have your Grandma put a petition across that room. Then they won't bother you."

We were near the shack and Grandpa stopped in the path and cupped his hand over his ear to catch the sound.

"Hush," Grandpa said. "I hear loud voices in the house!"

Grandpa hurried to the house; I hurried along behind him.

"Uncle George and I are entitled to somethin same as your drunken Mott," Aunt Vittie said to Grandma just as we opened the door.

"Let's don't have any furse," Grandpa pleaded.

Uncle George and Aunt Vittie were a-sittin on the bench before the fire; Grandma was a-sittin in one of the chears Uncle Mott had bought her. She wouldn't let Uncle George and Aunt Vittie sit in them after she had called Uncle Mott a drunken sot.

"But you aint a-gettin nothin," Grandma said. "What is there to give you?"

"Land," Aunt Vittie said. "By the right of the Law, all this land is mine."

"Take to the Law and see," Grandma snarled. "You aint got the money to take it to the Law with!"

"Peace," Grandpa said.

"There won't be any peace here long as these varmints are in my house," Grandma said.

"*Your* house!" Aunt Vittie said. "It's *my* house and I'm a-stayin. I'm a-eatin here and Uncle George is a-eatin here long as there's a bite. I'll show you; I'll take it to the Law the minute you try to put me out!"

"We are entitled to sleep in this house and eat here long as there's a bite in this house," Uncle George said. "I know enough to know that. Mott's money that's a-payin for the grub that we eat is, by rights of the Law, our money. You let Mott have our timber and he's a-puttin it down his bull neck as fast as a man can drink saw logs!"

"Peace, peace," Grandpa said. "I've got something to say here."

"Say it then, Press," Grandma said. "You are the head of this house."

"It won't pay you to get hooked with the Law," Grandpa said. "It brings you a heap of misery when you do. Look what's happened to me! I've lost my relief; I've lost my pension. Look what a shape we are in!"

"But how did you lose it?" Aunt Vittie screamed. "You lost it by takin what belonged to me!"

"Just a minute, Vittie," Grandpa said. "I'm not through talkin. I aint a-gettin in any messes. I don't want you to furse when we can settle things peacefully. Now what do you want?"

"I want this farm," Aunt Vittie said.

"We'll take it to the Law before we'll let you have it," Grandpa said. "Will a piece of land big enough for a house and garden do you?"

"That's all we want," Uncle George said.

"With fifty dollars to help us build our house," Aunt Vittie said.

"I'll see Mott," Grandma said. "If he aint spent all his money, I can get that much. I'd give a hundred dollars to get you out if I had it."

"It's better to do things right," Grandpa said. "Keep the Law outten it. I don't like the Law."

"Take five acres anywhere you want it, Vittie," Grandpa said. "You know that's enough for a house and garden."

"Just so you don't take five acres close to us," Grandma said.

"Don't worry, Ma Tussie," Aunt Vittie said. "I know where I want it now if it's all right with Uncle George."

"Where, honey?" Uncle George asked.

"In that flat above the sawmill," she said.

"That's a fine place," Uncle George said. "We can get lumber from the sawmill to build our house."

When Grandma knew that Uncle George and Aunt Vittie were a-goin to leave the house, she seemed pleased. She was friendly with Aunt Vittie again, talked with her and laughed while they worked in the kitchen together. Uncle George chopped stove wood and firewood again for us. He worked as much as he had worked before he married Aunt Vittie.

"Vittie, I think there ought to be a petition in the room upstairs," Grandma told Aunt Vittie. "You and George need more privacy."

"But we don't have much longer to stay here," Aunt Vittie said. "It'll be a lot of work for nothin, Ma Tussie."

"But it doesn't look right to put a young boy in the same room with you while you're in your bridal days," Grandma said.

"But he's in the fur end of the room," Aunt Vittie said.

"I'll put a petition there anyhow," Grandma said.

Grandpa has told Grandma what I told him, I thought as

I listened to them talkin in the kitchen while I sat before the front-room fire.

"I don't want you to do a lot of work for nothin, Ma Tussie," Aunt Vittie said.

I was away at school the day that Grandma built the petition upstairs. I'd been sleepy at school all day. And Miss Clark told me if I didn't sleep so much in school that before school was out I'd stand a chance a-bein promoted to the fourth grade. I couldn't tell her the reason that I slept in school. I couldn't tell her that Uncle George and Aunt Vittie kept me awake most of the night. And I wanted to tell her that I'd stop sleepin in class pretty soon for Grandma was a-goin to put a petition in our big upstairs and give Uncle George and Aunt Vittie the lower end of the room. She would put a petition there so Uncle George and Aunt Vittie could go to their room at dark and close the door behind them and all the pet words they said to each other and their love noises would be fastened up in the dark room with them. I wanted to tell Miss Clark all this but I couldn't.

I didn't know that Grandma had been workin on the house when we ate supper and laughed and talked like we used to laugh and talk. Aunt Vittie and Grandma talked friendly to one another; Grandpa and Uncle George laughed and talked but they had always been friendly. And after supper Aunt Vittie helped Grandma wash the dishes while Uncle George sat before the blazin fire and tuned his fiddle. Uncle Mott was in town; he wasn't in the shack to bother Uncle George with his fiddle. And just as soon as Grandma and Aunt Vittie came into the front room, Uncle George started to play his fiddle.

"I've played summers for you," Uncle George said. "I've played autumn for you with the wind a-rustlin down the dead leaves from the trees and a-blowin through the dead grasses; I've played the last notes of the grasshoppers, the katydids and the beetles. Now I'm a-goin to play winter for you. You'll be able to hear the winter wind around this shack—the winter wind a-blowin high among the leafless oak tops and a-moanin among the thick needles on the tall pine trees. Winter is a sad time and I love to play winter tunes. Listen for the snowbirds a-chirrupin among the dead ragweeds and pickin up ragweed seeds from the snow. Listen to 'em a-nestin in the fodder shocks."

And while we sat before the fire and listened to Uncle George play his magic fiddle, I could understand what Uncle Mott had said to me the day that he showed me how to set the steel traps. He said that Uncle George's fiddle had played his way into the hearts of many women. And he said that he didn't stand a chance with Vittie because of Uncle George's fiddle. He said he couldn't get the music from his banjer that Uncle George could get from his fiddle. I loved the sad moans of winter Uncle George played on his fiddle. I wondered how on earth this big rough-lookin man like Uncle George could drag from his fiddle strings such pretty music by just fingerin the strings with his long fingers and a-drawin the bow across the strings. How could he get such pretty music from the winter world? You could hear the fallin of the snowflakes as they preened against the oak leaves still a-clingin to the tough-butted white oaks. You could hear the hungry snowbirds a-chirrupin as they found ragweed seeds upon the snow and picked them up to fill their craws. You could hear the birds' tiny bills a-peckin against the hard crust of snow and after a while you could hear their satisfied chirrupin. Then you heard 'em a-flyin to the fodder shocks, through the icy winter wind. And as they roosted in the fodder shocks, you could hear them rustle the fodder blades. Uncle George could make these sounds on his fiddle for he went to the cornfield in winter and heard the wind among the fodder shocks and mocked it with his fiddle. And it was lonesome to hear the high wind in the leafless oak tops and to hear it blow among the thick pine needles.

I could understand why Uncle George had played his way into Aunt Vittie's heart. She loved the music of his fiddle; I loved the music of his fiddle more than anyone but Aunt Vittie. And while he played his winter songs I saw Aunt Vittie wipe the tears from her eyes. Grandpa and Grandma wiped tears from their eyes when he played the sounds of the snowbirds a-findin somethin to eat. I couldn't help if Uncle George wasn't good to work. I couldn't help if people did talk about him for marryin his niece. Aunt Vittie wasn't any blood kin to Uncle George. But people talked everywhere about it. A lot of people even said that we were a "low-down" trashy set. One boy told this to me at school and he told me about Aunt Vittie a-marryin her Uncle George. And when he said this I mashed his mouth until his lips bled. "I won't let you talk about my people," I told him. "I won't let you talk about Uncle George. You never heard 'im play his fiddle." I didn't want Uncle George to stop playin his winter songs on his fiddle. But he stopped shortly before midnight and took Aunt Vittie upstairs to bed.

"There's a petition in that room tonight, Sid." Grandma said.

"That's what we've needed all the time," Grandpa said, laughin until his tall thin body bent like a saplin in the wind.

"Why didn't you put it there then?" Grandma asked him. "You think it's funny, Press. You're a nosey old man."

"I'm glad you put it there, Grandma," I said.

I'll never be able to sleep tonight even if the petition that Grandma has built shuts away their sounds, I thought as I walked upstairs with a lamp to light my way. That music is still a-goin through my head. I still can hear the snowbirds a-peckin ragweed seeds on the crispy crusted snow. "Peck, peck, peck, peck." And then their flight through the icy wind to a fodder shock and the rustle of the dry fodder blades and their cheerin chirrups when they nested for the night safe from the winter's blasts. Who on earth but Uncle George would think of sich a music? And who on earth could fiddle this music like Uncle George?

When I reached the head of the stairs, I saw on my left a petition built of quilts. They were stretched from wall to wall and from top to bottom of the room. The quilts weren't nailed to the floor and all Uncle George and Aunt Vittie had to do was raise one up and walk under it into their room and then to bed. This petition was just a little better than none for I could hear 'em whisperin to one another now. I could hear Uncle George a-callin Aunt Vittie a lot of pet names of wild flowers and birds. I'd heard them so much I was a-gittin plenty tired of hearin 'em now. And when I blew out the lamp and crawled in bed, I plugged my ear-holes with my fingers to stop the sound since the quilt petition didn't keep their secrets of their nights of bride-and-groom love enclosed in their little room.

Somehow the pet names got into my head. They got a-past my fingers into my head and they made their way into my brain no matter how hard I tried to keep them out. To hear them got me riled and when I got riled I couldn't go to sleep and when I didn't get enough sleep I went to sleep at school. I took my fingers from my ears and I thought I would think things to make me forget about the secrets of their love. I tried to think about school, the days I had spent there and how I felt, when I got a-hold of a new book and felt of its tiny size in my hand, that I ought soon to know everything in it for it was so tiny that I could eat it. I tried to go to sleep a-thinkin about the school, but every experience that I had in school hurried through my mind from the day I had entered school until the last day that I had gone. I thought about my steel traps and each possum, mink, fox, coon and polecat that I had taken from them. And I thought about how wrong it was to kill little animals for their skins. And I thought about the way the pretty coons had fought to the last for their lives and how the cunning foxes had tried to hide from me with traps a-holdin their legs. I thought about the way the possums would lie down beside the traps and go to sleep with their numb legs still a-holdin them prisoners in the traps. Possums would lie down and wait to be rescued. And I thought about how many of the polecats had eaten their legs off and got away. I didn't like to think about these dead animals.

I thought about huntin in the woods with Uncle Mott. I could see 'im when a rabbit jumped from a greenbriar stool and took up the hill—how Uncle Mott would put his double-barrel shotgun to his shoulder, shoot, and how the rabbit would go end over end. Then I'd run and grab the kickin rabbit—I'd see his red warm blood drippin from his nose to the wet oak leaves and mix with the water on the leaves. I thought about the way that I had killed rabbits with Uncle Mott's gun. And how I wondered what Uncle Mott would say when he found out that I had used his gun and shot his shells. I knew that a gun was one thing that a Tussie never loaned. And a gun was one thing that a Tussie loved. But I couldn't love a gun the way they loved their guns. And I didn't love to hunt and kill like the Tussies. Uncle Mott never batted an eye when he put a mattock handle over a possum's neck and put his feet on each end of the handle to hold it down while he yanked up on the possum's tail until he broke its neck. And Uncle Mott didn't care about cuttin the trees and leavin their tops piled high on Grandpa's black land. Trees didn't mean anything to him. Soon as the timber was cut and sawed, Uncle Mott would have all the money he'd received for it down his short bull neck.

"My little snowbird," Uncle George whispered. "Love me, honey?"

"You bet I do, Uncle George!"

If Uncle Kim could only hear 'em, I thought.

✕

CHAPTER XXI

"Not only will I give you fifty dollars of my timber money to get 'em outten this house," Uncle Mott told Grandma after he'd sobered and had come home late and Uncle George and Aunt Vittie had gone to bed, "but I'll furnish nails, hammers, saws and axes. I'll buy 'em a winder for the durned house and help 'em build it if Uncle George just won't bother to speak to me."

Uncle Mott's lips trembled when he spoke.

"Not so loud, Mott," Grandpa said. "They might hear you!"

"Let 'em hear me," Uncle Mott said. "I mean what I say. This is not my home with 'em in it. I'll be glad to get 'em out."

"When you get your hand in a bear's mouth," Grandpa said, "you'd better work easy until you get it out."

"I've larned to do that with 'em, Press," Grandma said. "The night when you give 'em five acres of ground, I was ready to fight Vittie. I would've clawed 'er like a wildcat."

"We couldn't let this go to the Law," Grandpa said. "I've always got the worst end of the Law."

"Somebody would a-been hurt if this had a-gone to the Law," Uncle Mott said. "A-lawin over the last remains of Brother Kim would've looked bad."

And it looks bad that Grandpa, Grandma, Aunt Vittie and Uncle Mott ran through with all of the Uncle Kim money too, I thought. But they hadn't thought about this. Grandpa told them to "dance and be merry for tomorrow they may die." And they did dance and they were merry. They laughed, talked, drank, danced and loved until the dust came up from the polished dance-hall floors and down from the wallpapered ceilin. They danced until they kicked holes in the hardwood floor. And they bought good grub, rotgut licker and fine clothes. And no man would bother to work. Not one would go to the woods and chop kindlin. It was easier to burn the coalhouse, the fence posts and a locust shade tree than it was to walk a hundred yards to get a pole of wood for kindlin. And Uncle Mott didn't think about himself when he spoke of Uncle George; he didn't remember how he'd kissed Aunt Vittie, how he had tried to love her, marry her. Now that Uncle George had won her, maybe with his fiddle, Uncle Mott would talk about her and Uncle George.

If Uncle Kim could only know how the money they got for 'im has been spent, I thought, he would rise up from his mountain grave. He would come to our shack and tell Grandma, Grandpa, Uncle Mott and Aunt Vittie that they should have held some of the money for a rainy day. Then I thought: Would Uncle Kim have done this? Maybe he would have told them that they had spent it wisely, for money didn't mean anything to Uncle Kim. And maybe he would have told Aunt Vittie that she had done well by herself to marry Uncle George after he'd heard Uncle George play the fiddle. If Uncle Kim could've come back to've seen what was left of the money they got for 'im, he would've seen fifty acres of land left with most of the timber cut. And he would have found two saw logs of rotgut down Uncle Mott's gullet.

Miss Clark told me to go into the fourth grade next year. I would've made it this year if I'd a-got enough sleep at home. And when our school year ended, I climbed the mountain to the rock cliffs and gathered my traps. I'll come back to this same school next year, I thought. But I'll not need these traps. I'll not trap again next year; I can't stand to kill little animals for their skins. Then I wondered if we'd be a-livin in the shack next year. If Uncle Mott got dry enough for rotgut and he didn't have money to buy it with, he was liable to take Grandpa's land from him. And I thought Uncle George and Aunt Vittie may take a notion for more than five acres. We may be on the road again, and if we were on the road again, I hoped we'd never haf to live in another rock cliff.

As I walked over the mountainside, down my little well-worn path toward the sawmill for my last time that winter, I saw Uncle George, Grandpa, Grandma and Aunt Vittie a-walkin behind Surveyor Fred Madden. I'd heard Uncle George say that he would survey the five acres so it could be recorded in the deed book. Uncle George said that Surveyor Madden had caused a lot of fusses over his surveyin-line fences and had got a lot of men killed but he'd get 'im to do his surveyin because he worked cheaper.

"I'm glad your school is out, Sid," Grandpa said as we walked down the path. "We all aim to chip in and help George and Vittie get their house built. They want to be moved into it in a couple of weeks."

"I want to help Uncle George and Aunt Vittie with their house," I said.

Uncle George walked in front a-carryin a double-bitted ax and a crosscut saw. Uncle Mott followed 'im a-carryin a box of tools. I had all the nails that I could tote in a sack across my shoulder. Grandpa walked behind me a-carryin a mattock, sproutin hoe and a brier scythe.

"If we keep steady on the job it won't take us long to get it done," Uncle Mott said.

I knew the reason that Uncle Mott was with us. He had drunk up his payment on the timber and he had two weeks to wait before the next payment was due. Uncle Mott was a little pale around the eyes and his eyeballs were still red over his two weeks' toot. We were lucky to have 'im a-helpin us. And while he was sober, we wanted to get all the work done we could.

Uncle Mott used a double-bitted ax to chop the treetops apart. Uncle George cut the sprouts with a mattock while Grandpa used the brier scythe to cut the greenbrier stools and saw-brier clusters. I piled the brush and treetop branches in heaps. When Uncle George wanted Uncle Mott to chop down a bruised young sapling he would say to Grandpa, "Press, you tell Mott to cut down this sapling." Uncle George would point to the sapling. Uncle Mott would work at the job he was a-doin as if he didn't hear Uncle George until Grandpa would say, "Mott, cut down this sapling." Grandpa would point to the same sapling that Uncle George had pointed to. "All right, Pap," Uncle Mott would say as he walked up to the sapling and started choppin it down level with the ground.

"It's a handy place here to build a house," Uncle George said to Grandpa. "I'm glad we took our five acres here. Plenty of culled lumber close."

"It's a handy place all right," Grandpa said. "After the sawmill's moved away you'll have a slab pile for wood that'll do you two 'r three years."

"I like to have plenty of wood handy," Uncle George said. "I aint able to carry wood from the ridge tops any more."

It took us two days to clear the brush, briers, tree laps and small bruised saplings away, to pile them and burn them. And then we laid the foundation of Uncle George and Aunt Vittie's shack in a day. We carried field rocks and put down at the corners and we carried sleepers and sills from the culled-lumber pile. Ben Hinton told us to help ourselves to whatever we could find that would fit into the foundation of the shack. We took advantage of the invitation for it was better to find a foundation sill with all four sides sawed, though it did have a rotten heart in it, than to cut a sound sapling and score and hew it with our double-bitted axes. It took work to score and hew sound wood. We were in a hurry to build the shack and we skipped as much work as we possibly could.

While we worked on the shack Aunt Vittie went to town every day. She'd come back to the shack at night a-carryin a load big enough for a strong man to carry. She'd bring old well-worn carpets, dishes, pots, pans—once she carried home three chears. One had a broken rocker, one didn't have a back, the other had a broken round.

"Where are you a-gettin all your house plunder, Vittie?" Grandma asked.

"People just give it to me when I ask 'em," Aunt Vittie said.

"I'd call that beggin," Grandma said.

"But that's the only way I got to get it, Ma Tussie," Aunt Vittie said.

I knew that there was something in the minds of the hen crows in the spring that told them to build their nests. I'd watched them fly down and pick up sticks and carry them in their bills away through the blue air a-wingin their way to a distant pine grove. They would fly among the dark pine boughs and would be hidden from my eyes. The nest was their secret. It was a hidden thing. And I'd seen wrens, robins, martins and sparrows a-buildin their nests in the spring. Even the rabbits dug little holes in the ground and the mother rabbit tore fur from the father rabbit to line the nest so it would be soft and warm for the little rabbits. And if the father rabbit didn't have enough fur on his body to line the nest, he tore fur from the mother rabbit to finish linin the nest. Even the terrapins dug nests in the sand to lay their eggs and the snakes made nests in the hot loam around rotted stumps and logs. And I thought whatever it was in them that told them to build their nests in the spring was in Aunt Vittie. She was a-buildin a nest for Uncle George.

In one week we had the framework up, the boxin nailed to the framework, the winders and doors sawed. And we had the sheetin nailed to the rafters and the floor laid. I'd never seen Uncle Mott work like he was a-workin now. Maybe he knew that soon as he got his next payment on his timber that he wouldn't be able to work and that he wanted to work now to help build the shack so he'd get Uncle George outten our shack. I think Uncle Mott would've liked to've had Aunt Vittie stay on in our shack. Aunt Vittie was a-gettin her house plunder collected; she was a-carryin it upstairs to her and Uncle George's room. Grandma said they had a heap of plunder in the room. Said she didn't see how a woman tiny as Aunt Vittie could carry sich loads from town. I didn't wonder since I'd seen her carry loads of relief grub from town. Grandma had forgotten about that.

We had started our second week's work on the shack. All we had to do was to cover the roof with long culled planks, nail them on like you would clapboards and make a small chimney and fireplace with field rocks that covered the slope behind the shack. We had to bat the cracks between the boxin with narrow planks. And after the first day of the second week, we had come home, had eaten our suppers and were restin around the fire. Grandma and Aunt Vittie had finished washin the dishes. Uncle Mott had picked his song on the banjer; Uncle George had played his tune on the fiddle. It was Grandpa's time to tell us a story.

"Tell us somethin about Michigan, Press," Grandma said, wheezin on her pipe, blowin clouds of smoke toward the fireplace that were caught in the draft and pulled up the chimney.

"Can't tell anything funny," Grandpa said, a-holdin his ter-backer behind his jaw. "I'll haf to talk of a speretual nature!"

"What's the matter, Press?" Grandma asked. "Have you had a change of heart?"

"Not exactly," Grandpa said. "I've just been a-sittin here a-thinkin tonight, while I listened to Mott's banjer and George's fiddle, that my work is nearly done. The last work that I'll get to do is on George and Vittie's shack. I had hopes that Sid and I could set fire to these tree laps this spring and let the fire clean us a new ground and I could git a mule and Sid could double-furrow the ground and I could use a hoe. We could raise us a crib of corn from this black leaf-rot loam. But I got my land too late."

"What are you a-talkin about, Press?" Grandma asked.

"What happens when a Tussie talks like I'm a-talkin?" Grandpa asked Grandma. Then he spit into the fire and watched the spittle sizzle on the embers. "What happens when a Tussie has lived his threescore years and ten and begins to get his tokens?"

"Don't tell us that, Press," Grandma wailed, a-pullin her long-stemmed pipe from her mouth and holdin it in her nervous hand.

"I know that sure as I'm a-sittin before this fire I won't be a-listenin to fiddle music and banjer music much longer," Grandpa said. "I've been a-hearin voices in the wind. One said, 'We're a-comin after you, Press. Be ready.' I heard it plain as I hear your voices when you speak here tonight. I'm not deef; you know that. I'm still in my right mind; you know that. You know that I've been as tough all my life as a tough-butted white oak."

"My God, Press," Grandma wailed.

Uncle Mott lifted his eyes from the hearth and looked at Grandpa's white-beardy face. Uncle George looked at Grandpa and Aunt Vittie's lips trembled like she was about to cry.

"I've been a-dreamin of burnt new ground," Grandpa said. "That's the sign of a hard death. Every night I dream of burnt new ground. I can see piles of white and brown ashes; I can see black charred stumps. And I keep on a-walkin through the deep piles of ashes a-tryin to find a mountain path until my feet get so heavy that I can hardly lift them and I get tired enough to fall in my tracks. And there's no end to the new ground. I just keep a-goin and a-goin. To dream of ashes and a long journey is a bad sign."

"Pap dreamed of burnt new ground before he died," Grandma said as she wiped tears from her eyes. "Pap was sick a month before he died."

"I'm a-goin to have a long lingerin spell," Grandpa said, "before I go home."

"Maybe not, Grandpa," I said.

"But I know that I will, Sid," Grandpa said, turnin his head toward me and lookin at me with his soft kind eyes.

"Where did you hear the voice?" Grandma asked.

"Between here and the sawmill," Grandpa said. "I aint for sure but it sounded a lot like Ma's voice. It was a woman's voice. It's been a long time since I've heard Ma's voice. I could hardly tell."

"Then you won't be a-workin any more on the shack, will you, Pap?" Uncle Mott asked.

"I'll not be a-workin any longer, boys," Grandpa said.

While we made the chimney and fireplace for the shack and nailed a plank roof on the sheetin and batted the cracks, Grandpa and Grandma walked to town together. Grandpa wanted to see a few of his old friends. He went about shakin hands with them and a-talkin but he didn't tell them what was a-goin to happen to 'im. He went to see Sheriff Whiteapple and shake his hand; he wanted to shake hands with George Rayburn but Rayburn wouldn't shake hands with Grandpa after Grandma lambasted him about the furniture. When he came back to the shack that night he would tell us where he had been and everybody he had seen.

"I don't like to see Press a-shakin hands with everybody and a-sayin good-by when he leaves 'em like he's a-goin someplace," Grandma said. "They don't know what to think of Press. They think he's a-losin his mind. It hurts me to go along and to hear all this but I want to be with Press long as I can."

"Have you seen young Ben and Dee Tussie?" I asked Grandpa.

"They are two that I don't want to see," Grandpa said. "They'd be a-tryin to send some bad news about me on to the next world."

"I've got a debt to settle with Dee and young Ben one of

these days, Pap," Uncle Mott said. "Remember, I'll never forget what they've done to you. I'll talk as sweet to them as they talked to you before I run my knife blade into their hollows."

"Forgive 'em, Mott," Grandpa said.

"I can't forgive 'em, Pap," Uncle Mott said. "I never forgive and I never forget."

"Sheriff Whiteapple will understand why I went to him and said good-bye in about a month from now," Grandpa said. "Among all the men in this county, I'm one that he'll remember."

CHAPTER XXII

A UNT Vittie and Uncle George moved their house plunder
into their two-room shack near the sawmill. I think they
were as happy to get in their little shack as Grandma and
Uncle Mott were to see them leave our shack. Grandpa told
them when they went away with the last load of plunder that
he wanted them to come back and see him as often as they
could.

"Pa Tussie, you've been like a father to me," Aunt Vittie
said. "And when I can do anything for you, I'll be glad to do
it. I'll never be able to do enough for you. If you ever had
anything, I had it. And if I ever have anything, you'll have a
part of it."

Grandma didn't talk so kindly to Aunt Vittie when she
left. Grandma was too glad to see her go. Grandpa never
cared whether he had anything or not and when he did have
something everybody was welcome to it. I'd never seen
another man like Grandpa. The only thing he'd ever had he
didn't want to part with was his land. I knew that if he was
a-dyin and it took all the grub he had to save him and that if
somebody was hungry and asked 'im for part of it he'd give
'im half of it.

Before Aunt Vittie and Uncle George reached their shack
with their last load of house plunder, Grandpa went to bed.

"Do you want me to heat rocks and wrap 'em in sacks and
put 'em at your feet, Press?" Grandma asked 'im.

"All the hot rocks in a chimney around my feet wouldn't
help me. Arimithy," Grandpa said. "I'm a-seein things and
a-hearin voices."

"How about me a-goin after a doctor, Pap?" Uncle Mott
asked Grandpa.

"No use to do that, Mott," Grandpa said. "Save the money

you'd pay the doctor and give it to your ma. She'll need it."

Uncle Mott will never do that, I thought. Just as soon as Ben Hinton pays 'im his monthly payment on his timber today, he'll go straight to town to get drunk. I could always tell when Uncle Mott wanted whiskey. He was as nervous as a white-oak leaf in the winter wind. Now Uncle Mott was a-runnin around over the front room like a grasshopper a-jumpin from weed to weed on a hot day in July. Uncle Mott would go to the winder and look down the path toward the sawmill every few minutes to see if Ben Hinton was a-comin up the path to pay him.

What will we do now? I thought. Grandpa down in bed. Uncle Mott will go to town. Uncle George and Aunt Vittie gone. Just Grandma and me here with Grandpa. What will we do for somethin to eat if Uncle Mott doesn't send us somethin? And what will Uncle George and Aunt Vittie do? They didn't have a bite of grub to take to their shack with them. They could not live on the wind they breathed and the water they drank. They could not live on love. Love, wind and water would make their bodies lean as the tall thin saplins a-tryin to grow from the crevices among the cliffs.

I stood by the winder and looked toward their shack. I saw smoke a-comin from the chimney and gusts of wind swept it down to the ground. I knew that this was a sign of bad weather. February was still with us and it was the worst month of the year. The earth looked dark and barren. And the naked trees that had once looked so good around our shack were slaughtered and there were tree laps piled higher in places than our shack was high. And now there was a great moan of February wind that swept over our shack and howled like a hungry dog since the trees had been cut. As I stood watchin the smoke swirl to the ground around Uncle George and Aunt Vittie's shack, I saw Ben Hinton a-comin up the path.

"I see Ben Hinton a-comin," I said.

"Oh, you do," Uncle Mott said with a new light a-comin from his worried eyes.

When Ben Hinton knocked on our door, Uncle Mott opened it.

"Here's your check, Mott," Ben Hinton said.

Uncle Mott crumpled it in his hand so I couldn't see it. He didn't mind for Grandpa and Grandma to see it. But he knew that I had learned to read and write and cipher some at school. Though Uncle Mott couldn't read it himself, he knew the amount it was for. And he would be the only one to know.

"Thank you, thank you, Ben," Uncle Mott said.

When Grandma heard Uncle Mott a-thankin Ben Hinton, she left her work in the kitchen and hurried to the front room.

"Mott, honey, you got your check," Grandma said. "I just want to tell you I'm uneasy. We aint got much grub to go on. Just enough flour for biscuits in the mornin. Just enough meal to last two days. And the middlin meat is too fat for Press. Fetch us some grub, honey, if you go to town. Send a box of groceries and a sack of meal and flour on the next timber wagon that comes back to the sawmill. What will we do with Press down sick if you don't?"

"Don't worry about me, Arimithy," Grandpa said. "I'm a-worryin about you and Sid."

"Not one of you will haf to worry," Uncle Mott said. "I'm a-goin to town and I'll send the groceries out this afternoon on the last tie wagon!"

Uncle Mott, bundled in his ragged overcoat, his fur cap and his mittens and brier-scratched boots, slammed the front door behind him and made out the path over the frozen ground in a run. I could hear his boots whettin against the frozen ground for a minute after he left the house. Will Uncle Mott send the groceries? I wondered. He's a-wantin a drink more than anything on earth. If he could only get the groceries and the meal and flour before he gets his rotgut! If he gets Toodle Powell's rotgut first, he won't send them. Uncle Mott will not turn loose of the jug until he is so full that he can't remember. I may be wrong about Uncle Mott, I thought, since Grandpa is down sick. Surely Uncle Mott will remember that we are in this shack without much to eat.

When I carried wood inside the house from the chimney corner, the February wind drove hard flakes of snow against my face that made the flesh sting. Now I knew that I would haf to get the wood, build the fires and do everything about the shack. It would keep Grandma busy a-waitin on Grandpa and a-doin the cookin. I would get the wood all right, if only Uncle Mott would send us the grub. I watched for the last tie wagon to go down the creek below our shack toward the sawmill. As darkness hovered over the silent dark hills, I saw the last wagon roll toward the sawmill. It was an empty wagon. I knew that Uncle Mott had seen Toodle Powell before he got our groceries.

"Must I go to town and look for Uncle Mott?" I asked Grandma since the night had passed on and the gloom of another winter day spread over the dark land.

"Aint no use to go, Sid," she said. "Poor little Mott has let the bottle get 'im since your Aunt Vittie jilted 'im."

"The bottle had 'im long before Uncle George married Aunt Vittie," I said. "He's been a sot ever since I can remember."

"You shouldn't talk that way about your Uncle Mott," Grandma said.

"He ought not to go away and leave us like this," I said.

"I worry so about poor little Mott," Grandma said. "I wonder if he's a-layin out in this blizzardy weather."

I wouldn't worry about 'im, I wanted to tell Grandma but I didn't. I wouldn't care if he did lay out in the blizzardy weather. If he didn't think any more of Grandpa and Grandma and me than to leave us in the shack with only enough grub for three days, then I didn't care if the blizzard did freeze Uncle

Mott stiff as a possum's tail. He would be better off frozen stiff than he would be a-layin out limber drunk when Grandpa was a-layin in bed a-listenin to the voices a-beckonin for 'im to come.

"I'll go down to the sawmill to see if any of the team drivers have seen Uncle Mott in town," I told Grandma.

"All right, Sid," Grandma said. "Don't stay long."

"I won't," I said.

I could tell that Grandma was scared. Her lips trembled when she spoke to me. And I knew why she held to Uncle Mott. He had always lived with them. He had never married. He and I were all that Grandma would have to look to when Grandpa died. Anything that Uncle Mott did was all right with Grandma. As I walked down the path toward the sawmill, I met Uncle George and Aunt Vittie a-goin to see Grandpa.

"How is Brother Press?" Uncle George asked me.

"About the same as he was yesterday," I said. "He's just a-layin in bed and a-talkin about the voices a-jabberin around his head!"

"Poor old Press is gone," Uncle George said.

"Has Mott come back yet?" Aunt Vittie asked me.

"No, he aint," I said. "I'm just a-goin down to the sawmill to see if any of the team drivers have seen 'im in town."

Uncle George and Aunt Vittie walked up the path so close together that they could walk side by side on a path wide enough for one. Uncle George had his left arm around her and she had her right arm around him and he was a-holdin her left hand with his right hand. They walked slowly over the frozen ground where a sprinkle of hard snow grains lay here and there to whiten the bleak forsaken earth.

"Had any of the drivers seen anything of your Uncle Mott?" Grandma asked me as soon as I'd reached the house.

"Pert Ailster had seen 'im," I said. "Said he saw 'im yesterday afternoon. Said he'd just about had time to get to town. Said he was a-walkin down the street with Toodle Powell. Said he was a-takin both sides of the street."

"That's Mott all right," Grandpa said.

"You're about outten grub, aint you, Ma Tussie?" Aunt Vittie asked Grandma.

"We got a little grub left," Grandma said. "But it aint good grub to feed Press. Sid and I can eat it all right. But corn bread is hard on Press for breakfast—corn bread, and not much to go with it."

"What would you like to have to eat, Pa Tussie?" Aunt Vittie asked Grandpa. Grandpa was a-lyin flat on his back in bed a-watchin a spider spin her web from the wall to the loft.

"I'd like to have some red apples," Grandpa said. "Seems like my stummick craves fruit. Apples would be soft to bite. My teeth are two rows of roots and snags."

"I'll get you some apples," Aunt Vittie said. "If you wait for Mott to come home with grub, I'm afraid you'll starve to death."

"I'm afraid so too, Aunt Vittie," I said.

"Vittie, where'll you get the red apples?" Grandma asked. "You aint got no apples, have you?"

"But there's red apples in the stores in town," Aunt Vittie said.

"I didn't think you had any money left," Grandma said. "That's what you kept a-tellin me."

"I don't have a copper penny in my pocket, Ma Tussie," Aunt Vittie said. "Uncle George doesn't have a penny in his pocket. But I'll get the apples. I'll get them like I got my furniture."

She begged that furniture, I thought. She went from house to house in town and asked people to give her the old broken-down furniture that they had thrown away. She wanted to line the nest that we had helped Uncle George build like the rabbits tore fur from one another to line their nest. And then it flashed through my mind: Wonder how Aunt Vittie feels now to go back there and beg red apples for a sick man. I wouldn't want to see her do it. Something would hurt inside me if I had to do it. But I'd do it before I'd see Grandpa want red apples and not have them.

"George, you go back to the shack and stay until I get back," Aunt Vittie said, a-gettin up from her chear. "I'm a-goin to get Pa Tussie red apples! I'll bring 'im back a poke of fruit!"

Wonder what Grandma thinks now, I thought. Wonder what she thinks after the way she tried to put Aunt Vittie and Uncle George outten the house. Wonder what she thinks of Aunt Vittie's thoughtfulness of Grandpa in a time of need.

"No use of you a-goin outten the cold for me, Vittie," Grandpa said.

"The road will never be too long nor too full of muddy ruts and the night will never get too dark for me to go do anything for you, Pa Tussie," Aunt Vittie said as she closed the door behind her. And when she left, Uncle George wouldn't stay in our shack without her. Grandpa begged him to stay with us until Aunt Vittie got back. "I'll haf to go back to our shack," he said, "to look after everything until Vittie gets back."

When Uncle George left, Grandpa told 'im to be sure to bring his fiddle when he came again to see him. "I love your fiddle music, George," Grandpa said. "I'll want you to play some winter tunes at my funeral. Something like the snow-birds a-pickin up the ragweed seeds. Something like the winter wind among the pine needles and the October wind in the dry fodder blades."

But Uncle George didn't say that he would nor he wouldn't. Maybe he didn't want to think about Grandpa a-lyin there in bed a-waitin to die. I'd heard a lot of the Tussie men say that Uncle George was "chicken-hearted." I'd heard 'em a-talkin about 'im when he fiddled for our dances at the big house.

"George will be back and bring his fiddle, won't he?" Grandpa asked me.

"Yes, Uncle George will be back and bring his fiddle," I said.

"Mott aint here to play the banjer for me now," Grandpa said.

Grandpa lay flat of his back and he looked up at the rain-circled, newspapered ceilin. The spider had finished her web and she had caught a fly that was a-fightin to free itself but the little strands of web held the fly. Grandpa watched the spider race down a thread to the fly and stand over the fly and bite it. Grandpa watched the spider sap the life slowly from the fly—the fly's buzzin got slower and slower as the spider took more life from it. Grandpa wouldn't have watched anything like this unless he had've been sick in bed.

"I've just been a-layin here a-thinkin, Sid," Grandpa said, "that I'm a-gettin these tokens at the wrong time."

"Why, Grandpa?" I asked.

"I wanted you and me to farm this summer," he said. "I've just been a-thinkin about what a great fire the tree laps would make. And the fire would just about clean our ground. You could follow the mule behind a locust-beamed plow with a sharp root cutter in it and hear the roots pop. You could smell the fresh spring, new ground loam. It's got a good fresh smell in the spring. And after ye furrowed the ground we could plant it in yaller corn and stick in a few cornfield beans around the corn and pumpkin seeds around the rotted stumps."

"You've been a-thinkin about burnin the new ground so much," I said, "maybe that's the reason you've been a-dreamin of it."

"No, that's not it, Sid," Grandpa said. "A Tussie knows when he gets his tokens."

"Maybe you are mistaken this time, Grandpa," I said. "I

hope you are. I hope we can get a mule and we can farm this summer together. I'd like to work with you."

"No, I'm not mistaken," Grandpa said.

I took the wooden poker and punched a stick of wood back into the fire that had rolled down.

"I hate to leave land that has never been farmed," Grandpa said. "Land with rot-leaf loam as black as the land in Michigan. I'll tell you, Sid, we could raise some big ears of corn on this land. It would look like livin to be able to walk through the corn in September when the fodder blades start a-turnin and see the big ears of corn a-hangin down from the stalks— to see the ripe cornfield beans a-hangin down in long pods and big yaller pumpkins scattered over the ground like cornfield rocks. When we cut the corn, we'd stick the pumpkins back in the fodder shock to keep the frost from a-hittin 'em."

"I'd like to farm with you, Grandpa," I said. "I'd love to raise corn, beans and pumpkins."

"When you raise your own corn, beans, taters and pumpkins, you don't haf to depend on relief," Grandpa said. "You don't haf to wonder and worry about how long you are a-goin to hold your relief and about somebody a-reportin you. And you can vote the way you please. It's better than dependin on the old-age pension checks of nine dollars a month after you get sixty-five, fer ye and yer old woman—if you vote as you please. You don't get but seven dollars if you don't vote right. Farmin is the only sure way."

"Don't talk about farmin now, Press," Grandma opened the door and said. "I've been a-listenin and it hurts me to hear you talk. We ought to've done it long ago."

"But I didn't have land of my own," Grandpa said. "I didn't have dirt as black as a crow's wing."

Grandpa wouldn't let me leave the house to bring wood from the chimney corner for the night. He watched the spider eat the fly while he talked to me about farmin. Time had been the spider that had sapped the life from Grandpa, I thought. Time didn't haf to spin a web to catch Grandpa. Time could catch a man with a number of years. It made me sad to hear Grandpa talk about farmin next year when I knew that he would not be able to farm even if he missed death.

Why should Grandpa talk about the hands that had fed 'im, I thought. He had drawn relief from the first time it was given to the people. He was one of the first in our county to draw relief. I could barely remember a-goin with 'im to get relief grub. And the day he was sixty-five he applied for his old-age pension and got it. Grandma wouldn't be sixty-five until May and she was already a-plannin the things she would buy soon as she got her first pension check. Maybe one thing that had changed Grandpa was the way Sheriff Whiteapple had treated 'im after he'd helped elect 'im sheriff. There was no use for 'im to talk about beans, taters, pumpkins and corn now. The spider had eaten the fly.

The dark February clouds cleared away and the thin horseshoe moon hung low over the dark hill in the ice-colored sky when Aunt Vittie opened the front door. She was a-carryin a brown paper poke under each arm; her pale face was so red that it looked like the blood would break through the skin.

"Are you cold, Aunt Vittie?" I asked as she laid the two pokes down on Uncle Mott's bed.

"Just my toes got a little cold," she said.

"Did you see Mott?" Grandma asked, runnin from the kitchen when she heard me a-talkin to Aunt Vittie.

"I wasn't a-lookin for the old drunken sot," Aunt Vittie told Grandma. "I went to get apples for Pa Tussie."

Grandma didn't say anything more.

"And I got what I went after," Aunt Vittie said.

"Good red apples, Vittie?" Grandpa asked.

"Good red apples, Pa Tussie," she said. "And I got you some grapes, oranges, pears and bananas."

"God bless you, Vittie," Grandpa said. "My throat's been

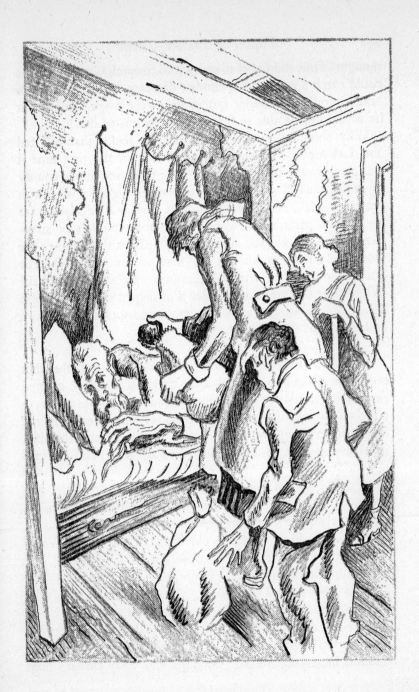

so dry I couldn't swallow cornbread. Seemed like the longer
I chawed it the bigger it got. But apples will slip right down
a dry throat, won't they? They'll be soft to parched lips, won't
they?"

"Do you want one now?" Aunt Vittie asked.

"Let Sid fetch me one," Grandpa said.

"Sid, if Pa Tussie wants anything, you run down to the
shack and tell me," Aunt Vittie said. "Uncle George and I
will be a-comin every night to see 'im."

"All right, Aunt Vittie," I said.

"Tell George to bring his fiddle when he comes," Grandpa
said.

"All right, he'll bring it," Aunt Vittie told 'im as she shut
the door behind her and hurried down the path.

"It's a real apple," Grandpa said. "Slips down my throat
too."

When Grandpa had finished the apple, he asked me for
another.

"You eat one too, Sid," he said. "They are sure good."

"We'd better save 'em for you, Grandpa," I said.

"Never mind that," he said. "I want you to eat apples
with me."

They looked good and I had wanted one but I hated to
eat the fruit Aunt Vittie begged for Grandpa. But I took a
bite from a red apple and it tasted better to me than wild
honey had ever tasted.

CHAPTER XXIII

❧

THREE days we waited for Uncle Mott to come home. I'd go down to the sawmill every day and ask the team drivers if they had seen any trace of him. Not one had seen 'im since the day that Pert Ailster had seen him with Toodle Powell. Then a big snow fell that was to my knees. Uncle George and Aunt Vittie didn't get to our house the evenin after the big snow fell. They had been a-comin every night and Uncle George had been a-playin the fiddle tunes that Grandpa wanted to hear. "It's a tune I want to hear again," Grandpa would tell Uncle George.

And now all the grub we had in our house was gone; all we had was the fruit that Aunt Vittie had brought Grandpa. We still had plenty of wood sheltered partly from the snow in our chimney corner. I had chopped the wood when I wasn't a-helpin Grandma and a-runnin to the sawmill to see if the team drivers had seen Uncle Mott.

All the night the snow fell, I knew that Uncle Mott wouldn't be home so I crawled into his bed. Grandma slept where she'd always slept, beside Grandpa. "Ye won't need hot rocks to your feet, Press," Grandma said. "I'll put my feet to your feet."

"Don't talk about your feet, Arimithy," Grandpa said, "when Pap and Ma are a-tryin to talk to me. Don't you hear 'em?"

"No, I don't hear 'em, Press," Grandma said.

"Well, I hear 'em," Grandpa said. "They've come back again tonight. Listen!"

I listened for voices; I didn't hear anything but the cold February wind a-swishin the snow from the tough-butted white oaks that grew behind our kitchen. I wondered if this was what Grandpa heard. All night long Grandpa would wake me by callin out names of the Tussies that had died long ago—Tussies that I had never known but I had heard 'im talk about. Grandpa would talk to this one and that one just like they were a-talkin to him and he was answerin them.

I was glad when this winter night was over and I heard the caw-caws of early mornin crows a-flyin over our shack to some distant cornfield to get their breakfasts. I got out of bed, stirred livin embers from the ash heap and laid dry kindlin down to catch from the embers. I could see gray twilight through our front-room winder soon as the heat from the fire had melted the jackfrost that was a-clingin to the panes. I didn't build a fire in the kitchen stove for Grandma since we didn't have anything in the house to cook. All we had, and we had very little of it, was the fruit Aunt Vittie had brought Grandpa.

When Grandma got outten the bed, I looked toward the blazin fire so I wouldn't see her dress.

"I aint had much rest," Grandma said. "Press has been a-goin on all night."

"I heard Grandpa a-talkin most of the night," I said.

"It teches a body to hear 'im a-talkin to the old people who's been gone for many years," Grandma said. "He talked to many of his dead kinfolks I knew when I was a little girl. I'd about forgotten about 'em until last night when he started a-talkin to 'em."

"I wonder if they were real people, Grandma," I asked.

"Sure they were real people," she said. "His father and mother were after 'im about a week ago and they didn't come back until last night. Didn't you hear 'im tell 'em he wasn't ready to go yet? Said something was a-holdin 'im back?"

We thought that Grandpa was fast asleep, since he hadn't rested well durin the night; we thought that he was now a-gettin some mornin rest. He lay flat of his back in bed with his closed eyes turnin toward the ceilin. And his long white beard lay spread over the quilts that Grandma had kept well tucked up to his chin. I looked at his face; the flesh that his beard didn't cover was pale as a frostbitten corn blade. And the bones in his face were a-tryin to break through the skin. Grandpa had never had much flesh on his face and what he did have was fadin away and leavin a well-worn, wrinkled skin to cover his bones.

"Don't come before midnight, Ma," Grandpa said. "I want to stay as long as I can."

I looked at Grandpa; then I looked at Grandma. The tears were streamin down her wrinkled cheeks.

"No, I'm not a-sufferin, Ma," Grandpa said.

"Poor Press," Grandma wept.

Grandpa is worse, I thought. Grandpa is outten his head. I'm a-goin down to Aunt Vittie's and Uncle George's shack to get Aunt Vittie to fetch a doctor from town to see Grandpa. Uncle Mott will be here soon as he gets rid of his money. Soon as he gets it down his neck, he'll be here. He's a-puttin a lot of saw logs down his neck this time to make up for the time he helped Uncle George and Aunt Vittie build their shack.

"He's outten his head," I whispered to Grandma so Grandpa wouldn't hear me.

"I aint outten my head either, Sid," he said. "I'm alive and in my right mind. I know what I'm a-talkin about."

"Sid, we're a-goin to haf to have somethin to eat," Grandma whispered. "Go down to your Aunt Vittie's and Uncle George's this mornin. See if they've got anything to eat. If they don't have anything tell your Aunt Vittie to help us if she can."

I knew that Grandma wanted her to go through the deep snow to town to beg somethin for us to eat. And it made me wonder if Grandma was sorry over the way she had treated Aunt Vittie. I wondered if Grandma would take her and Uncle George in our shack now to live with us if they wanted to come.

"When you have money," Grandpa said, "you have lots of friends. I've just been a-layin here a-thinkin since everybody's gone and let me alone, when we lived in the big house and had ten thousand dollars besides relief and my pension check, my kinfolks come and stayed with me until it was gone. They danced and they were merry. They had plenty to eat and good beds to sleep in. And they listened to good music and danced every night until nearly noon the next day. Where are all my kinfolks since I'm sick in bed? Not a one has come. They don't want to come now."

"Aunt Vittie comes," I said.

"But she's no blood kin to me," Grandpa said. "She seems closer to me than all my blood kin. She'd do more for me. But I've been like a father to 'er and she aint forgot."

Now I knew that Grandpa wasn't outten his head. He was a-talkin in his right mind.

The snow was nearly to my boot tops but I waded through it along the place where I thought the path ought to be. I could tell where the tree laps were for the snow had drifted over them to form small white mountains of snow. When the February winds blew, great flakes of snow that had lodged upon the tough-butted white-oaks' branches slithered from their restin places to the thick quilt of snow that blanketed the earth. Overhead the crows flew close to the brush tops, their wings a-fannin against the wind, their necks outstretched, with caw-caws that sounded of hunger. I could understand how hungry crows felt on this winter mornin. I went toward the shack where a cloud of wood smoke was a-comin from the chimney and thinnin on the gusts of wind.

Just as soon as I knocked on the shack door, Aunt Vittie opened it. "How's Pa Tussie?" was the first thing she asked me.

Aunt Vittie was dressed in a heavy coat with a scarf about

her neck; men's boots that came up to her knees were on her feet. She had heavy mittens on her hands.

"Grandpa went on all night last night," I said. "Grandma and I didn't get much sleep."

"Has he got any fruit left?" Aunt Vittie asked.

"Just a little," I said. "His fruit's all we got in the house to eat."

"We don't have anything to send up there," Aunt Vittie said. "But I'm on my way now to get somethin. I couldn't sleep last night for a-thinkin about 'im. I was a-thinkin about all of you in that shack without anything to eat."

"But you can't get to town this mornin," I said.

"Oh, yes, I can," she said. "I'll follow the wagon road. I may be able to catch a ride on a loaded wagon after it leaves the ruts and gets on the turnpike."

"Aunt Vittie, it will be a hard trip," I said. "Maybe I could go to town and you could stay with Grandpa and Grandma."

"You can't do what I can do," Aunt Vittie said. "I'll send Uncle George up to stay with you."

Uncle George and Aunt Vittie couldn't walk with their arms around each other through the snow. Uncle George, a-carryin his fiddle, walked in front, a-steppin in the tracks that I had made to the sawmill. I followed Uncle George, a-steppin in the tracks that he had made much bigger, and Aunt Vittie followed me. When we reached the sawmill, Uncle George held Aunt Vittie close and kissed her.

"Be careful, honey," he said.

"Don't worry about me, Uncle George," she said.

We stood there watchin her walk along a groove that a wagon loaded with lumber had made through the deep snow. We watched 'er until she was ready to go beyond sight around a dark pine grove whose long limbs with needled fingers were weighted with snow. Aunt Vittie waved to us; we waved to her and then Uncle George and I walked slowly up the hill through the deep snow to our shack.

While Uncle George played his fiddle for Grandpa, I kept wood on the fire. Grandma puffed clouds of smoke from her pipe. She smoked faster than I'd ever seen her smoke. I knew that it was worry about Mott and Grandpa that made her do it. And once I heard her say that when she was real hungry that she could smoke her pipe and kill the hunger that gnawed at her stummick. But we waited for Aunt Vittie to return. That was our last and only chance of gettin somethin to eat. We could depend on Aunt Vittie more than on blood kin or friends we knew.

Often I went to the front-room winder and looked out the path. I'd watch the path so much that it was a habit for me. I knew that the little drains were filled with snowdrifts and no one could walk the path. Aunt Vittie couldn't walk on this path because she was too thin to carry a load through drifts well over her head. Anybody who reached our shack would haf to come the wagon road to the sawmill and then come up the bank. I could see the wagon road and the deep grooves that the wagon wheels had cut through the snow as far as the pine grove where we had waved good-by to Aunt Vittie. And when I saw a team a-comin toward the sawmill, I watched to see if Aunt Vittie was on the wagon or if there was a box of groceries on it.

"I've seen two wagons come to the sawmill empty, Grandma," I said as I watched the second empty wagon roll over the snow to the lumber pile.

"But you are too eager, Sid," Grandma said. "Vittie aint had time to get to town unless she's been lucky enough to catch a ride."

"It's a bad day for a woman to be out," Grandpa said. "Hate for Vittie to do this."

Uncle George didn't say anything. I wondered why he didn't go instead of Aunt Vittie. But he couldn't do what Aunt Vittie's a-doin, I thought. People will give to a woman before they will to a man. That wasn't exactly my own

thought—I'd heard Grandpa tell Grandma that, the day Aunt
Vittie went to town to get 'im some fruit.

"Sid, you are too anxious because you're a-gittin hungry,"
Grandma said.

"But yander comes another wagon in sight," I said. "And
I believe it's got a man on it beside the driver."

Grandma and Uncle George came to the winder and
looked. And I wondered if they weren't just as hungry as I
was. They looked through the windowpanes with eager eyes
that searched the wagon like a crow's eyes search a winter
cornfield.

"That's Mott all right," Uncle George said.

"I'm glad to see some grub come into this house," Grandma
said. "We aint a-gittin it before we need it!"

Grandma walked back and sat down before the fire. Uncle
George watched a minute longer and sat down. I stood by
the winder watching the team stop at the sawmill. I
watched Uncle Mott slide from the wagon and walk slowly
up the hill, carefully steppin in the path that we had made.
Uncle Mott didn't have any groceries; he carried a small box
in his hand.

"I told you Mott would be here," Grandma said proudly.

Just then Uncle Mott opened the door.

"Mott, Mott, my darlin boy," Grandma said, runnin to the
door, throwin her arms around Uncle Mott's neck. There
were tiny icicles frozen in Uncle Mott's beard.

"Did you bring us some groceries, Mott?" Grandpa asked.

"No, I didn't, Pap," Uncle Mott said with a worried
look in his eyes.

I didn't ask Uncle Mott what he had in the box. I knew
he had a box of candy. When Uncle George saw the box of
candy in Uncle Mott's hand, he stopped playin his fiddle and
looked at it. He didn't speak to Uncle Mott and Uncle Mott
didn't speak to Uncle George. He's brought the candy for
Aunt Vittie, I thought. Uncle George knows he's brought the
candy for Aunt Vittie.

"What's kept ye so long, Mott?" Grandpa asked in a soft voice.

"Trouble, Pap," Uncle Mott said.

Grandpa and Grandma didn't ask Uncle Mott about his trouble; they waited for Uncle Mott to tell them. Uncle George sat pluckin his fiddle strings and turnin the keys to draw them tighter. I watched the water run from Uncle Mott's beard as the warm fire melted the icicles. Water dripped from his chin to the floor like water from a soft summer rain drips from the green leaves on the trees to the ground. Snow and ice he couldn't kick from his boots melted and ran across the floor in a little stream. The part of Uncle Mott's face that his beard didn't cover was red as a turkey's snout in November.

"Sheriff Whiteapple is liable to be here any time," Uncle Mott said. "I sent 'im word he'd better bring all his deputies with 'im when he come to arrest me."

"Oh, Mott," Grandma wailed.

"I had a debt to pay to young Ben and Dee Tussie," Uncle Mott said. His eyes snapped and his lips snarled. "You know what they did to Pap! They won't do anything more."

I wondered if Uncle Mott had shot them or had knifed them to death. I wanted to know but I was afraid to ask him. And I wondered if he was drunk or sober when it had happened. Uncle Mott was sober now; I wondered if he had paid his debt to them when he was drunk. I knew that young Ben and Dee Tussie were customers of Tootle Powell. I wondered if it had happened at Tootle Powell's shack in Greenwood. And I wondered if this was what it had taken to sober Uncle Mott from his long drunk.

"Sheriff Whiteapple will get ye, Mott," Grandpa said. "I'd hoped never to see 'im around here again."

"He'll never take me," Uncle Mott said.

"You'd better leave, Mott, darlin," Grandma said. "Hide among the rock cliffs."

"But they'd track 'im in the snow," Grandpa said.

"I'm not a-leavin this shack," Uncle Mott said as he put the box of candy on his bed.

Uncle Mott walked to the middle of the room and reached up and lifted his double-barrel shotgun from the joist where he kept it hangin. All the Tussie men kept their shotguns in the front room. They hanged them to the joist alike—the gun barrel restin on a long spike nail driven into the joist, the trigger guard hangin over a smaller nail. They hung them so they could have them in a handy place and so they could get them down easily at a second's notice.

"He'll never get me long as I've got this old friend," Uncle Mott said. "If I haf to die, I'll die with my boots on."

Uncle Mott is talkin like Uncle Kim used to talk, I thought.

Uncle George didn't pay any attention to anything Uncle Mott said. He didn't get excited when Uncle Mott said that he had paid his debt to young Ben and Dee Tussie. He may have been thinkin a lot as he sat tunin his fiddle but he didn't say anything.

While Uncle Mott broke the double-barrel at the breech to see if it was loaded, Uncle George pulled his bow across his fiddle. It made a low mournful sound. It sounded like the autumn songs he had played at the big house when the corn turned buff-colored and the leaves turned brown. He played a note of death.

"That's the son of a bitch that's caused all my trouble," Uncle Mott yelled, aimed his double-barrel at the fiddle at close range and pulled the trigger before a cat could bat its eye.

The fiddle fell from Uncle George's hand and shoulder to the floor. There wasn't enough splinters left of it to start a fire. The roar of the gun inside the house made my ears ring like tiny bells. Grandma screamed; Grandpa waved his weak bony arms for Uncle Mott to stop.

"I've blowed that son of a bitch to smithereens," Uncle Mott said fiercely. "It'll never steal any more women!"

Uncle George sat shakin like a tough-butted white-oak leaf in the winter wind. In one hand he held his fiddle bow. I knew that Uncle George felt like that he had lost the best friend he had on this earth, but he couldn't say anything for Uncle Mott had a loaded double-barrel, had only fired one shell and was standin over Uncle George.

Uncle Mott leveled his double-barrel at the fiddle bow that Uncle George was holdin in his tremblin hand. He shot it in two, leavin half of it in Uncle George's hand; the other half fell to the floor.

Grandma screamed again and Grandpa waved his hand and said somethin I couldn't hear for the roar of the gun.

"I'll fix that damned bow too," Uncle Mott said, breakin his gun at the breach, takin out the smokin empty shells. Two tiny streams of black smoke was leavin his gun barrels. One of Uncle George's hands fell limp at his hip while in the other he still held half of his fiddle bow.

I don't know how it happened. Uncle George's hand that had fallen limp at his hip worked so fast I must not've seen it. I never saw 'im draw his pistol from his hip pocket. I didn't know where it came from. All I heard was the crack of the pistol. And then I saw Uncle Mott fall like a tree, his face down, his head toward Uncle George; he hit the floor with his double-barrel in his hands, his body quiverin. Uncle George never aimed his pistol at Uncle Mott. He shot from his hip where he still held his pistol. The long pistol barrel spit a tiny stream of smoke.

"Oh, my God," Grandma screamed as she threw herself down on the floor beside Uncle Mott. "Has he killed ye, Mott?"

Uncle Mott didn't answer. His body slowly relaxed like a squirmin black snake with its head cut off; soon he was still.

"I didn't practice shootin rats over on Lost Creek for nothin," Uncle George said. "I've kilt a rat."

Grandpa tried to get outten bed but I held him. He was

so weak that he was easy to hold in bed. Tears came from his eyes and dripped down on his pillow. Grandma was down on the floor a-takin on so, I thought the men workin at the sawmill could hear her.

"If I had a gun, I'd blow yer brains out," Grandma screamed at Uncle George, shakin her fist at 'im. "Ye've kilt Mott! My darlin boy's heart has stopped."

Grandpa grew tired of tryin to get outten bed; then he lay still, weepin like his heart would break. Uncle George put his pistol in his hip pocket, now that he knew Uncle Mott would never rise again to give him trouble.

"Hep me turn Mott over, Sid," Grandma said, weepin harder than ever.

When Grandma and I turned him over, there was a little hole between his eyes a clot of blood had covered. There wasn't even any blood on the floor.

"Get outten this house, George!" Grandma screamed.

"Not until Vittie comes," Uncle George said.

Uncle George wouldn't go.

"I hope Sheriff Whiteapple comes now," Grandma said. "I'll tell ye there's a time when a body needs a sheriff no matter how much a body hates one!"

I'd love to see Sheriff Whiteapple come now, I thought. I'd love to see him come and bring all his deputies. And then I thought about the times when I had hunted with Uncle Mott and how he'd killed rabbits. I thought about how he had taught me to set traps and how he had given me all the hides from the little animals I had caught to sell and buy things I needed at school. It made me feel sorry over the things that I had said about Uncle Mott. I was sorry now that I had even thought in my mind that I didn't care if Uncle Mott froze stiff as a possum's tail some winter night when he was a-layin out drunk. I was sorry for all these things now that Uncle Mott was dead. I had seen Uncle Mott so full of life, huntin the brier thickets with his double-barrel; I'd seen him walk the paths through the woods with his gun across his shoulder; I had heard him laugh and cuss; now he was silent. Life had gone from him like life had gone from the rabbits he had slipped up on and shot when they were asleep and like the possums whose necks he had put under a mattock handle and stood on the mattock handle with his feet while he pulled on their tails with his hands to break their necks. Uncle Mott has taken the lives of men and animals, I thought. Now his life has been taken.

"I wish Sheriff Whiteapple would come," Grandma wept.

"Ye didn't want him to come when Mott had kilt his two cousins," Uncle George said. "But ye want 'im to come for me. I'm a-waitin for Vittie! Let Sheriff Whiteapple come and bring his deputies. I'm not afraid!"

"But ye're afraid," Grandma sobbed. "You're a coward!"

Grandpa lay on the bed and sobbed; Grandma stayed on her knees, bent over, with her arms around Uncle Mott's neck and her face against his beardy face. There was so much sobbin in the shack that I didn't think that I could stand it any longer. Grandma couldn't fight Uncle George; and I wondered what Grandpa would've done if he had been able to fight. I wondered if he would have killed Uncle George, his brother, who had killed his son, Uncle Mott. I walked to the window and looked over the snow-covered earth about our shack.

While I stood at the window lookin at the snow-covered world, the sobbin in the shack lessened so I could hear great sweeps of February wind roar from the pines upon the hill and over the shack. It was a cold lonesome winter wind and its moanin and all that had happened in the shack made me wonder if I was asleep and dreamin or if I was awake. It was hard for me to believe that Uncle George had killed Uncle Mott, and our shack didn't seem right when Uncle George was in it without the sound of his fiddle.

"Look down the road, Sid," Grandma said. "See if ye can see the Sheriff a-comin!"

"I don't see 'im, Grandma," I said.

"Tell me soon as ye see 'im a-comin," she said.

"All right, Grandma," I said.

As I stood listenin to the winter wind howl over this February earth, I saw two people a-comin in the distance by the pine grove where the heavy February snow had weighted the pine boughs. They were walkin close to each other. They were so far away I couldn't tell but it looked to me like they were walkin side by side in the same wagon rut the timber wagons had made through the snow.

"I see two people a-comin, Grandma," I said.

"Sheriff Whiteapple and a deputy," Grandma said. "Thank God, they're a-comin."

"It's a man and a woman, Grandma," I said.

"Maybe it's Vittie," Uncle George said, gettin up from his chear and walkin to the window.

"If it's Aunt Vittie, she's a-walkin awful close to another man," I said.

"Walks like 'er but I don't guess it's 'er," Uncle George said, slowly walkin across the room and sittin down in his chair. "She wouldn't be a-walkin that close to another man."

"I'm not so sure about that," Grandma said. "If she aint, she ort to. She aint got a piece of a man for a husband."

Then Grandma started weepin again.

"I wish I had a gun," Grandma wept.

Uncle George would be too quick on the draw for Grandma, I thought.

"It's a soldier boy with a sack of groceries on his back with Aunt Vittie," I said. "Come, Grandma, and look!"

"Wonder who he is?" Grandma said.

Grandma took her arms from around Uncle Mott, wiped her tear-wrinkled eyes with the corner of her apron and walked toward the window.

"He walks *pliam-blank*, like Kim used to," Grandma said as she looked through the window at Aunt Vittie and the soldier boy as they started to climb the steep hill from the wagon road to the shack. "Ye cowardly hellion, George, ye'd better draw yer pistol; he has his arm around Vittie!"

Even before Grandma snarled at Uncle George somethin went plunk through me like a bullet goes through the guts of a rabbit. I felt all weak and my knees sagged.

I knew I was lookin at what wasn't so. It *couldn't* be. But they came nearer. My stummick started to turn over.

"Grandma," I sort of squeaked, for my breath wouldn't come the way it ought to, "Grandma!"

"Yes, honey," said Grandma, still lookin mean at Uncle George.

"Grandma"—and somehow I put it into words—"it's Uncle Kim," I said. "I know 'im! I know 'im!"

"It can't be Kim, honey," Grandma said, her eyes still on Uncle George. "He's buried on the mountain top."

"But it's *Kim*!" I screamed.

There must have been somethin in the way I said it. Grandma swung around toward the winder with a kind of loud gasp. Uncle George jumped up and ran to the winder and tried to brush me aside. But I clung on with hands and feet and everything I had. I could see now that Aunt Vittie was walkin close to the soldier boy, whose arm was round her back and whose hand was claspin her hand—just the way Uncle George himself had walked over the mountain paths with Aunt Vittie.

Uncle George looked for a minute, and then slowly gave a long curse deep down in his throat in a kind of groan. Grandma's hand was on my shoulder, as she pushed her face close to the glass. Suddenly I felt her fingers stiffen and claw into my flesh like iron hooks. "*Kim!*" she screeched right in my ear. Then she dashed to the door and out, screamin, "Kim, is it you? Is it you?" But Grandma didn't reach them; she fell headlong on the snow, her face buried, and her arms stretched out.

"Uncle Kim, it's you," I yelled as I ran toward them, while Uncle George came out of his spell and turned and ran back through the shack.

"It's Kim, Sid," Aunt Vittie said, tears streamin from her eyes. "I can't believe he's back! Kim! Kim!"

"Uncle Kim," I said.

But he didn't speak to me; he bent over and picked Grandma up from the snow. Aunt Vittie brushed the snow from her face.

"She's fainted," Aunt Vittie said.

"No wonder," Uncle Kim said. "You bury me on the mountain top, shed buckets of tears over me, and then I come home!"

Color came back to Grandma's face; she threw her arms around Uncle Kim's neck and he held her close to him in his powerful arms.

"Yes, I'm Kim, Ma," Uncle Kim said. "I'm back with you!"

"Kim, don't go in the house," Grandma said.

"Why, Ma?" Uncle Kim asked.

"Your Uncle George has just kilt yer brother Mott," Grandma screamed.

"Did he?" Aunt Vittie asked without sheddin a tear.

"Mott's dead and Uncle George deserves to die," Uncle Kim said.

Uncle Kim didn't shed a tear over Uncle Mott. He didn't seem to care.

"Where is Uncle George?" Uncle Kim asked.

"He's in the shack," Grandma said.

"I want to see 'im," Uncle Kim said.

"He'll kill ye," Grandma said. "Don't go in on 'im, Kim! He's got a pistol!"

"I'm not afraid of his pistol," Uncle Kim said. "Pistols are my friends. I've used so many of 'em. A pistol won't even shoot at me!"

Uncle Kim went inside the open door. Grandma, Aunt

Vittie and I pushed in behind him, all a-tryin to be the closest to him.

"Where is he?" Uncle Kim asked, passin Grandpa a-layin almost lifeless on his bed and Uncle Mott dead, a-layin flat of his back on the floor before the fire. Uncle Kim had his hand in his overcoat pocket when he went into the kitchen.

"Cold air is comin into your kitchen, Ma," Uncle Kim said. "Uncle George didn't take time to open the door. Didn't take time to raise the winder. Took sash and all with 'im when he left."

Uncle George had jumped through the winder and there were shattered glass and pieces of broken winder sashes on the kitchen floor. I walked over to the winder and looked at the tracks he had made through the deep snow. His tracks were far apart like he had run up the steep hill through the deep snow toward the pines where the snow was not so deep.

Uncle George had gone to the rock cliffs, I thought when Uncle Kim hurried back to the front room to see Grandpa. I heard 'im a-talkin to Grandpa while I stood by the winder and looked at Uncle George's tracks in the deep snow. I wondered what Uncle George would do and night not far away, old as he was, out in the deep snow and the blasts of icy winter wind. And then I thought how easy it would be for Sheriff Whiteapple and his deputies to track Uncle George through the snow. And then I thought that it must be a dream. All of these things couldn't happen at once. But I touched the kitchen wall with my hand and the wall had a strange feelin. And I could see Uncle George's tracks in the snow; I could hear Grandma cryin with joy one minute over Uncle Kim's comin home and then I could hear her speak of Uncle Mott and start wailin. I could hear Grandpa a-talkin just above a whisper to Uncle Kim. I could hear Uncle Kim and Aunt Vittie a-sayin love words to each other. I could hear the winter winds sweep over the shack; I could hear their mournful sounds as they shook snowflakes from the tall pine boughs.

It wasn't a dream, for I was awake with my people in a world where we lived, breathed and died. The worried winter wind blew through the open winder and chilled me until my lips trembled. I hurried back to the front room to the fire.

"I'll put Mott in the bed, Ma," Uncle Kim said.

"Can ye lift 'im by yerself?" Grandma asked.

"He's not heavy to lift," Uncle Kim said.

Uncle Kim lifted Uncle Mott from the floor with as much ease as if he were liftin a half bushel of meal, carried him to Uncle Mott's old bed, laid him on it beside the box of candy he had brought for Aunt Vittie, and covered him with a sheet.

"I've lifted a lot of dead men heavier than Mott," Uncle Kim said.

"Can't believe ye're here, Kim," Grandpa said. "Seems like ye've been resurrected from the dead!"

"No, Pap, I've not been resurrected from the dead," Uncle Kim said. "You just thought you buried me. I'd like to know the unknown soldier you buried. I've never even been scratched in this war!"

"Wish I'd a-opened that coffin," Grandpa whispered. "Wish I'd a-done it instead of Mott. But I thought Mott would have knowed ye!"

"He didn't want to know me, Pap," Uncle Kim said. "He had somethin in the back of his head. He had other plans. He didn't shed any tears over me, did he?"

"Come to think about it," Grandpa whispered, "I don't think Mott did do a lot of weepin."

"No, he wouldn't do a lot of weepin," Uncle Kim said. "He's got what was a-comin to 'im. Uncle George will get what's a-comin to 'im."

"I won't be here to know about it," Grandpa said. "I'll be a-leavin ye tonight, Kim. Just so glad you got here and I got to see ye alive!"

"When a brother wants your wife I can't shed a lot of tears over his dead body," Uncle Kim said. "That's why he died! Look, he even brought her a box of candy, and her married to my uncle."

"I told you everything, Kim," Aunt Vittie said. "Let's don't talk about Mott and Uncle George."

"All right, honey," Uncle Kim said, "I promise you, I won't talk. But it does make me mad. Fightin over the land that was bought with some poor soldier's dead body. It's hell to think about it. Now I wonder whose land this is?"

"It's yourn, Kim," Grandma said. "I've allus told 'im this land was bought with Kim money."

Grandma dried her tears as Uncle Kim talked. But when she looked toward Uncle Mott's bed, she started weepin again.

I wondered as Uncle Kim talked if he's a-goin to treat me like he treated me before he went to war. He had seen everybody and talked to them but he hadn't noticed me yet. I looked at his broad shoulders and his brown face. I looked at the gold teeth in his mouth. I looked at the medals pinned on his coat, a sharpshooter's medal and two medals for bravery. I watched him wave his big hands. I wished that I was as big and as powerful a man as Uncle Kim was. I had always liked Uncle Kim but he had never seemed to like me.

While he talked to Grandma, Grandpa and Aunt Vittie, I walked up closer to him and looked up at his sun-tanned face.

"Sid," Uncle Kim said, takin a step toward me, placin his hands under my arms and liftin me up in front of him like I was a peck of meal, "you're growin up like a bean pole. You'll soon be a man! You're taller than your mother now!"

"My mother, Uncle Kim?" I said. "You mean Grandma?"

"No, I mean your mother," he said.

I didn't say anything for I didn't know who my mother was.

"Doesn't Sid know who his mother is yet?" Uncle Kim asked Grandma.

Neither Grandma, Grandpa nor Aunt Vittie said a word.

"I think it's time we told 'im who his mother is," Uncle Kim said.

Grandpa, Grandma and Aunt Vittie still didn't say anything.

"Vittie's your mother, Sid," Uncle Kim said.

"Aunt Vittie," I said.

"She's your mother," Uncle Kim said. "She's not your aunt."

It's hard for me to believe, I thought, but I didn't say anything. I'll never be able to call her "mother."

CHAPTER XXIV

✕

GRANDMA hung a quilt over the window that Uncle George had jumped through when she and Aunt Vittie started to get our suppers. We were all hungry but we had forgotten that we were hungry. And while Aunt Vittie and Grandma cooked supper for us, Uncle Kim and I sat before the fire and talked. Uncle Kim had never been so friendly with me before. I told him about goin to school and the good grades that I had made. I told him how I had trapped animals and sold the hides to buy things I needed in school. And Uncle Kim listened to me talk. He had changed until he didn't act like the same person. He had changed or I had changed. I thought that it was the war that had changed him or that it was my growin older that had changed me.

"You've changed a lot, Uncle Kim," I said.

"You mean I look different?" Uncle Kim laughed.

"No, you talk different," I said. "You never would talk to me before. I didn't think you was a-goin to talk to me this time."

"I never treated you right, Sid," Uncle Kim said. "I won't lie to you now. I'll tell you the truth about everything. I never treated you right because you were not my son!"

"But I've always wanted to be your son," I said. "I've thought about you more than anybody since they brought you back and buried you. Never a night I didn't think about you. When we lived at the big house and had the dances, I thought about you. I went to bed thinkin about you. I thought about everything we had, even to the clothes I wore, had come from money that we got for your dust!"

"Your father is a Seagraves," Uncle Kim said. "Your father's father owned the Blue Creek Mountain Coal Mine in Harlan County. He got your mother in trouble when she

297

was fourteen. And I was bummin over the country and got a job at the coal mine. Seagraves wouldn't marry your mother because her pappie was a coal miner and his pappie was a coal operator and it was fixed for me to marry your mother and take you and her away so he could marry another girl. I got paid for it. I didn't care about your mother then; I didn't want to settle down! I didn't care for anybody—least of all you. And Pap and Ma took you when you were a little baby. You're old enough for me to tell you these things now. I'm not your father but I'd love to be."

"He's tellin you the truth, Sid," Grandpa whispered. "I've allus laid off to tell ye but never could do it!"

Grandma fed Grandpa while I sat at the table with Uncle Kim and Aunt Vittie. I knew that it would be hard for me to call Aunt Vittie "mother" since I had never used that word in my life. I had never used the word "father." They sat side by side on one side of the table and I ate on the other side. Uncle Kim would feed Aunt Vittie with his fork from his plate and she would feed Uncle Kim with her fork from her plate. It almost made me laugh and I would have laughed if I could have kept from thinkin about Uncle Mott, who was dead, lyin in his old bed in the corner with the box of candy beside 'im that he bought for Aunt Vittie. But it didn't make me as sad to think of Uncle Mott as it did to think of Grandpa. I remembered what Grandpa had told his mother this mornin, that he would go tonight at midnight with her and his father.

Uncle Kim didn't seem to mind about Uncle Mott's death. He was hurt over Grandpa, but he looked so deeply in love with Aunt Vittie that nothin else seemed to bother 'im and so happy to be home again that he laughed most of the time. He could hardly stay away from Aunt Vittie while she got supper. And never had Uncle George and Aunt Vittie been the love-birds that Aunt Vittie and Uncle Kim were, now they were reunited. I remembered as I watched them feedin each other how I had often wished for Uncle Kim to come home again to see what he would do to Uncle George and Uncle Mott. I had wondered if he would pull his pistol and shoot up the place. And that is what I thought that he would do. But Uncle Kim hadn't done what I thought that he would do. Maybe he'd had enough fightin, maybe he was tired of fightin.

Before we had finished supper there was a knock on our front door. I heard Grandma leave Grandpa's bed and open the door.

"Sorry, Mrs. Tussie, but we've come after Mott," I heard Sheriff Whiteapple say. "Is he here?"

"He's here," Grandma said.

"Where is he?" Sheriff Whiteapple asked.

"In bed," Grandma said.

I heard many feet trampin on our floor and many voices a-talkin in low tones.

"You know what he did, Mrs. Tussie?"

"Yes, I know," Grandma said. "You've allus wanted Mott. Here he is."

"Is he asleep?" Sheriff Whiteapple said.

"He's asleep to sleep a long time," Grandpa said.

"Mott," Sheriff Whiteapple said. "We've come after ye! Come on, we don't want any trouble!"

"You won't have any trouble with 'im, Sheriff," Grandma said.

"Mott," Sheriff Whiteapple said. "Come along now! We're takin ye back with us!"

He's tryin to wake Uncle Mott, I thought. But Uncle Mott will not awake.

"What's the matter with 'im?" Sheriff Whiteapple asked Grandma.

"He won't go with ye this time, Sheriff," Grandma said. "He's dead."

"What happened?" Sheriff Whiteapple asked.

"You won't need yer guns, Sheriff Whiteapple," Grandma

said. "Yer deputies won't need theirs. Old George Tussie kilt Mott! Mott is free of all his troubles!"

"One son resurrected from the grave," Grandpa said, "and one sent to his grave."

"Where's George Tussie?" Sheriff Whiteapple asked.

"He went out at the kitchen winder," Grandma said. "He's gone to the rock cliffs up on the mountain. Ye can track 'im in the snow. He's got a pistol on 'im and he's right handy with it! Shoots from the hip!"

"But we'll get 'im," Sheriff Whiteapple said. "We've got too many men and too many guns. Come on, men!"

I heard 'em leave the shack and I went over to our kitchen winder and pulled the quilt back to watch them. There was a thin moon in the star-filled sky. With the snow on the ground, the night was almost bright as day. I saw Sheriff Whiteapple and six deputies, armed with big guns in their hands and pistols stickin from their leather hip holsters, start up the hill on Uncle George's tracks. They moved silently into the night, over the deep snow toward the pines, like a pack of silent hounds on a rabbit's tracks.

"Uncle George'll get what's a-comin to 'im," Uncle Kim said.

Uncle Kim and Aunt Vittie washed the dishes. Aunt Vittie would wash a dish and Uncle Kim would dry it; then they would hug and kiss before they washed another dish. I left them alone in the kitchen and went to the front room to be with Grandpa and Grandma. Grandma was tryin to feed Grandpa warm soup from a teaspoon. Uncle Kim had fed Aunt Vittie; Aunt Vittie had fed Uncle Kim and Grandma was trying to feed Grandpa.

"He can't eat it, Sid," she said.

"I don't want it now," Grandpa said. "Pap and Ma will soon be here."

I sat alone in the flickerin firelight while Grandma sat by

Grandpa's bed and tried to feed him. And thoughts ran through my mind as they had never run before. I thought about Uncle Mott, Uncle George, Grandpa, Grandma, Uncle Kim and Aunt Vittie; I thought about Dee and young Ben Tussie and wondered if they would be buried on the mountain top the same time that we buried Uncle Mott and Grandpa if he died—and if there would be more fights among the Tussies at the graveyard. And I wondered if Uncle George would get killed and be buried with them too. I wondered if Uncle George would die with his boots on like Uncle Mott had died. And I wondered what all the Tussies would think when they saw Uncle Kim. I wondered what Uncle Kim would think when he looked at his own grave.

Uncle Kim and Aunt Vittie came from the kitchen with their arms around each other and it disturbed my thoughts. Uncle Kim sat down in a chair before the fire, lifted Aunt Vittie into his lap. He sat with his arms about her, drawin her close to him and callin her pet names. He didn't call her the names of birds and flowers like Uncle George had called her, but he called her his "sweet little armful," his "little lump of sugar," his "quart of wild honey," and his "long sweetenin." Uncle Mott was dead, Grandpa was dyin and Uncle Kim was lovin, all in the same room. It all seemed so much like a dream to me and made thoughts go through my head and fade like mornin mists for more thoughts to come. It seemed like a dream, but it wasn't a dream for I felt life surge through my body and I felt warmth from the big fire.